*Tota*

Make Me Fall

# Fallbank

# MAKE ME FALL

## CASS SCOTKA

Make Me Fall
ISBN # 978-1-80250-550-4
©Copyright Cass Scotka 2023
Cover Art by Erin Dameron-Hill ©Copyright July 2023
Interior text design by Claire Siemaszkiewicz
Totally Bound Publishing

This is a work of fiction. All characters, places and events are from the author's imagination and should not be confused with fact. Any resemblance to persons, living or dead, events or places is purely coincidental.

All rights reserved. No part of this publication may be reproduced in any material form, whether by printing, photocopying, scanning or otherwise without the written permission of the publisher, Totally Bound Publishing.

Applications should be addressed in the first instance, in writing, to Totally Bound Publishing. Unauthorised or restricted acts in relation to this publication may result in civil proceedings and/or criminal prosecution.

The author and illustrator have asserted their respective rights under the Copyright Designs and Patents Acts 1988 (as amended) to be identified as the author of this book and illustrator of the artwork.

Published in 2023 by Totally Bound Publishing, United Kingdom.

No part of this book may be reproduced, scanned, or distributed in any printed or electronic form without permission. Please do not participate in or encourage piracy of copyrighted materials in violation of the authors' rights. Purchase only authorised copies.

Totally Bound Publishing is an imprint of Totally Entwined Group Limited.

If you purchased this book without a cover you should be aware that this book is stolen property. It was reported as "unsold and destroyed" to the publisher and neither the author nor the publisher has received any payment for this "stripped book".

# MAKE ME FALL

# Dedication

For Jana, agent extraordinaire.

# Acknowledgements

As with all things, this book would not exist without the love and support of so many people. My agent, Jana Hanson is such an amazing supporter, champion, and outstanding human being! Thank you for choosing to believe in me and my writing. I couldn't imagine a better partner as an author.

Anna Olson, Rebecca Scott and everyone at Totally Bound and Totally Entwined Group, thank you so much for taking a chance on my book and me as an author. Thank you, Erin Dameron-Hill, for creating a stunningly adorable cover that matches my book to perfection. You've all made this journey spectacular and so fun! The support and resources given to me for making my book a success have been invaluable and I am forever grateful.

To my writer crew! My agent siblings, Suleena Bibra and Claudia Ambrose, you keep me sane and inspired. I hope we get to meet in real life one day! The Romance and WF On Sub group chat—Joanne Machin, Suzanne Baltzar, Erin Rose, Laya Brusi, Jess K Hardy, Kimberley Ash, Despina Karras, Annia Dowell-Wiltshire, Noreen Mughees and Jannelle Drummond. You ladies keep me laughing, writing and pushing through this publishing life. I couldn't do this without all of you.

Gwynne Jackson and Ingrid Pierce, there are not words to say how much you mean to me. Thank you for reading and critiquing my work, for staying positive and encouraging, helping me work through mental blocks and plot questions. Thank you for trusting me to read your words and fawn over them before anyone else gets to. You two are amazing, wonderful, beautiful, brilliant writers who give everything you have to the writing community. I am so grateful to have you both in my corner.

Now for my real-life friends and family! The romance readers group chat—you make me laugh and smile and give the best book recs. The Elite Elevens, for not only hyping me up with my books, but also with my running. Our social club with a running problem is the best! I wouldn't trade our miles together for all the cheesecake. (LOL, we all know I'm lying... Sort of.) To the California Livin' crew, thanks for accepting me into the fold as a transplant and being the most awesome found family ever. My Colorado loves, Casey Kroepsch and Allison Simpson, you two are kindred and sisters from another mister. Thanks for always having my back and being awesome friends. My parents, sister, cousins and Aunt Linda, thank you for the lifelong support and love to shape me into the person I am today.

Angela Santello. A. My bestie. My ride or die. My no-questions-asked, where's-the-shovel, when-you-die-the-first-thing-I'll-do-is-dip-your-computer-into-acid best friend on the planet. No words are enough to describe my love, gratitude and happiness that you are in my life. Thanks for reading my words, telling me needs fixing, and overall being a badass. You are the BEST bestie.

All of YOU reading! An author is nothing without readers, and I am eternally thankful for each and every one of you. Thank you, thank you, thank you for reading and supporting me!

Lastly, to my children and my husband. Without you three, my life would cease to have meaning. I love you more than all the words that have ever been spoken, written or thought combined together. Your love, support, snuggles and laughter are everything. Thank you forever.

# Chapter One

The burst of crisp air lifted the hairs on the nape of Bridget's neck. She glanced toward the opening door as the bell above it chimed, and smiled out of habit. She froze her muscles in place as an old schoolmate who used to tease her walked in. "Hey, Julie. What brings you in today?" She knit her fingers together to keep from fidgeting.

Julie beelined her way. "Bridget! I'm glad it's you here today. Not that your gran isn't lovely, it's just that I'm hoping you can help me. You did assist me that one other time."

As if she could forget Julie wanting a love potion from her. She fought the urge to roll her eyes. Instead, Bridget tucked her dark curls behind one ear. "Of course, what do you need?"

Julie leaned in closer and glanced around furtively, despite no other customers being present. "Something for nausea," she whispered and touched a palm to her abdomen. "Because…you know."

She sucked in a surprised breath and widened her eyes. "You're pregnant?" Bridget kept her voice soft and cut her eyes over to the door for a split second.

Nodding, Julie beamed. "It's still early and we're going to wait to tell anyone, but the morning sickness is killing me." Her diamond ring glinted in the light as she brushed her bangs to the side. "It's been a rough couple of weeks since I found out. I thought since you had something for attracting Ben, then you might have something now?"

Uncomfortable warmth smoldered in Bridget's chest. "No, no. The lotion I gave you wasn't for attraction. It was for confidence. Lavender for relaxation, ylang-ylang to boost romantic thoughts and rosehips for feminine allure. All combined to give confidence in yourself. A natural inner glow is what attracts someone, not the lotion you put on. Soft skin and smelling good boosts self-assurance. Nothing more." She spun and stepped to the back wall with Julie trailing along.

"Whatever you say." Julie laughed and waved a hand. "All that matters is that you have something to solve my morning sickness problem."

Bridget snagged a tub from the third shelf in front of her then led the way to the left wall and picked up a tin. "Here you go." She held both out. "Lotion to put on pressure points when you're feeling nauseated. Rub it into those spots, and the massage plus the scent should help lessen it."

Julie examined the containers as Bridget continued talking.

"Tea to help keep things at bay. Ginger and lemongrass, plus caffeine-free." They crossed the well-loved dark wood floor over to the ornately carved mahogany counter with an heirloom cash register prominently displayed on it. Beside it rested a small white tablet and credit card reader. An assortment of colored leaves and tiny pumpkins dotted the length of the desk.

As Bridget rang up the items, she flashed a quick smile. "Hopefully these will ease your tummy troubles, but obviously I can't give any guarantees." She shrugged and opened her mouth to apologize, but Julie interrupted.

"Okay, whatever you say. I'll try anything at this point and even if it's just a little relief, I'll take it!" She tapped her card and grabbed the gold-embossed navy paper bag with her goods. "Thank you so much. I knew you'd have what I needed." She stepped back and arched one brow with a colder smile. "You're so magical." Julie turned back and headed out. "After all, you are the town witch!" Julie's laugh vibrated after her exit.

Bridget wanted to protest, but in the pit of her stomach, an icy void opened for a shaky moment. As Julie walked out of view, Bridget wiped her sweaty palms on her jeans and swallowed hard. "Not a witch. Not magical. I just sell herbal stuff. That's it."

Ugh, when would the people of this town learn? They never seemed to mind when they needed her products but wouldn't associate with her outside of the shop. To make herself feel less isolated, she shot off a quick text to her cousin, Becca, to see about grabbing dinner together this week.

Then she shook off her mutterings and anxiety, instead focusing on closing up the shop for the night. A quick sweeping of the floors, restocking gaps on the shelves and closing out the register and Bridget deemed herself ready to head home.

She poked her head out a side door and called up the stairs. "Gran, I'm heading home."

A lined face peeped into the hall. "Night, Bridgie! I'll open up in the morning and see you around midday."

Bridget furrowed her brow. "You sure? I don't mind coming in."

Gran waved her off. "Enjoy your morning. It's not as if I haven't been running this store for almost my entire life."

With a sigh, Bridget relented. There was no arguing when Gran made a decision. Like moving out of their little house together to live above the shop. Apparently, Gran wanted to live out her remaining years without a granddaughter "cramping her style" in case she had any "gentlemen callers." While Bridget couldn't fault her grandmother for wanting a bit of independence after raising two granddaughters, she still felt the sting. And the loneliness of the empty house.

"All right, Gran. I'll bring lunch then. Good night!"

"Night-night, dear."

After locking the front door, Bridget tucked her hand into the pockets of her hunter-green peacoat and walked up the block to the Harvest Street parking garage. The brisk fall wind lifted the heavy mass of long, dark curls from her shoulders. Tension released from her muscles as each step took her from Three Sisters Apothecary. She lifted her face to the evening sunlight, enjoying the warmth. Today had gone well. Sales were decent, the autumn decorations added a fresh breath of vibrancy and the customers were friendly...ish.

A beep from her phone revealed a response from Becca, suggesting Tuesday for dinner at her house. Happiness filled her chest as she smiled and sent back a message agreeing.

With September ushering in the pumpkin patches opening for the season and the leaves starting to turn, more and more tourists were trickling in. The upcoming annual harvest festival in two months would keep those numbers climbing. A grateful breath left her as a red truck rumbled down the road. She glanced at the brown-haired, bearded man inside the cab as he passed, but didn't recognize him. Maybe another tourist? New lumberjack in town for seasonal work?

A mother and child walked in her direction about half a block from her. Without thinking, Bridget lifted the corners of her mouth in greeting, but the woman took one look at her and jerked to halt. Then she tugged her child's hand and they scurried to the other side of the road.

The wind carried the child's voice. "Mommy, is that the witch?"

The woman rushed to quiet her son, but it was too late. Bridget's brief moment of confidence and contentment fizzled and died within her. She pulled the collar of her jacket tighter and tucked her chin into the fabric. Eyes down, she double-timed her steps to get to her car and get home. Alone.

\* \* \* \*

Jack scratched at his beard, still adjusting to having hair on his face, as he drove down the main road in Fallbank. What was he doing in the middle-of-nowhere Oregon again? Oh yeah, investigating whether this local logging company would be the next great acquisition for Thompson Incorporated. He tightened his fingers on the wheel of the red pick-up truck he'd purchased used as part of his "undercover boss" scheme. His grandfather's scheme. The one designed to "help find his path in life." Being groomed to take over the family business didn't count.

"I guess an MBA and landing all those deals for our current companies over the last five years isn't enough," he grumbled as he drove through the quaint downtown. All of the shops had fall-themed window displays and the sidewalks were lined with wooden flower boxes overflowing with chrysanthemums of all colors, with large pumpkins nestled between them. A massive sign stretched across two light poles advertising the "Forty-Third Annual Fallbank Fall Festival" on Halloween this year. Was that what counted as excitement around here? He shook his head. Well, at least this town wasn't completely devoid of any form of entertainment.

Jack had to admit a quieter pace for a few months would be a nice change from the high intensity of the office and hustle of Seattle. A way to reset the nagging sense of restlessness, of life slipping by with only shallow platitudes to show for it. Sure, money could buy a lot, but there was something missing from his life that Jack couldn't name.

The vehicle passed a woman in a dark green coat, then a mother and child duo. The kid waved as he drove by and Jack raised a hand in return. Maybe that was what was missing. Companionship. A relationship with a woman who didn't want him for his money and gilded last name, but for him as a person. As a partner in life. Not that he was going to find that here. He snorted. Nope, he was here to learn the logging business firsthand and see how it fit within the massive holdings of the family business.

Two lefts and one right turn later and his phone had successfully navigated him to the office of Timber

Logging Company. Jack hopped out of his truck and walked in. A tall, lanky guy with glasses met him.

"Hey, I'm Cornelius. You must be Jack?"

Shaking his offered hand, Jack nodded. "That's me. Nice to meet you. Sorry I'm late, traffic getting out of Seattle was even more ridiculous than I expected."

Cornelius laughed. "Well, that's one thing you won't have to worry about here. So, you're the new hire, huh? Ever done logging before?"

Heat crept into his cheeks and Jack found himself grateful for his newly grown beard. "Uh, not really. I've worked construction, though. I'm hoping that will give me something to go off. I'm a quick learner."

Cornelius lifted his eyebrows but didn't show any other surprise. "We'll do our best to keep you alive as long as you do the same for the rest of us."

"I can agree to that." He glanced around at the dated office interior. Linoleum flooring, faux-wood paneling, plain drop ceiling and well-used furniture. No wonder his father was eager about this deal. The business clearly needed an infusion of funds. Except the offices would shift up to Seattle once bought and they would bring their own teams to do the logging. As he looked back at Cornelius, a small stab of guilt hit him in the gut. Jack shook it off. This was business, not personal.

"You have a place to stay, Jack? Need anything to get you settled?" Cornelius nudged his glasses up his nose.

Jack cleared his throat. "I'm staying at the local hotel while I find a place to rent. I've got a couple of leads to check out. I think I'll be set by the weekend."

"Good, good. Let me know if you need any leads or want suggestions for things to do around town. This time of year, the tourist traffic picks up because of the crisp weather and fall celebrations happening in the surrounding area. There's got to be at least two each weekend within a fifty-mile radius. And of course, we have our own at the end of October." He grinned wide. "Fallbank is famous for our festival and lumberjack competition. Some great competitive games we've hosted. The festival boasts the largest turnout in the state for the last ten years since TLC sponsors it in conjunction with the fair." Cornelius waggled his brows. "The ladies love it."

Jack laughed with him and shook his head. "That'll be a sight to see. Who knows, maybe I'll have learned enough to enter a beginners' tournament. Although I'm not on the relationship market at the moment."

Cornelius hummed with a nod. "You have a girlfriend back in Seattle?"

"Nah, just taking a break after the last one." A year-long break, but who was counting?

"I hear you. I must admit, the fawning is nice. A little ego boost is never a bad thing."

"Right. Well, what time should I show up tomorrow? And where?"

Cornelius ran a hand through his sandy-blond hair. "I'd say around eight o'clock and you can meet me here. We usually ride up in teams with the equipment trucks."

"Sounds good." Jack nodded once more. "I'll see you tomorrow then."

"See you."

Back in town, Jack checked into the larger of the two hotels offered in Fallbank and crashed out on the bed. The hard mattress had him rethinking if he should have stayed at one of the multitudes of B&Bs around the area instead. He shook the thought off. He had several rentals to check out in the next two days so he could suck it up until he found a more permanent option.

With that in mind, Jack set an alarm on his phone and closed his eyes. Travel weariness settled in his bones and in no time, he was out.

\* \* \* \*

Bridget yanked at her hair and sighed. She'd been staring at spreadsheets all afternoon in between customers. Grabbing an elastic, she piled her curls into a messy topknot and rolled her head from side to side. The tightness in her neck eased for a moment and she focused back on the numbers in front of her. God, but she hated this part of running the shop. Her sister Sarah was always the one with a head for business. Of course, that was why she thrived in Seattle and why Bridget was here treading to keep her head above water and drowning at the moment. Her family had run this shop in some form or fashion since before the town had been founded and she wasn't about to be the reason it closed now. She'd figure it out.

"How's it going over there?" Gran asked as she dusted shelves across the shop.

Bridget smiled at her. *Brave face, don't let her see anything's wrong. She trusted you to take over, you can do this.*

*Not that you have any choice.*

Bridget winced at the snide voice in her head. True, Sarah had run off to Seattle. Her cousin Becca was still in town, but she ran her own farm, without which, they wouldn't have some of the ingredients to make their products. *So stop being whiny, Bridget.*

Gran had faith in her. So why couldn't she have that for herself? What was wrong with a little confidence?

The bell above the door chimed and she straightened as a cluster of dirty, plaid-wearing men sauntered through the door. A head of sandy hair glinted in the sunlight. Bridget beamed and walked around the counter. "Hey, Cornelius!"

"Hi yourself, little B!" He threw an arm around her shoulders. "How's it going?"

"Same old, same old. You?"

Cornelius released her and walked over to hug Gran. "Can't complain. We've got a new project for the team that'll get us all in fighting shape for the lumberjack competition."

Gran shook her head. "You boys keep yourselves safe. Don't go showing off like a bunch of peacocks."

"Yes, ma'am," Cornelius answered.

"What brings in my favorite pseudo-grandson today?"

The flash of pain across Cornelius' face was so quick most would miss it, but Bridget had known him almost her whole life. He recovered and adjusted his glasses to cover his expression, but Bridget felt the pang in her own chest, too. At one time she'd believed he would be her brother in truth, but that dream had dissipated when Sarah had left town.

Turning away from their conversation, she glanced at the other three guys. Two were in the corner where most of their skincare ointments were grouped and she waved hello to the familiar faces. The third faced the shelves of bath and pampering products with his hands shoved into his pockets. Judging from the tightness in his shoulders, she didn't sense he was welcome to intrusion at the moment. Instead of bothering him, she returned to her stool where her computer and spreadsheets waited. After a few tallies, she picked up her pen to make notes about what products she needed to make more of this weekend.

"You have an error here."

She jumped at the low voice from over her shoulder. Whirling around, she leaned back at the nearness of the man standing there...the very large man.

His grin was sheepish. "Sorry, I thought you heard me walk over. I couldn't resist knowing what had you glowering at the screen."

Sweet buzzing bees, but he was gorgeous. All that thick dark hair and those deep brown eyes coupled with a tall, muscular body whose clothes couldn't seem to find an ounce of softness to emphasize. His tidy beard accented a strong jawline that made her fingers tingle to know the feel of it. Warmth spread across her belly. Plus those eyes...they kept drawing her back in. Velvety soft eyes that were currently squinting a bit in confusion.

"Hi!" Oh, jeez, why did she sound like an overexcited six-year-old? She cleared her throat and tried again. "I mean, hello. I was lost in all of this." She fluttered a hand in the direction of the computer. "Did you need help with something?"

"No, no," he answered. "I just saw that the number you have for jasmine bath salts up here is inverted in this formula at the bottom. It would make it look like you sold more than you had in stock."

"Oh," Bridget said as her cheeks heated. "Thanks." She adjusted the number and the resulting change in numbers had her heart sinking. *Shit.*

"I, um, I don't mean to pry, but you know there are some really great software programs available to help track your books easier than a spreadsheet and notebook." He scratched at his chin.

Who was this dude? What made him think he could waltz into her store that had been in her family for almost two hundred years and tell her how to run things? Such a *guy thing* to do. "Thanks, but I've got it." She crossed her arms over her chest.

He widened his eyes and lifted his palms up. "I'm sorry, that was rude. I had no right to insert myself in what's clearly not my business. I just…never mind. Sorry." He scratched at his beard again with a little more force.

She cocked her head to one side. "Does it itch?"

"Does what itch?"

"Your beard. You've scratched at it a couple of times."

He dropped his hand and gave her a lopsided smile. "Yeah, it's relatively new for me. I haven't gotten used to it yet."

Good grief, that smile with those eyes! She squeezed her thighs together. He was wreaking havoc on her lady parts. What had she been getting at again? His beard? "You should condition it," she said, then tempered her outburst with a smile. "That is, I have a skin and beard conditioner you can rub into it to soften the hair and soothe the skin. Keeps it from getting itchy and irritated."

"Uh, I don't know. I'm not into this sort of thing." He shoved his hands back into his pockets.

"You should try it out," Cornelius said as he and Gran walked up. "Everything here is magic."

Cornelius winked at her and she scowled back. Like she needed another person thinking that kind of stuff around here.

"Did you three meet?" Cornelius looked between them. "Little B and Gran, this is Jack Thompson. Jack, these lovely ladies are Esmerelda Wildes and her granddaughter, Bridget Wildes. Bridge here owns the store."

"It's Gran's store," she responded.

"It is not. You own it now," Gran said proudly.

She gave her grandmother a look of pure sass. "It's the *family* store."

Gran laughed. "Can't argue with that." She turned to Jack. "It's been in business since before the town was founded. We Wildes females ran it out of our homes originally, but then my mother decided to open up a brick-and-mortar storefront and here we are."

*Yes, here we are. Barely breaking even these days despite owning the property.* It shouldn't have been that hard, but it was. Production costs were killing them, even when making most of their items themselves. Packaging, additional ingredients, property taxes...the list went on and it grew each day. Pasting a smile on her face, Bridget yanked her mind back to the present. A quick glance showed Cornelius and one of the others holding her skin-healing salve. "Did you guys want those?"

"It's the only thing that will save our hands from cracking and bleeding during these cold months." Cornelius pushed his jar over to her for scanning.

She checked him out, then the other. She would always be grateful that Cornelius had dragged the other loggers into the store for a steady trickle of business. He knew there was nothing magical about any of the Wildes.

While she bagged the items, Cornelius shoved a tub of her beard conditioner at Jack. "You want this. Trust me."

Jack looked warily at it, as if it might jump up and bite him. "I'm not much for beauty products."

Cornelius and the other two guys cracked up. "Nah, this isn't that kind of thing. Besides, you're pretty enough already. Any prettier and we wouldn't be able to hire you on account of the insurance needed to protect us if something happened to that face of yours."

Jack rolled his eyes at Cornelius' barb, set the item on the counter and reached for his wallet.

Bridget stopped him. "It's on the house. Try it and see what you think. If you hate it, you've lost nothing. If you like it, you know where to get more."

"I can't do that," he protested, but she shook her head.

Laying one palm over his weirdly uncalloused for a lumberjack hand, she let herself get captured by those dark eyes again. Tried and failed to ignore the electric thrill at touching his skin. "I'm not after your money. I help people, that's what I do. If you want my assistance, here I am. If you don't, that's okay, too. No harm, no foul." She shrugged and pulled her arm back. "I don't want anyone uncomfortable because of me."

His answer was soft. "Thanks. I appreciate it." Picking up the jar, he flashed those white teeth at her again.

Mmm, what would those feel like nipping at the sensitive skin just below her ear?

"I'll try this stuff out." Jack nodded to the computer. "Let me know if you want suggestions for software. I could help you, too." He winked.

Her stomach fluttered in response. A wink like his could cause an all-out catfight between women. He turned to join the others waiting by the door and she couldn't help but check out the fit of his jeans over his butt. *Top-shelf keister on this guy.*

She and Gran waved as they departed then Gran spun on her. "Well, wasn't he a dish of a man! You and he'd have such pretty babies." She poked Bridget in the side. "Get on that, girl. Hmm, a tush you could sink your teeth into on that one."

"Gran!" Bridget gasped, a mix of scandalized and amused rushing through her. Her grandmother was definitely not one of those sweet little old ladies who baked cookies and knitted blankets. Well, she did do both of those things, but she did them while making very un-grandmotherly comments. "I'll thank you to stay out of my love life." Or lack thereof.

"Or lack thereof." Gran crossed her arms and smiled like she knew she'd just read Bridget's mind. "You need to stop worrying so much about this store and focus on your life outside of it. That's what matters most. Things fall into place outside the home when the inside is happy."

If only it were so easy. It wasn't as if anyone was beating down her door to woo her. Hell, even a drink at the local bar was asking too much of the men in this town. It didn't help that half of them thought of her as a little sister and the other half thought she was a witch. Come on, if she really were a witch, she'd be able to fold a damn fitted sheet, wouldn't she? No, she was better off focusing on the store and making it as successful as possible. Everything else could wait. Having enough income to keep a roof over her head demanded a top spot on her priority list.

"Sure, Gran. I'll get right on that." Bridget flipped the sign to "closed" then turned back. Her grandmother's expression was unamused. She sighed on the inside. "Really, Gran, I promise I won't say no to any guy who doesn't give off serial killer vibes or isn't old enough to be my father and asks me out. And in the meantime, I'll also focus on making sure the store doesn't close because over two hundred years of Wildes sisters' blood failed with me. Deal?"

Her grandmother narrowed her eyes, but let the discussion go for now. "That's all I ask, dear."

# Chapter Two

Jack walked out of the little shop and peered up at the sign. Three Sisters Apothecary. Interesting name, especially given that it was a grandmother-granddaughter duo now. He shrugged and headed toward Cornelius' truck. He guessed they couldn't have three girls in every generation, but the one his age? Damn, she was hot.

Not like a model or the fake rich girls he was used to seeing, but naturally beautiful. Effortless and very girl-next-door. The kind a guy stupidly wouldn't notice for years, then one day it would be like a punch to the gut, instant shift in blood flow to the south, fingers tingling to learn every dip and curve of her soft body. He wondered how long her hair was when it wasn't piled up. He wanted to see it spread out across his pillows as he kissed every inch of her.

"Hey! Yo, Jack." Cornelius waved a hand in front of his face.

Shit, he'd been caught with his mind completely in the gutter. "Sorry, man. I, uh, was lost in thought."

Cornelius chuckled. "Yeah, I figured that."

"My muscles are going to be screaming at me tomorrow. They're already starting to protest." Jack hoped this would throw him off the direction of what he'd actually been thinking about. Or who, rather.

"That's what has you so distracted?" Cornelius raised an eyebrow. "Uh-huh. If that's how you want to play it, I'll bite. Yeah, you sure as hell are going to be sore tomorrow. Logging is no joke and even doing construction work before won't prepare you for it. I'd take some ibuprofen tonight and get yourself back over to Three Sisters tomorrow. They have this amazing cream that has ginger or lavender or something in it and it'll fix you. Smells good, too. I should've thought of that before we left. But now you have a reason to go back." A grin spread across his face.

"I think I'll stick with regular over-the-counter stuff." He climbed into the truck cab, wincing with each movement.

"Suit yourself." Cornelius navigated the vehicle toward the office, elbow hanging out of the window. "You find place to rent yet or are you still living it up at old Harry's hotel?"

He groaned and shook his head. "None of my leads panned out. The first one had a water leak that will take weeks to fix. Second one got an offer to buy the house outright, and the third was just a bedroom in someone else's house. Who had three kids." Jack scratched at his beard again. Maybe he should try out the cream Bridget had given him. "It's not that I dislike kids, but I don't think I'm ready to live with three of them."

"Can't argue with that. Tell you what, if you don't mind a roommate, I've got space at my place. You'll even get your own bathroom."

"I'd hate to impose," he hedged.

"Don't worry, I'm gonna charge you rent, but at least you won't be at a hotel anymore. I'll even split the cooking with you."

Jack kicked up one corner of his mouth. "Well, if you really don't mind?"

"No problem. I'll text you my address and you can move in whenever you're ready."

\* \* \* \*

A week later, everything hurt a thousand times more. Each movement rippled with agony. Today he'd discovered what a giant yarder machine was. The massive piece of equipment was secured in place at the top of the hill so its giant claw could slide back and forth down multiple cables spread like bicycle spokes in the surrounding two-mile radius to haul felled trees from miles down the mountain back up to the top. Then those logs were piled onto trucks and driven back to town for sale.

As the newbie, he was lucky enough to get to physically run each of the five cables down the two-mile length they needed throughout their section of the mountain and secure them in place. He'd done so much running and chopping and stacking that every movement of his limbs added gasoline to the fire. The only thing that didn't hurt was the lower half of his face. Crazy enough, but that conditioner was amazing. The hair was softer and his skin felt cool and soothed. He was ready to head back to get whatever magical tonic Bridget had to help his body have even a fraction less pain. Plus, if he was being honest, getting another look at her was a bonus.

A tinkling bell announced his presence and he glanced around at the vacant store. Once again, he spotted Bridget at the side of the counter. This time, however, instead of peering at a computer screen, she was lining up labels on a tray of plastic jars in front of her. She sat up and a polite smile crossed her face.

"Hello, again," Jack said as he loitered like an awkward doofus by the door. Her hair was down today and those heavy curls fell halfway down her back. So that was how long it was. He liked it. The spirals were glossy and fell in stunning waves and coils, each with a mind of its own. The overall effect framed her face in a soft embrace before sliding around her shoulders.

"Hey there. You're back." She stood and he let his eyes trace the lithe form of her body.

The leggings and tunic sweater hugged her outline, emphasizing the ripe curves of her breasts and hips. Jack curled his fingers to keep his hands to himself. Jesus, but she was alluring. And he did not need that in his life. Romance only led to what his money could bring to the relationship. No woman had ever wanted him just for him. Why would this one be any different? Of course, he was incognito and hadn't blown his cover so far. She didn't seem to recognize him, but his face was often in magazines and some females were better liars than others. Clearing his throat, he said, "Cornelius told me you might have something for sore muscles?"

She nodded and those curls danced with the movement. "Over here." She gestured and walked to a table on the right. He joined her as she lifted up a pale purple container. "Our Saving Salve Muscle Easer is the one the other loggers swear by."

As Jack took it, their fingers tangled for a few scant seconds. Despite the brief contact, he felt the impact all the way down his spine. His breath stuttered as he stared into her eyes, an emerald green so deep he'd only seen the like when he'd visited Ireland a few years back. The open, rolling hills matched their color exactly. "Irish green."

A line appeared between her delicately arched brows. "Pardon?"

The tips of his ears grew hot and Jack was grateful for the beard he hoped was covering his embarrassed flush. Clearing his throat, he said, "Your eyes. They're the same color as the hills in Ireland."

Now her cheeks tinted a flower petal shade of pink. "Oh."

How was it possible she kept getting lovelier? That sweet flush of hers crept down to her neck and Jack wondered what it would take to get the pink to spread all the way down to her breasts. The resulting vision had his pants becoming uncomfortably tight. "Have you ever been?" He cast about for anything to distract his train of thoughts and the bodily reaction from them. "To Ireland?"

"No." She shook her head. "I've heard it's beautiful, but I don't really have time to take a vacation." She gestured around them. "The shop and all. Makes it hard to get away."

"You don't have other employees?"

"Just Gran and me. Helps keep overhead costs down, you know?"

"But surely you could hire one more person. Didn't Cornelius say you make all of the products for the store, too? Two people can't do all of this."

Her smile turned sardonic. "Oh, but two people can. My cousin Becca helps out, too. She runs a farm that gives us our milk for the goat's milk soap and a lot of the oils we mix in come from plants she grows. She makes some of the products for us. All of us were taught how." Bridget stepped back, her expression shifting into a mask of polite professionalism. "Anyway. Was that all you needed?"

He let the subject go. She didn't owe explanations to a stranger. "I think so. Unless you have anything else that helps aching muscles?"

Nodding at the shelf next to the register, she said, "This chamomile and yarrow root tea might give some additional relief, too. Let it steep for at least four minutes to let the leaves really release their essence."

"I'll do that." He dipped his chin once at her. "That cream for my beard worked wonders. I put it on the first night and like magic, it stopped itching."

"Plants can do a whole lot more than most people realize," she spoke, her words rushed. "Once a day should help keep the hair soft to prevent the irritation from returning. Nothing magic about it."

"Well, all I know is it worked." He paid and his gaze lingered on the full curve of her lower lip. He wondered if she would like it if he captured it between his teeth. Swallowing hard, he grabbed his small bag. "Thanks again, Bridget. I guess I'll see you around."

"Come back any time." She lifted a hand in goodbye. "See you, Jack."

\* \* \* \*

An afternoon off was a luxury Bridget had intended to enjoy, yet she found herself working anyway. Taking advantage of the sunshine that would soon be swept away by usual clouds and drizzle that heralded in October in the Pacific Northwest, she spent the time in her garden. She cut back her sunflowers and roses, weeded the ground between plants, raided her herbs that were ready to be harvested of leaves and seeds and trimmed back her multiple varieties of mint plants to keep those from taking over everything. She had to get more products ready for the store and also the upcoming festival she was showcasing at this weekend. No rest for her.

Instead she ground up plants, pressed leaves for oils and mixed ingredients together to create her most popular lotions, soaps and salves. Then she hung more flowers and plant trimmings in her shed and took down dried ones to create more teas. By the time she was done, the sky was streaked with pinks and oranges as the sun dipped closer to the horizon. As she walked back into her house, the scent of chili and spices tickled her nose. Giving the chili a quick stir, she frowned. Why did she make such a big pot? It was just her and even freezing half of it would be more than enough to get her through the colder months. Maybe...

She walked back outside to her side fence, stepped on a tall rock, and peeked over. "Hey, Cor. Want dinner? I made chili." She'd heard his truck rumble up not long ago and took a chance that he might be relaxing on his back porch. They often chatted through the slats on nice days.

He grinned at her. "I'd never say no to that. Only—"

His back door swung open and Bridget jerked in surprise. Did he have company? Was it a...date?

Jack Thompson stepped out holding two beers and a bottle opener.

"Oh," she squeaked.

Jack looked over at the fence, his own surprise evident on his face. "Uh, hey."

"Hi." She darted her eyes between the two guys. "What're you doing at Cornelius' house? Wait, that was weird and not my business. I'm just going to go back inside." She hopped down from the rock but froze at Cornelius' yelp.

"No way! I'm not passing up homemade dinner. Especially not your chili. We'll be right there, little B!" A scuffling sounded, then Cornelius called, "Jack, grab another beer. We're going next door."

Bridget raced inside, looking around wildly. Did she have socks on the floor or a bra dangling over the back of the couch? It wasn't that she was messy, per se, but living alone meant she could leave her shoes by the couch and not have someone barking at her to pick them up. Scooping up the fuzzy socks that had gotten too warm for her last night, she dashed into her bedroom and threw them in the hamper. A glimpse of herself in the mirror over her vanity had her cringing. Dirt streaked from her temple down across her cheek to her chin and her hair had taken on a crazy, frizzy life of its own. "Yikes," she whispered. A quick splash of water and a ponytail later, she was walking back into the living room as Cornelius opened the door.

He and Jack ambled in as Bridget stood there twisting her fingers together, unable to think of anything to say. No, no, this was not going to happen. She wouldn't be made uncomfortable in her own home. There was no reason to be weird around Cornelius and if Jack was in her house, then he needed to deal. Not her. "Hey, come on in."

They walked in and Jack held out a beer. "Want one?"

"Sure, thanks." She smiled and grabbed the bottle before walking into the kitchen. Bridget dished out the food and set it on the table along with topping options.

Cornelius dug into the food, growling his appreciation, and she couldn't help but laugh. He really was like a big brother. No manners and no attempt at entertaining conversation. Just slouching in the chair and shoveling food into his mouth.

As they settled into the meal, she looked up and caught Jack staring at her. Self-conscious, she wiped her mouth with her napkin and cast around for something to talk about. "So how's work going?"

Cornelius shrugged. "Same old, same old. Ask the new guy."

Jack curled the corners of his lips up. "Hard. Tiring. I'm enjoying it. It's not like anything else I've ever done before."

"What have you done before?"

"Construction, but mostly office work. Nothing exciting."

"Then why do it?"

He paused, spoon mid-way up. "I guess because my family expected it from me. That's what brought me here."

She rested her chin on her hand. "And how do you like it in Fallbank?"

His gaze traced her features and a frisson of heat danced down her spine. He swallowed and licked his lips. "From what I know, I like it. A lot."

Holy hell, was he coming on to her? Right in front of Cornelius? Her entire body grew warm under the intensity of his gaze. How amazing would that concentration feel with his body covering hers? An ache blossomed between her legs. *Calm down, girl*. She was reading too much into all of this. And apparently it had been too long since the last time she'd had sex which was…over three years ago? Wait, what? How had the brief fling she'd had been that long ago? Her vibrator needed her to find a boyfriend more than she did. Poor thing, it was a testament to craftsmanship, given it kept on working hard for her.

"That's good," she croaked. "So what brought you over to Cornelius' house tonight? I didn't mean to crash your bro time."

Cornelius chuckled and pinned her with one of his I-can't-wait-to-see-your-reaction grins. "Jack's my new roommate."

Her spoon slipped from her hand and the clatter against her bowl made her wince. "Oh. So you'll be next door. Living there."

"Yep." Jack's grin would've made her knees tremble if she'd been standing. She was going to live next door to all of this hot man-ness? She'd better watch out or she'd end up falling for him like one of his trees.

Jack was in so much trouble. He was flirting with the girl next door — that he hadn't known lived next door — and his new roommate treated her like a little sister. He needed to get a grip. He was here to do a job, figure out if this logging company was a good investment and go back home to Seattle. Not chase after a woman. Granted, she was one of the most beautiful women he'd ever laid eyes on and her shy nature intrigued him, but still, she wasn't in his plans.

"How long have you two lived next door to each other?"

Cornelius answered, "Pretty much forever. You were what, six or seven when you and Sarah moved here?"

Bridget nodded. "I was seven and Sarah was ten." She flicked her eyes to his. "My sister. She lives in Seattle now. Gran took us in after our parents died. We used to live in Connecticut."

"I'm really sorry." He wanted to reach out and touch her hand, but he couldn't tell if that would be welcome or not.

"It was a long time ago, but thank you." She nudged Cornelius' arm as she got up to clear the table. "Things didn't turn out too terrible."

Jack jumped up and grabbed bowls. "Let me help you."

She shot Cornelius a teasing smile. "Look at that, someone with actual manners. I'd love your assistance, Jack."

A phone rang as Cornelius opened his mouth to respond. "Saved by a call." He got up and walked out onto the porch.

Jack helped carry the dishes over to the sink, grabbing a towel to dry as she hand-washed the items. "Random questions, but I'm curious. You mentioned something about the Wildes sisters, and your last name is the same. How'd that happen?"

Her grin was playful. "We're a very progressive family and always have been. Wildes females don't change their last names if we get married, and we own the store. No men allowed." She winked. "Smash the patriarchy."

Jack threw his head back and laughed. "I love it. That's very cool. And you grew up in this house, huh?"

"I did. Me and Gran and Sarah. It was great. I always loved visiting here when I was a kid. Going with Gran to the store and 'helping.' Chasing around Sarah in the garden out back. Playing with my cousin Becca. When my parents passed, moving out here was the best possible option."

Her arm brushed his and he had to stop himself from leaning closer. She smelled amazing, of earth and lavender and sunshine. He wanted to press his nose into her hair and let the scent wash over him. "And now it's just you here?"

Nodding, she rinsed the last dish and handed it to him. "Sarah went off to U-Dub and never came back. Becca still has her parents' farm where she grew up a few miles outside of town. Then about a year or so ago, Gran decided she wanted to live out her remaining years independent. I think she was giving me space, but I never minded living with her. It didn't cramp my style or prevent me from doing anything."

He quirked his eyebrows. "No? You ever bring anyone home? Must be a helluva cool grandma. I know mine would be gasping and clutching her pearls if I ever sauntered out of my room with a girl I wasn't married to."

Bridget pursed her lips, but he could see the smile hiding underneath. "Okay, you have a point. I never brought anyone home and even staying over at a boyfriend's house was awkward coming home the next day." Her smile faded. "But I miss her. It gets lonely sometimes."

This time he didn't check his instincts and wrapped her into a hug.

She stiffened for a second or two.

He held his breath and hoped he hadn't overstepped. Jack didn't want things to turn weird between them. When she relaxed into him, he exhaled with relief. "We all feel isolated at times. It's okay. And hey, I know we don't know each other well, but I'm just next door if you ever want company."

She let out a shaky laugh and pulled back. "Thanks, Jack. I appreciate it." Color was high in her cheeks and she glanced around the room. "Wow, I sure can make things awkward."

A weird heaviness settled on his chest when she stepped away from him, but he ignored it. "No worries, you didn't make anything weird. I asked and you were honest. That's a rarity these days."

She quirked her brows in question. "Sounds like there's a story there."

"Nothing, really." He shook his head. "People like to tell you what they think you want to hear. Especially in business." No way was he ready to bare his soul on how often people lied to him. Particularly women who wanted a ring and access to his bank account. Thankfully, Cornelius walked back in and saved him.

"What'd I miss?"

Bridget rolled her eyes but smiled at him. "Just all the clean-up. Impeccable timing as always."

"I do what I can. Are you still going to that festival this weekend? Working a booth there?"

"That's the plan. Gran and Becca are manning the shop and I'll go over to the festival. I'm booked almost every weekend this month and in October. 'Tis the season." She shrugged.

"Do you need help?" Even Jack was surprised at his offer. Where had that come from? "Sounds complicated."

Shaking her head, she answered, "No, but thanks. I've done a ton of these before. You get there at the crack of dawn, set up and hope for light rain and heavy crowds instead of heavy rain and light crowds. If all goes as planned, breakdown is quick because you sold everything."

"Oh, all right." Jack needed to get a hold of himself. Why did her rejection sting so much? He barely knew this girl and here he was volunteering to work for free on the weekend then acting like a kicked puppy when she said no. Sure, she was gorgeous and had a hidden depth he didn't think she let many people see, but he didn't want involvement. His stay was temporary. Jack needed to keep that in mind.

"I hate to eat and run, little B, but I'm beat. We have an early morning tomorrow."

"Thanks for the company, Cor. Jack." She glanced his way. "I suppose we'll see each other a lot more frequently."

He nodded and tried not to read too much into the look she gave him. There was not a hungry edge to it. That was just him projecting. "Thanks for dinner. Have a good night."

She called out a goodbye as the door closed and he forced himself not to look back.

# Chapter Three

Bridget was ready to pull her hair out. No matter how hard she tried, she couldn't keep up with the store's spreadsheets. She could track the expenses and sales, which products were purchased, but she still never seemed to have enough to keep pace with the different items. She just couldn't predict what people were going to buy on any given day. Sometimes she'd think she saw a trend for a particular soap and make extra only to have a lotion be the next best seller. Or she'd think a particular lotion would do well at a festival based on the sales from the previous event, but have it sit on her table all day.

And of course, no matter what she did with trying to anticipate sales, it seemed she couldn't get more than barely making ends meet. Maybe she should think about taking out an ad in the local paper again. Although the last time had ended with a group outside with signs about her being a witch. Sales had plummeted for a month. She had to figure something out, but what?

The chime rang and she looked up at Jack entering the shop. Her heart stuttered in her chest. For a woman who'd never found flannel appealing, he sure did look fine in it. The cloth clung to his muscles in a way she found very stimulating. Blinking, she cleared her thoughts. "Hi, what brings you this way?"

He shuffled over to the counter with a smile. "I was checking out the downtown area and thought I'd say hello. And I need more of your beard stuff."

With raised eyebrows, she suppressed her smile and urge to say, "I told you so," to him. Instead, she crossed over to the shelves on the right and grabbed a tub. "Here you go." She held it out to him.

"Thanks. It really does wonders. Even if I skip a day, my skin doesn't itch anymore, but I like how soft my hair feels with it."

She almost reached up to touch his face. Almost. Her hand actually twitched at her side, but she curled her fingers into a fist. "I'm glad it works so well for you."

"What're you working on?" He gestured to her computer and she grimaced.

"Spreadsheets. I just can't seem to keep things in order no matter how hard I try."

He scooted around the counter and glanced at the screen. "Do you want some advice?" The look in his eyes was hesitant.

"I'll take whatever help I can get. I'm at my wit's end at this point." She glanced over her shoulder at the stairs to Gran's apartment. "Honestly, I'm barely making ends meet. I'm not sure how much longer I can keep this store going." Her eyes stung and she swallowed hard at the lump in her throat.

Jack reached over and grasped her hand. "It's going to be okay." His voice was soft and almost undid her. "I know this is hard, but I'm pretty good at this kind of thing. You won't be the reason your family store closes, I promise."

She bit her lower lip to keep it from trembling. Inhaling a deep breath, she nodded. "Okay," she said when she could speak without her voice shaking. "What do you suggest?"

"Well, if I may?" He pointed to her screen and she nodded. Jack angled it toward him and pulled up a web browser. After a moment of typing, he shifted it back to her. "The first thing I'd recommend is downloading this software. It's one that's good for tracking business expenses and sales and doesn't cost a crazy amount. This will help you track your outgoing payments, track invoices and bills, see sales figures. It can even help you plot trends of what products are hot, if there's any seasonality to them, that kind of thing."

"What about between events? Like I had one a couple of weekends ago and I thought since I sold my lavender soap so fast at that festival, the same would happen in St. Helens last Saturday. But it didn't. Instead my lemongrass one flew off the table."

"Did you go to that event in St. Helens last year, too?"

She nodded.

"Then yeah, it might have helped you see what was sold last year and be able to prep for what products to bring this year. Separate towns will draw in different audiences so the hot items might not be the same."

"I hadn't thought about it that way. I guess I should have paid better attention, but I also don't know that I could have teased the information out from my old spreadsheets." She gave him a sheepish smile. "I should have listened to your advice earlier. I'm sorry I didn't."

Shrugging, Jack smiled back. "You didn't know me back then. I was being presumptuous. I'm not offended." He blew out a breath. "Now, let's look at your revenue sources. What do you do besides the shop and festivals?"

She drew her brows together. "What do you mean? I make all the products myself to cut down on expenses."

"No, do you sell anywhere else? What about a website? You could ship products all over the country."

"Well, I could, but that would mean having customers all over the country. I don't have those."

"What about people who come to those festivals? They don't live nearby and maybe they want a refill once they run out of what they purchased at your booth. And maybe they have friends they rave to about Three Sisters' lotion. And you could hand out cards at these events with your website and store address on it. People are willing to go the distance when it's something they love."

"So now I need to have a website, too? I don't even know where to start with that. Aren't those expensive to create and maintain?"

"That depends. You can design a simple site on your own. There are websites specifically for that. Or you can hire a designer and have them put something together and help maintain it for you. Since you're just starting out, I would go with the simpler option and then you can always upgrade as things improve on the revenue front."

"Still seems to be daunting, but I guess I can look into it."

"I could come over on Saturday and help you with it?"

She shook her head. "I have a festival in Bacona. I'm booked every Saturday through the end of October."

"How about Sunday, then? We could tinker around with ideas and options? From there you could choose what you like, get it finalized and go live."

"You don't mind?" She felt bad that he was investing all this time helping her today then again on Sunday, too. Surely this wasn't that exciting to him.

Jack shook his head and lifted one side of his mouth into a smile. "I really don't. I enjoy this kind of thing. It's what I did as my main work focus before coming here. I've done more on the administrative side of businesses than physical work like logging. I have to admit as hard as it's been, I like being a lumberjack. It's a nice change of pace and I'm already in way better shape than when I arrived."

"Oh, I think you were plenty in shape when I first saw you. Although I will admit, I can see a bit of a difference." She ran her eyes over his shoulders and chest again. Yeah, that flannel treated him well. It really emphasized the size of him.

A low chuckle met her ears and she flushed. Damn, she hadn't been subtle about that, now had she?

"Well, hot damn. You've been checking me out." He puffed up his chest with a grin.

Bridget smacked his arm then winced. He was *built*. "Oh, stop it. Like you need a bigger ego."

"A man never gets tired of a woman, particularly one as beautiful as you, paying him a compliment. I'm not too proud."

Embarrassed, she ducked around the counter to distract herself from what she'd just said to him and what he'd told her in response. A guy could find a woman attractive—that didn't equate to him wanting to date her. She busied herself by straightening up and getting ready to close the shop for the night. "Sunday would be good. I'll make you dinner as a thank you. Cornelius can come over, too." Grabbing up her coat, she turned back to Jack. "I'm ready to head home. Thanks for all of your advice. I'll download that software tonight to get things changed over."

He joined her and she locked up behind them. "Where are you parked?"

He lifted his chin toward the parking garage ahead. "Up there. You?"

"Same. It's too convenient to not." They started walking and she inhaled the crisp, autumn air. "I love this time of year."

Jack glanced at her and nodded. "It is nice. Although the pumpkin spice overload is a bit much."

She pressed a hand over her heart. "What? You dare mock pumpkin spice? I love it!"

He laughed and stepped closer to her to let another pedestrian go by.

"Witch," the guy snapped as he passed them.

Bridget jolted in surprise and her spirits tumbled to the ground. She hadn't been on guard like she normally was when leaving or arriving at the store. Jack had provided a pleasant distraction and she never would have thought someone would make a comment to her with him next to her.

"Hey, asshole—"

She put a hand on Jack's arm, stopping his words. "Don't. It's not worth it."

"What's wrong with him that he would think it's okay to call you that?"

"I... Who knows? People are weird and rude sometimes. You learn to let things go or the anger will eat you up inside." Bridget shrugged and fiddled with her scarf. She couldn't meet his gaze, afraid he would see she was more upset than she let on. He didn't need to get dragged into her town drama.

"But he can't just say that to you." He glared at the man's retreating back.

She tugged him forward. "He can. And I can choose not to let it get to me. Yes, I'm putting on a braver face because you're with me. But thank you for being here. It does help me not get too in my feelings over this. Come on, don't let a stranger ruin your day. He's going to go around being a jerk for the rest of his life. You don't have to let that impact your evening."

He stared at her for a minute with an intensity that had shivers dancing down her back. "You're right. Spending this afternoon with you was great and that jackass isn't going to destroy that." He set his jaw and glared behind them once more. Then he gestured ahead and walked her to her car.

"See you on Sunday?" she asked. This encounter had left her uncertain of whether he'd want to hang out with her again or not.

He nodded and the tension in her shoulders loosened.

"I'll be there." The smile he flashed sent a giddy wave through her stomach. Goodness, but she needed to get a hold of herself. They were friends and she needed to focus on her business, not dating.

* * * *

The following Sunday, Jack stood sweating outside Bridget's door despite the cool, drizzly weather. Why he was so tied up in knots over helping Bridget out was beyond him. He was a wealthy, attractive, successful businessman who had women throwing themselves in his path to get his attention. He'd been named one of

Seattle's top ten most eligible bachelors, for crying out loud! Not that Bridget knew any of this. She thought he was another lumberjack in town for seasonal work and was more of an average kind of guy. He needed to locate that confidence he normally exuded to keep himself from letting a little crush get out of control.

He wiped his damp palms on his jeans and knocked on the door while plastering his thousand-watt smile on his face as it swung open.

"Whoa," a girl said and held up her hand in front of her eyes. "Dim the pearly whites, dude!" She laughed and winked. "You must be Jack. I'm Becca, Bridget's cousin."

"The one with the farm."

"You've been paying attention. Well done. Come on in, Bridge is just checking the pot roast in the oven. Where's Cornelius?"

"He's coming over closer to dinner time." He stepped in and the scent of delicious herbs and garlic and meat hit him right in the stomach. "Oh, man. That smells amazing." His belly gave a little rumble.

Bridget wandered in and smiled. "Thanks. It's looking good. A few more hours and it'll be perfect."

"A few more hours?" he echoed, lifting his brows halfway up his forehead.

"Low and slow, baby. Low and slow." She giggled and blushed. "Besides, it's only mid-afternoon."

A wide grin crossed his face. He liked her flirty attitude today. Becca snorted and walked into the living room, dropping down on the rug next to the coffee table. Bridget followed and he trailed after.

"We've been working on the site all morning," Bridget said as she sat on the overstuffed couch and turned her laptop toward him.

He was impressed with what they had come up with so far. "This looks good. I like the grayscale with pink accents. It works well with the pictures you've posted." He clicked through the different pages and nodded. "About, products, purchase, contact," he murmured and lifted his eyes. "Where's your calendar or events page?"

"I hadn't thought of that," Bridget said. "That's a really good idea. It'll tell people where I'll be for the festival season and any others."

"I'd add FAQs, too."

"I don't have any frequently asked questions though. At least not yet."

"Sure you do. What do you get asked at the store all the time? What about at the craft fairs? I'm sure people have tons of questions about your products."

"Oh." She sat back. "That makes sense. I guess I do have FAQs." She grabbed the computer and started clicking and typing and muttering to herself.

"She'll be busy for a little while," her cousin said and side-eyed him. "Tell me about yourself." She propped one elbow on her knee and rested her chin on her fist.

He let out a nervous laugh. He wanted to get Bridget's cousin to like him and be on Team Jack. "What do you want to know?"

"Everything," she said flatly.

"Well, I'm new to town, working at the logging company and doing this kind of work for the first time. I've done construction before, but this is another level of pain I've never experienced before. I came from Seattle and my family still lives there."

"Siblings?"

"I have a younger sister. She's married and has twin girls who just turned six years old a few weeks ago." He grinned, thinking about their wild-animal-themed party. Those girls were going to take the world by storm when they grew up and he couldn't wait to watch.

"Why do you look so familiar?"

"Huh?" A slow trickle of low-lying panic dripped through his veins. "I look familiar?"

Becca peered at him. "Yeah." She glanced back at Bridget. "Bridge, doesn't your Jack look familiar?"

Bridget jerked her eyes up with a startled jolt. "What? He's not mine."

But wasn't that a tempting idea? He could get used to being hers to do with as she pleased. Jack was pretty sure he'd be pleased, too.

Becca chuckled. "Whatever. His face is familiar, right?"

Emerald-green eyes framed by outrageous lashes traced his features. His heart pounded with each passing second. "I don't know what you're talking about. Jack looks like Jack."

Inside, he sighed with relief. "Maybe I just have one of those generic faces."

Becca narrowed her eyes and pursed her lips. "Maybe."

Something told him she wasn't buying it, but as long as she didn't recognize him from all the pictures the Seattle paparazzi took, he was happy. Time to change the subject.

"What about you? Tell me about your farm."

Lifting a shoulder, she said, "Not much to tell. I took over the farm from my parents, who've retired to Southern California. The farm has cows and sheep and goats, plus a few different crops. I sell most of it locally and give a fair amount to Gran and Bridget for products for the shop. Oh, and I'm the town lesbian."

He paused. Did she get extra prejudice from the people in town for being gay? "Do you enjoy running a farm? Or did you just feel obligated to take it over because it's your family's?"

"Both. I do enjoy it. I love the animals and the work is rewarding. And there's also a bit of family obligation. It's my dad's family's farm, so it's been around for a while. Not as long as Three Sisters, but almost eighty years."

"Now you get to uphold a double legacy."

She nodded once. "I guess I do."

Bridget turned the laptop around again. "How's this?"

They both looked over the new additions to the website and gave their approval.

"Beautiful job, Bridget," Jack said with a proud smile.

Another flush touched her cheeks, but she returned his expression. "Thank you. I appreciate your nudge to modernize the shop. I needed that."

Warmth blossomed in his chest and if her cousin hadn't been sitting right next to them, he'd have asked her out right then and there. However, Becca was watching, and he didn't let his feelings get the best of him.

\* \* \* \*

Bridget sat in idle happiness as she looked around at her full dining room table. Cornelius had joined their group and dinner had cooked perfectly. The roast was tender enough to fall apart at the slightest touch and the roasted potatoes' and root vegetables' seasoning was perfect. Bridget found the entire day to be one of the best she'd had in a long time.

Her new website had gone live, and that she could share the joy of that moment with friends made it all the sweeter. As they chatted around the table, a small yawn escaped her as the warm food, wine and long weekend caught up with her.

"I think we should head out and let poor little B get some rest," Cornelius announced as he caught her.

"No, no," she protested. "I'm fine. I'm enjoying having company tonight."

Becca stood anyway. "I do need to get home. Animals don't sleep in. Ever." She cast a sly glance at Jack, then turned to Cornelius. "Before I go, can you check something for me with my truck?"

Cornelius blinked at her from behind his black frame glasses. "Huh?"

She yanked at his arm. "Outside. I need your help." She dragged him toward the door. "Bye, Bridge! Talk to you soon."

"Bye." She waved, perplexed by her cousin's abrupt departure and kidnapping of Cornelius.

Then Becca flashed her a quick expression at the last moment. She waggled her brows and tilted her head in Jack's direction.

Thankfully, he wasn't paying attention. Instead he was stacking dishes for her.

"Go for it," Becca mouthed with a wide grin.

Bridget pressed her hands to her heated cheeks and shook her head in disbelief. How could her cousin be so obvious? And besides, Jack wasn't interested in her like that. He'd had plenty of opportunities to ask her out if he had wanted. "I've got the clean-up this time. No big deal."

He cleared his throat. "I guess I should head out then, too."

"Thanks again for all your help with...everything. The new software has been a game changer and I've had a lot fewer headaches over the past few days."

He flashed that smile that made her knees tremble. "That's great, but you're giving me too much credit. I just made a few suggestions."

"Well, I still appreciate it."

Jack stepped closer and she looked up at him with wide eyes. Would she ever get over how handsome he was? For a second he leaned in her direction, but then he scrunched and crinkled up his face. What the—

He whirled to the side, threw his arm over his nose and let out a thundering sneeze.

"Holy wow!" She yelped. "That was the loudest sneeze ever. Are you okay?"

Nodding, he rubbed the tip of his nose on his sleeve and lowered his arm. "Yeah, sorry about that." The edges of his ears turned red.

She chuckled. "No problem. I was wondering if I smelled funny or something when you squished your face up like that. I guess not. Or maybe yes given your reaction."

An awkward laugh escaped him. "Definitely not you. Just me. Always playing it cool." Jack rubbed the back of his neck. "Anyway, thanks again for dinner. I'll see you around."

"Good night," she said as they walked to the door. As it shut behind him, she sighed. So much for thinking he was into her.

# Chapter Four

As Bridget hauled herself out of bed the next Saturday, she thanked her previous self for having packed the car the night before to save time this morning. This week had been long with extra hours spent building her stock for the festival in Spitzenberg and keeping the store shelves full. They couldn't afford to have someone walk in and not be able to find what they wanted. At least today would be different from the norm, and with any luck, a booming business day.

After parking, she popped open her collapsible wagon, filling it to capacity with her wares and a foldable display shelf. She dragged it over to her spot and circled back to grab her pop-up tent. Two more trips back to bring her table and chair and she was ready to actually start putting everything together. An hour later, her tent, table and displays were ready for the first festival-goers to come through. She'd gone with an autumn theme and was enjoying her thick, cozy sweater given the chill this morning. Fall was in full force in the Pacific Northwest and she loved it.

A small trickle of attendees started to come through the line of tents. Families, couples, groups of friends. All smiling and excited to try the food and fare, see the crafts, pet the goats and lambs and maybe even get their faces painted. A dull pang throbbed in her chest as she watched them. But that was silly. It wasn't like she didn't have friends—she did. There was Gran, who was pretty much her best friend. And Sarah…who now had her own life off in Seattle. Becca helped with the store and came to dinner a few times a month and had practically been another sister growing up. Plus Bridget had other friends. She just didn't hang out with them a lot. Ever, really.

How had she gotten so far down this rabbit hole of being alone? Sure, the store needed her, but did she need to sacrifice everything in her life for it? Maybe Gran was right. Maybe she did need more in life. A boyfriend might be pushing it, but a night out would be good. She could make room for companionship of some sort.

She bent to pull her phone out of her bag and text Becca to see if she wanted to meet up. Maybe she could ask Serena, too? They used to hang out before Gran took more of a retirement role.

"Hey! Fancy seeing you here."

Bridget jerked upright at Jack's voice. "Um, hi. What are you doing here?"

He kicked up one side of his mouth and shrugged. "Nothing else to do today. I've never been to one of these fall things so I decided to check it out."

"You've never been to a fall festival? Where did you grow up?" Her mind was completely blown by his admission.

"Seattle."

"Seattle?" she parroted. "They have these kinds of events in the city all the time. How could this be your first time?"

"This wasn't exactly my parents' kind of thing, I guess."

A group of four people walked up and began browsing, pulling Bridget's attention away. "Sorry," she mouthed before answering their questions. The group bought three soap bars, one tin of tea and one lotion, which was pretty good for a festival customer purchase. By the time the group had moved on, another pair had walked up and Bridget found herself with a nonstop train of customers for the next hour. At some point, she noticed Jack had wandered off. She couldn't blame him. It couldn't be entertaining to stand there and watch her sell stuff. Still, she missed the eye candy and now that things had calmed down, she craved his conversation.

Sighing, she sat back in her chair, fired off a text to her cousin, then focused on updating her business software, tallying her totals from the morning. Movement caught her attention, and she plastered a smile on her face. "Hi, thanks for checking out the Three Sisters Apothecary booth. Feel free—" She stopped mid-sentence as she realized it wasn't a customer—it was Jack. She laughed. "Sorry, I was a bit distracted for a moment. Are you enjoying the festival?"

He nodded. "I am, actually. I didn't know what to expect, but this place has some cool booths." He lifted a bag. "I even bought stuff."

Bridget rubbed her hands together. "What'd you get?"

Jack flashed a small smile. "Presents for my twin nieces. One really likes elephants and the other's favorite is bears and there was someone who had knitted stuffed animals. I thought they might make a nice surprise. I'll put these in their stockings for Christmas."

Her heart thumped unevenly in her chest. He had wandered around trying to find gifts for his family? A stocking stuffer for his nieces? As if he wasn't hot enough, now she had to add thoughtful and kind to his list of attributes? Boy, was she getting in deep with her crush on him. "That's so sweet." She stood up and her body reminded her that she hadn't had any kind of break and it was after noon. "Uh, I hate to ask, but could you just make sure no one steals anything while I run to the restroom?" A loud rumble erupted from her stomach and she clamped a hand over it.

Jack burst out laughing. "Maybe you should grab some food, too. I can handle things here. Take a break and enjoy yourself a bit."

"Oh, but if anyone wants to purchase—"

"I've got it," Jack reassured her. He waved toward the computer. "I know how to work a Square and I've been told I'm pretty good with people. Go. Take a real break." He winked at her and scooted between her and her chair. Plopping down, he grinned. "It'll be fine, I promise."

With one last glance at him, she scurried off, making a beeline for the port-a-johns first, then to the line of food trucks.

\* \* \* \*

Just after Jack had wrapped up his tenth sale, Bridget walked back into the tent. Her cheeks were rosy and that smile of hers hit him straight in the chest. Every time he thought he'd gotten used to how beautiful she was, he'd look again and find himself blown away once more.

She held up a paper tray. "I come bearing funnel cake. I hope things weren't too crazy for you?"

"No, it was steady, but nothing I couldn't keep up with." He eyed the powdered-sugar-covered fried dough with appreciation. "But I won't say no to funnel cake."

"But will you say yes to sharing?" She held the treat just out of his reach with a teasing light in her eyes.

Laughing, he nodded. "I can agree to that."

With a smile, she set down the tray and leaned her hip against the table. Snagging one of the forks, she speared a section and lifted it to her lips.

He stared at the unconsciously sensual movement of her mouth as she closed her eyes and hummed with pleasure. She peeked her tongue out to capture the lingering sugar and he swallowed back a groan. He wanted to lick away those remnants then kiss her senseless so those little sighs and moans were because of him. He wanted to see what it took to make her scream with ecstasy.

His cock jumped as an eager volunteer. *Down boy*, he reprimanded it. The last thing he wanted was for Bridget to notice his erection in the middle of a family-friendly event. His attraction to her was growing way too fast for his comfort. He needed to put some distance between them.

He cast around for something to talk about. "Did you get a chance to look around?"

She shook her head. "Mostly the food trucks, but those are always my favorite part. I love street food. There's nothing else quite like it. How was the booth? I hope it wasn't too stressful."

"Not at all. Ten sales, I think. All logged in your computer, too."

"You didn't have to do that! And wow, ten sales is great. Maybe I need to have a hot guy manning my booth at all of these events."

A slow grin spread across his face. "You think I'm hot, huh?"

The blush alone was worth teasing her. Damn, the things this woman did to him. Pleasant warmth seeped through his limbs as he watched her skin turn a delicious shade of pink all the way past the edge of her cream-colored sweater.

"I don't—That is, I mean…" She stood and plunked her hands on her hips. "Like you don't know you're gorgeous. You've probably had women and men falling all over themselves to catch your eye."

Laughter bubbled up in his chest. "I will admit to being told I'm easy on the eyes. Although I could say the same for you. It's a wonder you're single."

She looked away and started rearranging items, shifting things around to hide gaps where products had sold. "Not much left, which is great. A handful or so more buyers and I might sell out entirely."

"What will you do with your time if that happens?" Jack pushed aside the disappointment at her evasion about her personal life.

Bridget trailed her fingers across a stack of three soaps. "Maybe a little shopping. Head home early and relax."

An older couple walked into the tent and she turned to give them her attention. She and the woman began an in-depth conversation, joined by a trio of girls who were strolling by. The older man ambled over to where Jack now stood, ready to jump in with assistance if needed.

"That's a lovely young lady you've got there."

Didn't he wish. Shaking his head, Jack replied, "We're just friends. Neighbors, actually. I met her a couple of weeks ago."

The other man grunted. "Better get a move on. A girl that pretty *with* business smarts? Someone will come along and sweep her off her feet."

Bridget glanced at him with a questioning expression while still talking with the women surrounding her. He gave her a smile and nod, letting her know all was well on his side of the tent. "Yeah, but I don't know that she's open to dating. A bit of a tough exterior." Her admission from dinner the other night came to mind. "But I think deep down she's lonely."

"Well, if that's true, then all it could take is the right attention from the right person." The man turned to focus his faded brown eyes on Jack. "And the way I saw her looking at you when we were coming up, she thinks you might be that person. Don't mess that up, son." He clapped a hand on Jack's shoulder. "She hasn't friend-zoned you yet."

Jack laughed with the older man. "I'll take that under advisement, sir."

"Good. Now hand me one of those tubs of good-smelling stuff so I can buy my bride a present and keep myself out of the friend-zone, too."

\* \* \* \*

Sometime around half-past-two, Bridget sold out of items at her little booth. And Jack was still hanging out. She wasn't sure which one made her happier. As the last customer left, she grinned wide and bright. "We sold out! I can't believe it. I even brought more than usual and still sold out."

"Congratulations, then. Today was a pretty good 'light rain and heavy crowds' kind of day, huh?"

"For sure," she agreed. "Thanks for the company, too. It was nice having someone else around for a change." She glanced around and sighed. "I guess I should break this all down and get it to my car." She wondered if she'd have time after to walk the lanes a bit and see what else was being sold. Maybe she could find Christmas gifts, too.

"What needs to be taken down first?" Jack asked.

"Oh, you don't have to stay and help. I've already worked you hard today as it is." As soon as the phrase "worked you hard" flew out of her mouth, her mind went to all the ways she would rather have worked him hard. Mortification poured over her and she wished the ground would open up and swallow her whole.

If he had noticed her unintentional innuendo or resulting embarrassment, Jack didn't let on. "I don't mind at all. Did you really carry all of this out here yourself? The tent and table, too?"

She nodded and started putting decorations back into her plastic bins then untying the Three Sisters Apothecary sign she'd affixed to the front of the table. "It usually takes me several trips back and forth to my car, but I have this foldable wagon that helps a ton."

Covering one of her hands with his, he said, "At least this afternoon you'll have me to help haul things back."

The low, rough edge in his voice did warm, achy things to her body. She wanted to hear him growl dirty, sexy words in her ear as he thrust hard into her. Feel the rumbling vibrations of that voice as her naked breasts pressed against his chest. Hear how he sounded when he groaned her name as he came. And —

Good God, what was happening to her? Clearly her battery-operated boyfriend was not satisfying her needs these days. Exhaling a slow breath to get control over her rioting thoughts and raging hormones, she faked a smile and hoped he couldn't see the hungry desire in her eyes. "Thanks. I'll take you up on that."

Within thirty minutes, her car was packed and her work for the day was done. The festival still had another two hours and Bridget stared at the tents, debating. Go home early, take a bath and relax? Call Serena to see about meeting up for drinks tonight? Or should she finally take the time to meander the festival lanes and see what else happened at these events outside of her booth and the food trucks?

"Come on, let's go walk around." Jack laughed. "I can see it written all over your face that you want to."

"I do, but I also want to go home and relax. Maybe meet up with friends."

"Why not everything? It's only three o'clock. Plenty of time to do all of that. Plus, won't it be relaxing to just be a festival goer instead of a booth saleswoman?"

His smile was infectious, then he held out his hand. She was a total goner. Looking into his eyes, she slid her palm against his. His skin was warm and the slightest bit rough and felt amazing. It had been too long since she'd had the simple joy of holding hands with someone. "Okay, let's go be festivalers."

They walked hand-in-hand back from the vendor parking lot to the open field filled with tents and laughter and scents of street food in the air. Her heart pounded in time with her steps. What was she doing holding hands with Jack? Was this a friend thing he did with all girls, or was this a subtle sign he was interested in her? Bridget wished she weren't crap at things like men and dating. She hadn't the first clue what she wanted in a relationship, let alone what a man wanted.

*Enjoy it*, she told herself. All he'd said that he wanted was for her to relax and have fun. She didn't need to overanalyze the fact that her hand was warm and encased by his larger, rougher one. No reason to think about what that toughened skin would feel like caressing across the softer, feminine parts of her.

She swallowed and pushed those thoughts aside. *Focus on the here and now and have fun, Bridget.* They ambled along the paths, checking out quilters, woodworkers, stonemasons and plenty more homemade body products like hers. With each booth, she let go more and more of her work troubles and embraced the airy delight of the atmosphere surrounding her.

When they passed a face painter, she squealed. "Oh, I want to do this. I haven't gotten my face painted in almost twenty years."

"How old are you?" Jack chuckled. "It can't have been that long."

She stuck her tongue out at him. "I'm twenty-seven and I haven't gotten my face painted since I was eleven? Maybe twelve? Come on." She tugged at his hand.

The saddest part of getting her face painted was that she had to let go of Jack's hand. The loss of his big, warm fingers around hers was visceral. The sparkly, whimsical unicorn on her cheek cheered her spirits. Then Jack sat down on the stool and got a dragon placed high on his cheek above his beard, making her laugh harder than she had in recent memory. When he leaned in and took a selfie of the two of them, her heart stuttered. The scent of fresh-cut wood and eucalyptus wafted over her. She wanted to nuzzle closer and bury her nose in his neck to see if the smell was strongest there. She wanted the fragrance of him on her pillows.

"So, where to next?" she asked as he slid his phone back into his pocket. "Petting zoo?"

"Petting zoo, for sure."

This time they walked close to each other and their hands brushed against each other a time or two, but he didn't reach out for her. Did that mean he hadn't wanted to hold hands in the first place? Was he waiting for her to make the move? Should she—

"Look at that, they even have pet adoptions from an animal shelter."

"Wait, what?" She did a double take. Sure enough, there was a set-up with groups of dogs lounging in a large penned-in area and another spot with a few cats in easy-view kennels. "Oh, how cute!" She beelined for the shelter group with Jack trailing along.

Once there, she knelt by the cats. There was one cage which held a trio of tiny kittens and a second with a larger black cat with one white ear. "Hey there, sweetheart," she cooed. "Can I pet you?" When she glanced at an adoption worker, he gave her the nod to go ahead.

"That's Candle. She's a sweetheart who was found abandoned in a parking lot. She had some pretty significant fleas and skin conditions, but our vet's given her a clean bill of health."

Bridget opened the door and the cat stood, sniffing delicately at her fingertips. With a deep purr, she stretched her two front paws out, setting them on Bridget's shoulders. Then Candle rubbed her head under her chin. "Oh my goodness, her fur is crazy soft!" Tears sprang to Bridget's eyes as the cat continued to cuddle. Scooping her up, she asked, "How old is she?"

"We think she's around two. We've had Candle longer than most cats because she's a black cat and they don't get adopted as easily. People still believe those old superstitions."

Bridget was far too aware of how silly myths and fears hung around. The poor cat wasn't responsible for having black fur and people being dumb. She scratched the top of Candle's head and was rewarded with an extra burst of happy purring. Twisting around, she looked over at Jack with a wide grin. "I think she likes me."

He held up his phone and took another picture of her. "I'd say so." He held out a hand and Candle offered her single white ear for scritches. He obliged and widened his eyes. "Wow, she really is softer than most cats."

The shelter aide smiled. "Yeah, she's got the fluffier, extra-soft hair that most short-haired cats don't have. We call them cats with rabbit fur. Another more common black cat trait."

"How do I adopt her?" Bridget's question surprised even herself. She hadn't been thinking about getting a pet, yet she couldn't imagine letting her go. She peered in Candle's green eyes and knew they were meant to be together. Hadn't she just thought about needing more companionship? Not wanting to feel so alone at home? Candle was the perfect solution.

The aide grabbed a clipboard and pen. "There's some paperwork and the normal rate is a twenty-five-dollar donation, but for black cats we lower that to ten."

"I'll donate a hundred dollars. She's worth way more." She kissed the top of her cat's head then turned to Jack. "Will you hold her while I fill out the paperwork? She can't go back into that cage."

Before Jack could say anything, she plopped Candle into his arms with a grin. His eyes were wide with his eyebrows halfway up his forehead, but he swiftly recovered and cuddled the cat close. To everyone's surprise, Candle stretched and climbed up, lying down across his shoulders and neck. As soon as she had settled on her perch, she blinked at Bridget as if to say she'd made a good choice in men who also doubled as a cat tree.

Bridget cackled at the sight and scrambled for her phone to get a picture before either of them moved. Once she had it, she reached up and patted Candle's head. "Good girl. This won't take me long at all."

Jack couldn't help but think this whole cat thing had escalated quickly. Somehow it had gone from pointing out how nice it was that the local shelter had a booth here to a cat now making his shoulders her new bed. As long as she didn't decide his neck was a scratching post, he supposed he could make this work. The pure elation on Bridget's face made it all worthwhile.

He reached up and rubbed his fingers over the rabbit-like fur and was rewarded with a squawky meow and purr. "Keep your claws to yourself and we'll get along just fine," he murmured.

Bridget finished up the paperwork then relieved him of cat chair duty. "I have so much I need to do. Things to buy for her! A litter box, actual cat litter, food, some toys, maybe a puffy bed to put by a window? Oh, a collar with a name tag! Maybe a green one to match her eyes. How am I even going to get her home in my car?" She spun back to the very amused-looking shelter worker. "Is she microchipped?"

The helper laughed. "Yes, all of our animals get chipped and you can take this kennel with you for transport. On the last page of your copy of the paperwork is a list of common items needed for cats."

"Thank you!" Bridget grinned up at him and Jack forced himself not to lean in and kiss the hell out of her. She was too cute with her giddy happiness, and the way she cuddled her cat stabbed a pang of jealousy through him. He wanted her to snuggle and love all over him the same way. Damn, but he was losing his battle to this crush. Holding hands earlier had felt like a major step forward, but she hadn't reached out again after their face painting. At least he had their selfie together plus the ones he'd taken of her with Candle. He did have to admit, the cat was adorable.

"Why don't you take her home and I'll run by the store on my way back and get those things for you?"

"Jack, that's so nice, but you don't need to do that for me. I can get her settled and then duck out to get everything. I could have Gran or Becca come by to stay with her if I need to."

He shook his head. "I don't mind. I want to do this. Think of it as a congratulations on your new cat gift.

Like cat shower presents instead of baby shower presents."

Her laugh was worth every penny he was about to spend on an animal that wasn't even his. "Okay, if you insist. But don't purchase everything. I need a litter box and some food to get me through tonight. I'll get the rest tomorrow, after she's settled in more."

"Sure," he lied, knowing he was going to buy anything and everything for her cat. If it made her smile at him like she was right now, he'd do whatever she asked. Hell, he'd run naked through this entire festival if she wanted him to. They walked back to the car, Candle protesting pitifully inside the carrier.

Bridget made lots of soothing noises and kept holding the case up to peer into it. "It's okay, baby. I'm still here, we're going home! Just you and me, okay? I promise I'll give you extra scritches and kisses when we get there."

Ugh, the jealousy was killing him. How could he be this envious of a cat? Because he wanted her petting and kissing him all over, that was how. He'd be more than happy to return the favor if she'd let him. They reached her car and after placing the carrier into the passenger side, she threw her arms around him and hugged him tight.

"Thank you again. I can't believe how amazing this day turned out because of you. I never would have wandered the grounds otherwise."

He held her close and once she couldn't see, stuck his nose into her curls and inhaled her flowery, feminine scent. Every part of his body tensed. He wanted to toss her over his shoulder, take her back to his bedroom, and make love to her until they were both too sated and exhausted to move. *How very lumberjack of you, Jack.*

He cleared his throat of the desire clogging it. "I didn't do anything that someone else wouldn't do for you. You're the one with the magic that made today so special."

She stiffened and stepped back, pushing her hair out of her face. "Well, anyway. Thanks. I'll see you back at my house." With that, she turned and went around her car to hop in.

What the hell had he done wrong there? He had paid her a compliment and she had shut down completely. He trudged back to his truck, hunched against the late afternoon chill setting in. He was never going to understand women.

On the way back to Fallbank's general store, he tried to enjoy the scenery around him. Lush, thick Douglas firs with the occasional brightly colored deciduous tree mixed in while the road meandered in long, slow curves helped take his mind off his parting with Bridget. It really was beautiful out here. As much as Seattle pushed for environmentally sustainable businesses and homes and tried to keep nature a part of the city, it had nothing on this little section of Oregon. Here nature was the deity in charge and allowed little pockets of humans to gather together as long as they remembered who was the boss. It reminded Jack of his place within the tapestry of the universe.

Twenty meditative minutes later, he pulled up to the store and jumped out. Jack located the pet aisle easily enough and soon had a cart full of cat supplies. Everything from litter to food dishes to toys to catnip, he had it all. And since he was here, he decided to make a loop for anything else he might need at his place. Though he smiled politely, he couldn't quite shake the feeling that the other shoppers were giving him weird stares for some odd reason. He checked his clothes — and his zipper fly — but everything was in good order. Shaking it off, he lined up to cash out and tried not to engage too much with the flirty checkout cashier who made bizarre cat and dragon jokes. No need to encourage crazy to follow him home.

Then he was parked at his place and hauling the bags with the cat items. He walked over to Bridget's house and rang the bell.

Her guarded expression cracked when she opened the door and burst out laughing.

"Okay, what gives? People looked at me like I was crazy at the store and now you're laughing at me, too."

Bridget sucked in a breath and calmed her laughter. "It's just that you still have that dragon painted on your face!" She broke into giggles all over again. "I can't believe you forgot you had your face painted and walked around town."

A meow sounded from behind her and Jack looked over her shoulder. "Are you mocking me, too? After I bought you all this stuff?"

Bridget backed up and gestured him inside. "I'm sorry, but not really sorry. You have to admit, it's pretty funny. How many grown adult males get their faces painted at all, let alone walk around in stores that way?"

A smile crept across his face and he let go of his laughter. "Okay, I agree, it's hilarious. I'm glad I could give entertainment to the town today." As he set the reusable bags down on her kitchen table, she scooped up Candle and joined him.

"Oh my God, Jack! How much did you buy? I told you not to get everything, just a litter box and some food." She looked at him with wide eyes and his choices were validated. The happiness and surprise and something else. Maybe a little crush? Not love, but like? As in *like* like?

"I might have gotten a little carried away, but I'm invested, too. I kind of feel like we found her together. I'm her… I don't know? Dad? Uncle? Cousin?" He reached out and massaged behind the cat's ears and she stretched her paws to jump over into his arms. Then she leaped up onto his shoulders again. "See?" He grinned and so did she.

"Candle has spoken. She's claimed you for her own. Congratulations, you're a daddy."

A sudden image of her saying those words in an entirely different context filled his mind. The breath in his lungs seized. Holy shit, he wanted that. Wait, *he wanted that*? Kids? With Bridget? What the…no, no way. He barely knew her. It had only been a few weeks. They hadn't even kissed, yet here he was picturing her having their child? He was insane.

What kind of crazy voodoo magic spell was happening to him?

"Um, you know, I think I'm going to head home. I'm suddenly really exhausted." He extracted Candle from his shoulders and set her down.

"Are you okay?" She crinkled her forehead.

The frown on her face almost had him backpedaling, but even that waffling moment reaffirmed his decision to leave. "Yeah, yeah. I'm fine. Tired. It's been a long day and an even longer week. I think you've got whatever you should need here." He waved toward the bags then ran his fingers through his hair. "Good night. I'll see you around."

As he turned to leave, he caught her bewildered expression but he couldn't back down. Not when she'd shaken him so hard with a simple sentence. One he'd prompted her to say in the first place.

Sure, he wanted kids one day. In the future. With someone. Eventually. He was only thirty-one…plenty of time for a family later. His feet carried him swiftly back to Cornelius' house and to his room there. It was just a stupid crush. Nothing more. Focus. Jack needed to focus on the logging and deciding if the business was the right investment. Not playing some lovesick guy chasing after the girl next door.

# Chapter Five

Bridget stared after Jack's hasty departure. What had just happened? She was left confused and trying to sort out what she'd done wrong. They'd been joking around, then poof! He had practically run away. She looked over at Candle. "I guess it's just us tonight." She shrugged and tried to shake off the feeling of loss. After all, she wasn't alone anymore — she had a cat now. And pets were way better than humans anyway. They weren't going to just up and leave without any indication about why. She dove into the bags and set up the litter box and food dishes, placed the cushy pillow bed next to a tall window, tossed a few toys out — which Candle immediately pounced on — gave her a few treats and hid the catnip for another day when it wasn't so close to bedtime. Instinct told her to text "thank you" to Jack, but when she grabbed her phone, she realized she didn't have his number. Bridget resolved to say thanks when she saw him next.

As she curled up that night with a purring ball of fluff cuddled up against her chest, Bridget let out a contented sigh. She wasn't alone. Her cat loved her already. And she didn't have to worry that her cat might think she was a witch. Although...now that she had a familiar, did that make her a witch?

The following evening, a knock on her door had Bridget ushering in her cousin for dinner. "Becca, how are you? It's been days since I heard from you. I was starting to get worried." She hugged her tight then pulled back to examine her cousin's face. Nothing seemed amiss.

"I'm good, Bridge. We had a cow deliver a calf, so that's why I've been staying close to home the past few days. I had to be there for the labor and I knew it was getting close to time. Show me your new cat! I want to meet her in person. The pictures you texted were adorable." Becca tucked her chin-length blonde hair behind one ear as she looked around.

Bridget found Candle curled up on her little pillow by the window and waved Becca over. "She's right here. I'm just going to check on dinner."

After they'd eaten and each had had a couple of glasses of wine, they settled on her living room couch that looked out through the French doors to her garden and the fence to Cornelius' house. Where Jack now lived. And Bridget stared at it constantly.

Becca asked, "What's up with you? You seem distracted. Is it the store?"

Bridget jumped on the topic. She didn't know if she wanted to talk about Jack. "Sorry, Becca. Yeah, the store has been a bit slow and I'm worried. What if I can't keep it open? I feel like I'm always needing to make products and restock inventory, and constantly looking at spreadsheets of numbers to make sure everything adds up. It's exhausting."

"Maybe Gran or I should—"

"No," Bridget interrupted. "Absolutely not. Gran is retired and works part-time for fun and you have your farm to take care of. I appreciate your offer, but you help enough with the ingredients for products and at the store when I'm doing the festival weekends. I'm whining, that's all."

"You're not. You are allowed to feel anxious about this and be stressed and express that. If you need help, just ask. I can be at the shop more or help make the lotions and soaps and teas. You know I know how to do all of that. I grew up in this family, too." She grinned.

Bridget felt a little of the stress fall away from her shoulders. "Thanks, I appreciate your offer. I'll let you know when I need help."

"What else is going on with you? You've glanced over at the fence between you and Cornelius something like four thousand times now. Is it that Jack guy?" She flashed her no-BS look at Bridget. "Is there something going on with you…and Cornelius?"

"Oh my God, no," Bridget shouted. "Ew! I just can't even. Ew, ew, ew. Gross." She shook her head wildly. "It's *not* Cornelius."

Her cousin grinned like a cat with a bird in sight. "So it is about the new logger next door, then?"

Well, she'd walked right into that. "Okay. Yes, I might have a tiny crush on him."

"And? Tell me everything!" Becca sat up and wiggled in glee. "You never talk about guys."

"Fine, but you're going next. We hung out at the event last weekend, and he helped with getting some stuff for Candle. There. End of story."

"Not buying it. What else? Have you two made out yet? I know you must think he's hot."

She put her heated face in her hands. "Yes, I think he's hot. Like, really, really, *really* hot. No, we haven't kissed." She sat up again. "I can't figure out where I stand with him. Sometimes he flirts and looks at me with this heat in his eyes that makes me go all squishy inside."

"I like where this is going!"

"And he showed up at the fall festival in Spitzenberg last weekend. He hung out at the booth for *hours* helping me. Then when we were walking around the other tents, he held my hand. We even got our faces painted together! I can show you." She grabbed for her phone and pulled up the pictures of the two of them with their faces painted. "See?"

Her cousin took the phone and swiped through the photos. "These are adorable! He truly is smoking hot!"

Irritated heat rushed through her. Bridget plucked her phone out of Becca's hands. "Yes, he is and you don't like men. Stop eyeing him like candy."

"Jealous much? I'm a lesbian, not blind. I can appreciate male beauty even if I'd rather not have him in my bed. What gives?"

"I don't know! There're other times when he flips this switch and acts like he can't get out of my sight quick enough. After the festival, he went and bought all this stuff for Candle. When he came here to drop it off, he ran out of here so fast it was like I'd tried to murder him. And I haven't seen him since."

"Did you text him?"

"I don't have his number." She sighed. "Maybe he's not into me like that and thought I was getting the wrong idea. Or someone told him I was the town witch and to stay away. Who knows?"

Becca narrowed her eyes and shook her head. "I don't think so. Not with the face painting and letting your cat perch on his shoulders. The look in his eyes in that photo you took says 'I want you.' I don't know what happened, but he was into you."

A hard lump dropped into Bridget's stomach. "Maybe someone *did* warn him off, then. It wouldn't be the first time I've gotten dumped because of the family reputation."

"If that's the case, then fuck him. He's not worthy of you if he's going to believe some made-up trash from bigoted jerks in town who can't understand women being successful and smart." She pinned Bridget with a look. "But I think you should speak to him first. Maybe whatever was going on had nothing to do with you."

"Maybe."

"Talk to him. At least give him the chance to explain."

"I don't even want a boyfriend. I don't have time for one." She sipped her wine and avoided her cousin's eyes. "I'll talk to him, but that's it. It's not going any further. He'll be my neighbor and we can be friends."

"Uh-huh."

\* \* \* \*

Jack pulled into the drive of his sister's house and sighed. Despite the three-hour drive, he was looking forward to seeing his two nieces for a small getaway. At least he had been excited to see his sister and her family until he'd had that wild thought about having kids of his own. What was that?

His sister and her girls stepped out onto the porch and waved at him. Well, the girls jumped madly while flailing their arms. Enough woolgathering. He'd done enough of that on the drive up. Now he wanted to spend time with his family and take a break from this alter ego he'd taken on. "Hey, Allison!" He hopped out of the car "Hi, Luna and Lily! How're my two favorite girls?" The twins swarmed him, jumping all over him and squealing with glee.

Three hours later, the girls were tucked into bed and it was just Allison, her husband and him. "So how are things in Oregon?" Allison asked. "Are you enjoying being a...lumberjack?"

Jack chuckled and nodded. "I am actually. It was a steep learning curve and I thought my muscles were going give out on me that first week, but then I got this salve stuff and suddenly it wasn't so bad."

"Salve stuff?" his brother-in-law, Hiro asked.

He rubbed the back of his neck as self-consciousness washed over him. "Yeah. There's a store in town that sells different body products. Like lotions and soaps and salves. And teas, Bridget also makes tea blends, too. She imports the leaves and then adds herbs and things to make her own blends."

"Bridget?" Allison lifted her brows.

Now he grew even more uncomfortable and awkward. "She's the woman who owns the store. And she's my neighbor, I guess."

"You guess?" she said and Hiro laughed.

"I'm renting a room from one of the guys I work with there. Cornelius. He's a cool guy and he had an extra room and bathroom. Anyway, Bridget lives next door. She grew up there with her grandma and sister. Her sister's here in Seattle and Gran now lives in an apartment above their store. It's just Bridget there. Oh, and her cat. She adopted Candle last weekend." He dug for his phone in his back pocket and pulled up the photo of Bridget with her cat. "I have a picture of them."

"Whoa!" Allison exclaimed. "Who are you? Where is my brother?"

He blinked at her as heat rushed up the back of his neck. He'd just word-vomited everything about Bridget in way more detail than he'd meant to. Clearly his sister had picked up on his crush. He refused to think of it as anything more. He forced out a clumsy laugh. "I haven't talked to a lot of people beside Cornelius lately. And the loggers at work, but that's business."

Allison snatched his phone. "Ohh, she's gorgeous. I see why you like her." She swiped her finger across the screen and burst out laughing. "Is that you with your *face painted*? You got your face painted for her? Holy cow, you have it bad."

"No, it's not like that. She's a neighbor. A friend."

Both Hiro's and Allison's faces screamed they weren't buying it. Allison stared at him and crossed her arms.

He waited for a beat of silence. "Okay, fine! I like her. She's pretty and smart and sweet. She's got great business sense, even if she doesn't think so. Plus the stuff she makes—it's all homemade. The salves and stuff are things her family's made for centuries. The store has existed for over two hundred years and now she's running it and doing amazing. She doesn't think so, but given she was using freaking spreadsheets and doesn't have a degree in business, she makes smart choices."

"Sounds like you could be a great mentor for her. Or a helpful boyfriend."

"Allison, stop. I'm not there for a girlfriend. Besides, women never want me for me. They want me for my money."

She snorted. "Don't I know it. Do you realize how hard it was for me to find Hiro? It took ages for me to say yes to a date because I thought he only wanted access to the bank accounts."

Hiro leaned in and kissed her cheek. "Worth every agonizing minute."

"How'd he convince you?"

"He came in with a legal contract stating he would pay for every penny of every date and that he wouldn't have a joint bank account or use any family money if we were to get married. It was signed and notarized already."

"A dating pre-nup? That is bizarre."

"It worked," his brother-in-law said with a smug grin. "Even though she burned the contract before our first date, I never let her pay for anything. I'm still paying off my student loans from my own paycheck." He looked at Allison and his features softened. "I was in love before we ever went out. It wasn't about the money."

Allison kissed him. "I never stood a chance against you, Hiro Takahashi." Then she turned back to Jack. "See? Not everyone is a gold-digger. Does this girl even know you've got money? I thought you were keeping that information classified?"

"I am, but that's not the point. I'm not there for a girlfriend. I need to learn about the logging industry and see if this is a good investment."

"And you can have some fun and maybe get laid at the same time! God knows you could use the relaxation. How long has it been since you and Daphne broke up?"

"A year and a half." But who was counting? Apparently, he was. Or maybe he was more aware of how long it had been since he'd made love to a woman since meeting Bridget. She'd become the leading lady of his fantasies, but those left him feeling hollow instead of satisfied in the end.

"So why not ask her out? You clearly like her and those pictures say she feels the same. Go on a date. Kiss her. See what happens. You don't have to marry her, just have fun."

"I'll think about it. That's the best I can promise."

His sister smiled. "That's all I want. Well, I want my big brother to be happy and in love, but I'll take this as a first step."

Hiro's phone rang and he rolled his eyes at the screen. "Work never sleeps and weekends aren't a thing. I'll be back in a few minutes." Leaning over, he pressed his lips to Allison's cheek then answered his phone. "Hey, Evan, what's up?"

Jack glanced at his sister and threw caution to the wind. "Okay, so it's maybe a little more complicated with Bridget than I let on. I've only known her a few weeks and I'm having these insane thoughts about her. Crazy things! Like she made this cat-dad joke—that I started, by the way. It's not like she brought up me being her cat's dad, I did first. And I'm suddenly picturing her having a kid. *Our kid*. What the hell is wrong with me?"

"Oh, Jack. You really do have it bad for her and you don't even know it. That's just love starting to grow. It makes sense. You're lonely even if you won't admit it to yourself. You are thirty-one and maybe at a point in life where you want to get married and start a family. That's not bad. Then this Bridget comes into your life and she obviously strikes a chord with you." She reached over and covered his hand with hers. "Let yourself enjoy this. Maybe it won't work out, but what if it does? What if she's the woman you're meant to spend the rest of your life with? Why does that scare you so much?"

"I don't know. It's fast...and what if she's not interested in me? We come from two different worlds. She's tied to that small town. Her business that's been in her family for over two hundred years. She grew up there, her Gran is there, all of her friends. Everything is tied to it. We have places here in Seattle, New York, Paris and Berlin. Dad's in talks to buy an apartment in Tokyo. We don't do small-town life. She and I are too different for anything to work out."

"Are you? Do you think she's against leaving Fallbank? Would you hate living there so much if she asked?"

Jack shrugged. He didn't have answers for anything.

"I think you might be happier there than you think. Those pictures and the way you've sounded on the phone tell a different story than what you're saying. You like the no traffic and close-knit friends in town. The hard work logging. The question is, do you like it more than your life in Seattle?"

"Like I could just walk away. Come on, Dad would never go for that."

"I'm not saying walk away because there's no way you're doing that. I mean, you could focus on life in Fallbank and adjust for it. The internet is a magical creation that connects people from literally anywhere on the planet. Pretty sure that includes Oregon. It could work."

He sighed. His sister made valid points. Each time he saw Bridget, it was harder and harder to deny his attraction to her. If he were honest with himself, he didn't want to be her friend. He wanted to be her boyfriend. To take her on dates and hold her hand and call and text her for no reason at all. He wanted to kiss the hell out of her and take her to bed and find all the different ways to make come over and over. To hear his name on her lips as she lost herself to the pleasure.

But...love? He hadn't kissed her yet and he was already falling for her? No way. Too fast, too soon. He shook his head. "Like I said, I'll think about it."

"Jack," Allison said in an exasperated tone. "Ask her out, for God's sake. One date! It won't kill you."

"Okay, okay." He threw his hands up. "I'll ask her out. Jeez, sis. Way to bully me."

"That's what little sisters are for. If I can't goad you into something, no one can."

\* \* \* \*

When Bridget still hadn't seen Jack or even Cornelius since the cat incident, she resolved to at least say thank you for all the stuff Jack had purchased. Taking matters into her own hands, she made a few dozen cookies and marched over to Cornelius' house.

A swift knock on the door revealed Cornelius in sweatpants and a sports jersey of some sort with mussed hair and at least a day's worth of stubble on his cheeks.

"Hey, little B! What's up?" He stepped back, inviting her inside.

"Hi, Cornelius. I made cookies to thank Jack for all the cat stuff he bought me. Is he here?"

He shook his head. "No, he went to Seattle yesterday. I think he'll be back sometime this afternoon or tomorrow. I'm more than happy to take the cookies though, I promise to save him a few."

"Sure. Thanks, Cor." She plastered on a smile and held out the plate. "You'll let him know I said thank you?"

"Of course." He drew his brows together and frowned. "Everything okay?"

"Yeah," she said with a touch too much enthusiasm. "I'm good! The store is keeping me busy and I got a cat. She's super sweet. You should come over and meet her sometime."

"Okay. If you're certain everything's all right?"

"Yep. All good with me." She took two steps back down the walkway from the house. "I'll see you later!" She waved and hightailed it back to her house.

# Chapter Six

Jack returned home to find a sparse plate of cookies waiting for him. "These are for me?"

Cornelius grinned and shrugged. "There were more, but there's a dessert tax in this house. Bridget brought them over yesterday to say thank you for all the cat stuff. I couldn't let fresh-made Wildes family cookies sit overnight."

Jack grabbed one. "That good, huh?" He bit into it and moaned. Sweet and chocolate and the slightest hint of salt burst across his tongue as the treat dissolved in his mouth. "Holy shit. This is the best ever."

"Now you know why I took my half." Cornelius laughed. "That family doesn't just have potions and lotions to cure all your ills. They know how to bake, too. Cookies, pies, cakes. You name it, they can make it. Those women are magic."

He took another bite and nodded. "Can't argue with that."

Later that evening, Jack decided to sit out on the back porch and enjoy the fall evening. He took a soda and the few remaining cookies out with him and was happily munching on them when a small black creature leaped over his fence and into the bushes.

"Candle!" Bridget called from the other side of the wood slats. "Come back, sweetheart."

The cat darted through the bushes and clawed her way up an evergreen tree. A few moments of shaking limbs and muffled yowling later and down she climbed. Bridget walked out onto the porch with Cornelius trailing her.

"Candle, what on earth was that?" She knelt down and held out her hand to coax the cat back to her. The small cat strolled up and dropped a mangled chipmunk at Bridget's feet, then sat down and purred at her master. "Oh. Uh, thank you...for the gift? I guess this means I need to make you an indoor-only cat if you're going to murder the wildlife for me."

Cornelius bent and scratched her behind the ears. "She's just doing what she's meant. I don't mind if you take out a chipmunk or two. They can be nuisances."

"No way," Bridget replied and scooped up her cat. "I'm not going to have my cat known as the wildlife killer. Plus, there's plenty of larger predators around. I don't need them to catch her scent and come investigate. I like my gardens and pets un-mauled. Sorry about the..." She gestured to the carnage.

"I'll clean it up," Jack offered.

She flicked her eyes in his direction but looked away quickly. "Thanks. I should probably get this menace back inside my house. Sorry again."

She turned to go, but Jack stopped her. "Thanks for the cookies, but you didn't have to make them." He wanted to test the waters to see if she might be open to a dinner invitation from him.

She shrugged and adjusted her hold on Candle so she could pet the cat easier. "It's no big deal. Thanks again for all of the cat stuff. It was way more than you should have done."

"I didn't mind. I like Candle, too. Anyway, those cookies were basically magic in baked form."

Her expression shuttered and she stepped back. "I have to go. Sorry again, Cor. See you both later."

With that, she pivoted on her heel and left them both standing there. Jack guessed that answered his question of how she was feeling toward him. He was in the doghouse for how he'd left so abruptly last weekend and the baked goods must be a point of politeness on her part. Nothing more.

Damn, how was he going to get back into her good graces? Did he even have a shot at asking her out? Wait a minute, was she this bent out of shape over him leaving that night? He'd spent all day with her, bought a boatload of cat stuff for her, gotten his *face painted* with her, and she was going to hold a grudge over a week later? About him having a freak-out moment and she didn't even know why? He didn't think she was that petty, but he also didn't know her that well. "Enough of this," he muttered and walked through the house and out to hers.

\* \* \* \*

A knock pounded on her door and startled the heck out of Bridget. She yelped and spun around, staring at the offending entryway. The banging sounded again.

"I'm coming," she called out. She grabbed the knob and yanked to see Jack standing outside. "H-hi?"

"Hey, can we talk for a minute?"

She stepped back and waved an arm inward. "Sure."

He followed her into the living room and sat on the opposite end of the couch from her. "Did I do something wrong?"

"Huh?" she said, playing dumb. She knew she'd run out on both him and Cornelius just a minute ago. He probably thought she was still sore over last weekend. And yeah, she couldn't figure out why he had left so suddenly, but so what? He wasn't obligated to her in any way.

"It's just that sometimes when we're talking or hanging things will seem good. Normal. And then you suddenly shut down and close off from me. I don't get it—am I saying something wrong? Because I can't figure it out."

She sighed. "No, it's not you. It's me."

He lifted an eyebrow and tightened his lips into a thin line.

"I mean it. Honestly, it's my own hang-up. I just… It's that I hate anything magic-related. When people refer to what I do or make as magic, it bothers me."

"You hate magic?"

"Yes. When your family has been called witches since the dawn of time, you tend to hate magic. We aren't witches and we aren't magical. We're in tune with nature and what it can do for humans. That's it. We're nature people."

"Oh, shit. Well, I'm sorry. I wasn't meaning anything related to witches when I said those things before. I mean magic like wonder, not like witches. I don't know, are witches bad? You use your knowledge and abilities with plants for good, so why would someone have a problem with you being a good witch?"

She snorted. "Because people are simple-minded assholes." She blinked then backtracked. "I mean, people can be very narrow-minded and only view things as black and white. All witches are bad. They put spells on you to make you do things against your will. They force men to fall in love and stray from their marriages. They help women trap men into relationships. They curse you. They poison you. They call upon evil spirits to hurt you."

Jack held his hands up. "Okay, I underestimated people's assholery." He flashed her a crooked smile. "My bad. And I'm sorry this has been a real-life problem that's plagued your family. That's awful."

She nodded and looked out through the French doors into the twilight. "It started in Salem, Massachusetts for us. After my many-times-over great-grandmother was hanged for being a witch, the daughters began moving farther and farther West. Over time, my ancestors landed here in Oregon and have had the least number of problems. Or maybe we just hit the ocean and couldn't go anywhere else. Either way, we settled here and took our stand.

"Like I said, Three Sisters Apothecary has been a business in some form or fashion for over two hundred years. Mostly out of our homes, but Great-Grandma opened the store at the turn of the twentieth century when she felt people had modernized enough to give it a real go. She chose the name for the three sisters who fled Salem in fear for their lives. It hasn't been easy. There have been very lean years and to this day, more than half the town distrusts us. It's part of why my mom moved away when she went to college. If I had a nickel for every time I've been called a witch, I'd have millions. So yeah, I hate all things magic."

He stared at her with a furrowed brow and sad eyes. "I'm sorry that was your childhood experience. That sucks."

"It really did." Bridget blinked away tears. She was touched by his sincerity and understanding of what her life growing up had been like. "It wasn't always that way. I was born in Connecticut and my parents had regular jobs and we were a normal family. I loved coming to visit. Loved the store and all of the different scents of the products. I helped Gran nonstop when we were here. I danced around the shop and thought it really was magic. I wished that we could move and stay here all the time. Be at the shop all of the time." How horribly fate had twisted her wish. She'd gotten to move out here and work at the store. She'd simply had to sacrifice her parents' lives and now every free moment she had to keep Three Sisters afloat. And taking on the mantle of town witch. Well, no one could say she hadn't gotten what she'd wanted.

Candle jumped up onto the couch and settled onto her lap with a loud, rumbling purr. She choked out a laugh. "I even have a black cat now. I guess I do fit the witch profile."

Jack reached out and covered her hand with his. She looked up and was caught in the snare of his soulful eyes.

"I think there's something magical about you, but you aren't a witch. Not in the traditional black hat, wart on the nose, floats-not-sinks in water kind of way. More of the helps people, is generous and kind, insanely forgiving—especially with all the adversity you faced growing up—is a gardening wonder and an incredibly smart businesswoman."

She felt her cheeks turn pink. "That's very sweet of you, but as you've experienced, I can also hold a grudge pretty well. I have a temper in my own quiet way."

"That I can tell." He laughed.

She stared at him, lost in his handsomeness until her breath froze. He leaned in an inch and she mirrored the movement.

Candle flipped onto her back and grabbed Bridget's wrist with her front paws while kicking up with her back legs.

"Ah!" Bridget cried and the spell was broken. "Hey, fluffball. Now is not the time for playing. Those claws are lethal." Letting out a shaky breath, she scooped up her cat and plopped her onto the floor.

Jack sighed and stood up. "I should go. It's getting late and I don't want to keep you up."

"Right, yeah. I do have to open the shop tomorrow so it will be a bit of an early morning. And you too, I'm sure."

"Loggers do love to get a jump-start on the day."

She walked him to the door and bid him goodbye. After closing the door, she pressed her forehead against it. What was she doing baring her soul to a man who was practically a stranger? She needed to get a grip on herself. Focus on work. The store needed her attention more than anything else.

\* \* \* \*

After another grueling day in the woods felling trees and trying not to get himself killed, Jack headed over to the local hardware store. Last night after the cat had denied him kissing Bridget—he'd been certain she had been leaning in, too...hadn't she?—an idea had popped into his head. Candle needed more play equipment so she would stop using Bridget as a jungle gym. Maybe. Cats were unpredictable little creatures, so who knew? At the very least, this might score him a few more points with Bridget.

After getting supplies, he drove the red pick-up truck he was becoming fonder of every day to go to work. He relied heavily on Cornelius' tool stash and Cornelius' assistance a few times, but over the course of the next few days, Jack built a three-tiered cat tower with a little condo cubbyhole for hiding and sleeping, too. The entire thing was covered in a soft, pale green carpet and he'd wound thick rope up the first foot of the stand as a built-in scratching post. Two higher levels offered platforms for playing or lounging. He thought it would fit well by the huge window next to the doors that led out back. Candle could stare outside or sunbathe while napping.

Finally, he deemed it ready. He and Cornelius carried the unwieldy cat tree down the sidewalk to Bridget's house. When she opened the door, her pleasant smile morphed into amazement. "Holy cow! Where did that come from?" She bounced on her toes and clapped. "I can't believe this! You guys, this is too much!"

Jack couldn't stop his grin at her excitement. It was exactly why he'd gone through all of the trouble to build this. He wanted to see that smile on her face all the time. To give her reasons to feel this giddy happiness. "Should we see what Candle thinks?"

"Oh, yes." She squealed and pulled the door fully open. "Do you need help getting it inside?"

"Nope." Jack grunted as he and Cornelius picked it up again and hauled it inside. "Where should we put it? I was thinking by the window in the living room, but just say the word and we'll get it there."

"That sounds perfect. Candle will love looking out at the birds she wants to kill." She grinned again. "I can't believe this! Where did you find it? Did you have to order it?"

"Jack built it," Cornelius announced with a smug grin.

Bridget turned to him with a gasp and delighted smile on her face. "You built it? For me? I mean, for Candle?"

"For both of you," he answered. "Last time I was here, it seemed like she could use a little extra play space and I thought you might appreciate it, too."

"That's...really sweet of you. Thank you, Jack. It's too much, though. You already bought all the other stuff for her and now this? How much did this cost? I can pay you back."

Cornelius shook his head and waved as he walked out of the house, which Jack appreciated. "You don't have to pay me back for any of this. I wanted to do this. I'm a cat-dad, right?"

A frown crossed her face and she eyed him warily. "I don't know. I wouldn't say that exactly."

"Listen, I know I freaked out a little the other night. And I know I was the one who started the joking. I don't have a good excuse, but I promise not to do that again. I was thinking—"

A blur of black skidded into the room with an accompanying meow. The cat froze in the middle of the two of them, looking back and forth. Then she sauntered up to Bridget like she hadn't just raced in like her tail was on fire. After a quick rub against Bridget's legs, Candle investigated the new addition to the room. First she stretched out and dug her claws into the scratching post, then she jumped onto the edge of the little condo and sniffed inside. Finally, she leaped up the second and third platforms to perch from her new viewing spot. Amusement filled Jack. At least she was already making herself at home with her new toy. He'd been right to go tall. Based on how she enjoyed lounging on his shoulders, he'd thought she might enjoy the height.

He crossed the room and reached up, scratching her behind the ears. Nose to nose with him, Candle purred then climbed onto his shoulders to sit. "See? She's definitely not letting me out of my responsibilities."

A small smile crossed Bridget's lips. "She is taken with you."

God, he hoped the cat wasn't the only one. "I was wondering if—"

Her phone rang. She looked down and said, "Oh, it's my sister. I'd better take this. Sorry."

"No problem. I'll let myself out." He tried not to let his disappointment get the better of him. He'd have another chance to ask her out, even if it wasn't tonight. He placed the cat back onto the tower and waved as she answered.

"See you," she mouthed and lifted her hand in return.

He plodded home in defeat and collapsed in his bed, wondering how to create another opportunity to ask Bridget out.

* * * *

Humming along to the music, Bridget pushed her cart through the grocery store in a more buoyant mood than she'd been in for a while. Having a cat put a spring in her step that she'd missed. Her loneliness abated a little more each time her sweet little black ball of fluff greeted her at home. As she rounded the pet food aisle, she smiled at a passing shopper.

The woman looked around with a frantic expression. "Please don't hex me."

Bridget stopped in her tracks and the good vibe she had going incinerated into ash. "I wouldn't... I don't do tha—"

The woman rushed off, muttering about witches under her breath, before Bridget had a chance to defend herself. Heaving a heavy sigh, she grabbed the cat treats she needed and headed toward the front. No reason to linger where others might say something to her. After completing self-checkout, she made it back to her car where she called her sister, who answered on the second ring.

"Hey, Bridget, how's it going?"

Hearing Sarah's voice caused Bridget's tears to erupt.

"I'm okay." Bridget swiped at her eyes as she navigated home.

"The hell you are. Why are you crying? What's wrong, baby sis?" Sarah's voice soothed Bridget from the car speakers. Somehow her sister had always known how to make Bridget feel better.

"Ugh, it's nothing. Stupid people in this stupid town calling me a stupid witch. I mean, not a *stupid* witch, just a witch. The rest is still stupid."

Sarah laughed softly then sighed. "You need to let yourself get mad for real. I'm sorry, Bridgie. People in

Fallbank suck sometimes. You have to stand up for yourself. I know you get the worst of it."

"Yeah, why is that?" Bridget shoved at her hair then turned left. "Why not you or Becca? What is it about me?"

"I don't know. Maybe it was me being with Cornelius for so long and he's beloved by the town. Becca's the town lesbian and they support her to not look bigoted? Nothing that's a reason for being prejudiced asshats and treating you this way. You have to stop taking this crap from the town."

"I know," Bridget mumbled. "I don't want to alienate myself more. I don't want to put Three Sisters in jeopardy."

"The store isn't everything. You can't let it be your entire life. You deserve more than that," Sarah replied. "I don't mean to sound harsh, but this isn't healthy for you. Maybe you should take a step back from the store. Let someone else take over for a bit. I'm sure Gran wouldn't mind."

"Absolutely not," Bridget said. "Gran earned her retirement and I'm not stealing that from her. Maybe I do need to look at hiring someone else, though. I'll think about it, okay?"

"And get out of the house besides work stuff? Do something fun for once?"

Bridget pulled into her driveway. "I will." She spied Candle's head peering out of the front window at her. "I gotta go. I'm home and need to get my groceries in. Thanks for the pep talk, Sare-Bear."

"Anytime, Bridgie. Love you. Come visit?" she asked.

"Let me get through festival season and I'll come up. Love you, too." After ending the call, she grabbed her reusable bags and walked to her door.

"Hey, Bridget."

Jack's voice startled her and she almost dropped a bag. Glancing over her shoulder at his approach, she smiled. "Hi, Jack. What're you doing out here?"

"Went for a walk to check out the neighborhood more." He shrugged and lifted her shopping from her hands. "Let me help you."

"Thanks," she replied as she opened the door. Candle raced over and meowed at them both. She knelt and scooped the cat up. "Aww, did my baby miss me?" She dropped a kiss between soft, fuzzy ears as she walked into the kitchen.

Jack set the bags on the counter and Candle jumped from Bridget's arms to twine around his legs. Taking his cue, he lifted the cat. She settled on his shoulders and purred. "Nice to know I'm good for something." He laughed and scratched behind one of Candle's ears.

"Oh, I think you might be useful at more than that," Bridget joked as she put away groceries.

"Oh yeah?" He grinned and her tummy swooped at the sight. "Like what?"

Heat prickled over her skin. "I don't know. You're good at sales." She finished putting away everything and shifted to step around him toward the living room.

Jack snagged her waist and the heat from his palm felt searing through her shirt. He tilted his head. "Anything else I might be able to assist you with?"

The low rumble of his voice sent sparks though her body. She ached in the most delicious way. How did he make her forget the world so easily? She'd never responded to anyone this way before. "I'm sure I could think of something." She bit her lip at how needy she sounded.

He dropped his gaze to her mouth then back up at her eyes again. "I've been meaning to ask you something. For a while now, actually."

"Oh?" He was so close she couldn't seem to make her brain function.

He reached out and put his other hand around her too. "Would you want to go out sometime? With me?"

Her breath whooshed out of her. He wanted to go on a date with her? He wanted to go on a date with her! Excitement flooded her limbs and she wanted to dance through the house. *But hold on*, her brain piped up. Should she do this? Didn't she always say she didn't have time to date? Although she had promised Gran she'd say yes if asked out. And everyone else in her life kept telling her not to make the store her only priority.

Plus, Jack was wicked hot and she would be an absolute fool to turn him down. "Yes. I'd love to."

His answering grin was almost blinding and she couldn't help but smile in return.

"Does Thursday work? There's a drive-in theater not far from here. They're playing Halloween-themed films right now. I thought it might be fun?"

She almost melted into a puddle. He'd researched this before asking. He was making the effort not to just take her to the local pub but do something completely different. "That sounds amazing."

"Perfect. I'll pick you up around six. Just in case I don't see you before then." He squeezed her hips and leaned in to press a kiss to her cheek.

Her eyes slid closed as she savored the softness of his lips and the warmth of his breath on her skin. She angled her head to catch his lips—

"*Meow*," Candle squawked and climbed from Jack's shoulders and onto Bridget's chest.

Bridget's arms came up automatically to hold the cat. Laughter bubbled up from both her and Jack. "I guess she wants attention."

Jack stepped back, still chuckling. "Seems like it. I should go, it's getting late."

She walked him to the door, still holding Candle. "Good night. I'll see you Thursday?"

"Wouldn't miss it. Sweet dreams." He winked as he headed out.

Her lady parts sighed in appreciation as she watched him go. After she closed the door behind him, she counted to ten then squealed, causing Candle to jump a foot in the air.

# Chapter Seven

Thursday evening could not come fast enough for Bridget. The entire day dragged at a snail's pace. She couldn't keep still and found herself flitting from one wall to the next, adjusting and filling and tweaking the displays.

After the third time she'd moved the collection of silk autumn leaves on the table holding an array of soaps, Gran smacked her hands on the checkout counter and said, "What is going on with you, Bridget? You are antsier than an eight-year-old on Halloween. Sit down and tell me why."

She turned wide eyes toward Gran. Did she want to tell her about the date with Jack? Gran might decide to start naming grandkids or something and they hadn't even gone out yet. There was a ton of room for things to go wrong between the two of them and she didn't want to crush Gran's daydreams.

"Stop right there." Gran pointed at her with narrowed eyes. "I can see the wheels turning to come up with a cover story. It won't work. Spill it, little girl."

"How did you...?"

"You think after raising you, I don't know when you're trying to cover for something? Oh, please."

A nervous laugh bubbled up from inside Bridget. "Okay, Gran." She crossed over and sat on the second stool behind the counter. "I just didn't want you to get too excited. Keep your expectations in check, all right?"

Gran fixed her with A Look. "I am seventy-three years old. I know what to expect of the world and how to keep my assumptions bound by reality."

"I might have a date tonight." She clasped her hands together. "I mean, not maybe. I do. Have a date. Tonight."

The grin that spread across Gran's face lit up the store despite the gloomy clouds outside. "That's great! Why didn't you want to say anything?"

"It's new. A first date and I don't even know if this will work out or not. I didn't want to get your hopes up."

"Are *your* hopes up?"

Bridget squirmed a little. She hated admitting to her feelings when it came to men. Things hadn't worked out in the past so she never wanted anyone to know how invested she was or wasn't in a relationship. She didn't need fawning over when things inevitably went wrong. And yet... "Yes," she said in a soft voice. "I'm optimistic."

"So you like this boy?" Gran bumped her shoulder against Bridget's.

She couldn't stop her smile. "I do like him. Probably more than I should, given we haven't gone out at all yet." She was surprised Gran hadn't asked who the date was with, but she'd be grateful for small favors.

"It's okay to be excited. Even if it doesn't work out, at least you'll enjoy the ride. There's nothing wrong with savoring the little things in life and not being afraid to take a risk. Love is worth it. If you never venture into dating, you'll never find anyone to spend your life with. And having a partner by your side makes life worthwhile. I miss your Gramps every single day, but I don't regret a moment of our life."

She hugged her grandmother tight. "I miss Gramps, too." He'd passed about ten years ago and it still hurt not to see him each day. He'd been a great male role model for her growing up.

"So, you go on home. Get ready or just get out of my orbit. You are driving me batty with all of your pacing. I'll close up the store today."

"Are you sure? I'll do better at keeping still. I don't want to abandon you."

She waved her away. "Go. Be excited at home and come back ready to tell me details tomorrow. No oversharing because there are still some things I'd rather not have painted in my head—"

"Gran!" she exclaimed and shook her head.

"Oh, stop it. I know what I got up to when I was your age. I'm not naïve. I just don't need to know all about it. But I do want details about the date."

"Okay. I'm going." Bridget hopped up and grabbed her coat, scarf and purse. She pressed a kiss on her grandmother's cheek. "See you tomorrow. Call me if you need me." She made it all the way to the door before Gran called back out.

"Be sure to tell Jack I said I love the new business software when you go out with him tonight."

She spun and sputtered at Gran. "How— Did you— Wha—"

Gran cackled. "I told you I know you. When you said you had a date, there was only one person who came to mind." She winked. "That's a fine-looking man you've got there. Make sure you take full advantage of the evening."

Bridget choked on thin air and shook her head. "Good night, Gran."

\* \* \* \*

The evening was chilly and the sky laden with heavy, gray clouds. The perfect October evening for a drive among the pine trees with a pretty girl. Jack almost skipped over to Bridget's front porch. She answered the door and took his breath away. It wasn't as if she'd dolled herself up for their date, but her hair fell in loose, lush curls around her shoulders. The cream of her cable knit sweater that fell to the tops of her thighs set off the green of her eyes and the leggings she wore clung to her legs and tapered into her knee-high brown boots. She looked like the best fantasy dream brought to life.

"Hey." Hey? That was the best he could come up with? *Hey?* "You look beautiful." There. That was marginally better.

"Thanks. You don't look too bad yourself."

She smiled and it was on the tip of his tongue to blurt out they should forget the drive-in and go make out on the couch instead. The lower half of his body fervently agreed with his train of thought. "W-we should go. Don't want to miss the start of the movie. It looks like it might rain and it's chilly, so I packed a blanket. The good news is that we won't have to get out of the car."

"I'll grab a jacket and be right back. Come in and say hi to Candle. She's on her tower surveying her kingdom."

He laughed and walked over to pet the cat, who purred in appreciation.

Once they were in his truck and on the road, she asked, "Have you seen this movie before? I remember watching it as a kid. I loved the three witches. I wanted to be Winnie, but my sister always teased that I looked like Mary."

"I have seen it. It was a fun movie and my nieces just discovered it last year. My sister was obsessed as a kid. It'll be cool to see it on the big screen again."

"I've never been to a drive-in. This will be my first." She shot a smile in his direction.

His brain short-circuited over her words, interpreting them in the most sexual way possible. Damn, he needed to get his head out of the gutter. "My parents took us a couple of times as a kid. It's a neat experience. I'm glad I get to escort you to your first drive-in."

The truck wound through the curvy roads lined thick with firs that his headlights lit up. They joined the line of cars outside the field to get the tickets for the movie. He found a spot mid-way back from the screen and adjusted the radio to the frequency for the movie broadcast. As the opening scene played, a server knocked on their window to take orders for concessions. A large popcorn and two sodas later, they were comfortably enjoying the nineties teenaged angst playing out before them.

Bridget shivered after about ten minutes and he reached to pull out his blanket. He shook it out, stretched it across the bench seat then scooted closer to her. Bridget in turn did the same. Taking the bull by the horns, he draped his arm across the back and closed the small gap between them. As if she was meant to be there, Bridget nestled right into the crook of his side and rested her head on his shoulder.

"Warm enough?" he murmured.

"This is perfect," she said with a small smile. A low rumble of thunder sounded as the clouds above briefly lit up deep within their thick depths.

His brain, and other parts of his anatomy, screamed at him to kiss her, but he didn't want to rush things. He didn't want to scare her off. The long game was what mattered here. If he sprinted too fast, too soon, it could cost him in the end.

Halfway through the movie, she peeked up at him and when he met her eyes, he couldn't look away. Was he imagining the desire in those depths? She pressed into his side even more and the tip of her tongue licked across her lips.

He swore under his breath, leaned down and kissed her. The moment their lips met, he was done for. She matched his movements and his control snapped. With a strangled groan, he dipped his tongue into her mouth and stroked inside.

She reached up and slid her hands into his hair, holding him tight to her, and angled her body toward him. Jack gripped her hip with one hand and cupped her jaw with the other. Her skin was so soft as he traced the line of her jaw down her neck, and he wanted to follow the path of his fingertips with his lips. Instead, he contented himself with learning all the different nooks and dips of her mouth and seeing how he could elicit those little sighs she was making. He found if he rubbed his tongue along hers, she would hum. If he nipped her lower lip then soothed it with a little suck, she shivered and moaned into his mouth. The air around them grew heated and heavy and the windows fogged at the edges.

Bridget wiggled against him and pressed her breasts against his chest. He dug his fingers into her hip and tugged her to straddle his lap. This new position gave him better access to touch her the way he wanted. He tangled his hands in her hair, marveling at the silkiness. Then he caressed down to brush along her ribs, his thumbs learning the outer curve of her breasts. He forced himself to keep moving down, over the dip of her waist and flare of her hips. He squeezed at the softness there with a grunt of satisfaction.

Bridget responded by circling her hips against his as their mouths remained fused together.

His erection pressed painfully against the zipper of his jeans and with each little rock of her hips, he hardened more. He arched up and was rewarded with a breathy moan from her.

She broke their kiss and rested her forehead against his as she ground down once more. "Oh, my God," she whimpered and captured his mouth again.

Keeping one hand at her hips, he lifted the other to slip beneath her sweater to touch the warm skin of her belly. This girl was so damn near perfect, she might have him acting like a teenager and coming in his pants. He slid his palm up until he encountered the edge of her bra.

*BOOM!*

They both jumped hard at the loud crack of thunder, then the heavens unloaded from above. Rain dumped in heavy sheets, obscuring the view from the front windshield. Despite the fogged windows and their heavy make-out session as dead giveaways that they weren't paying one iota of attention to the movie, they broke apart. With a sinking heart, he knew this would mean the movie would be suspended and everyone would head home. With a downpour like this, no one would be able to have a clear view of the picture.

Pushing her hair away from her face, Bridget laughed nervously. "I guess this means the drive-in is over?"

Cars around them rumbled to life and started pulling out of their parking spots. "Yeah, looks that way. Sorry." He flashed a sheepish grin.

From her seat back on the passenger side of the truck bed, she reached out and laced her hand with his. "Don't be. I'd say that beats any other first drive-in experience I could have imagined."

And, just like that, his spirits danced to life again.

# Chapter Eight

A week later, Bridget was still buzzing from her date with Jack. They'd texted back and forth, but she hadn't seen him again despite living next door to each other. The massive festival she had this weekend had been keeping her busier than ever. She spent her days at the store while her evenings and nights were filled with making and packaging a stockpile of products to sell there. This event usually drew more than double the number of attendees than the typical festivals she attended and Bridget was determined to maximize her profits.

Thankfully she had plenty of extra energy to burn off. She alternated between being mortified that she'd almost begged him to have sex with her right then and there — in his truck! At the drive-in! — and floating on air because holy mother forking shirt balls, Jack kissed like a damn fantasy come true. Their make-out session had left heat simmering in her veins and her nights pulsing with all sorts of vivid dreams that left her aching. Bridget desperately wanted to see him again, but she couldn't afford to get distracted this week. God only knew if she threw absolute caution to the wind and jumped into bed with Jack, she would be utterly useless right now. And this event tomorrow was too important for their cash flow this month for her to not be one-hundred-percent focused.

She should probably give it at least another date or two before hitting the sheets with him. With all of her previous partners, she had tended to be careful about that sort of thing. So what if that had caused a guy or two to call her a prude and dump her? That just proved she'd been right not to go too fast with them.

Still, she couldn't help but imagine what it would be like with Jack. She'd never had such instant physical chemistry with anyone else. With how well he kissed, she was laser-beam focused on what his mouth would feel like between her thighs. How his soft beard would stimulate her most sensitive places. Not to mention, based on the bulge she'd so clearly felt, there was very little chance he'd disappoint down below either.

*Ding-ding!*

The chiming of the bell rattled her thoughts and yanked her back to reality. A woman and a set of adorable identical twin girls entered.

Bridget smiled and waved. "Hello! Welcome to Three Sisters Apothecary. Feel free to look around or if there's anything you're looking for in particular or you have questions, please let me know."

"Thanks," said the woman as one of the girls tugged her toward the colorful soap display. The three of them shopped for twenty minutes and every so often the mother would glance back at Bridget.

A sense of self-consciousness began to creep over her skin. Did she have something on her face? Her sweater? As discreetly as she could, she glanced at her clothes and found nothing amiss. Another check of her reflection in the side window didn't reveal anything out of the ordinary.

Sneaking a peek back at the trio, a sensation of familiarity washed over Bridget. Maybe she had met this woman at a festival before?

"Do you make all of this or do you have a source?" The woman sidled closer while keeping an eye on her twins who were now sniffing the scented candles.

"We make almost everything we sell. We locally grow or produce most of the ingredients needed for the products. My cousin has a farm just outside of town and I have a substantial garden and workshop behind my house."

She stared with wide, round eyes. "That's impressive. I can't imagine taking on all of this on your own. It must be so time-consuming."

"It is and it isn't. I have my cousin and my gran who help, and my family has been doing this for over two hundred years." Bridget shrugged and smiled. "We've got it down to an art at this point. Was there anything you wanted to know more about?"

"Oh, no, that's all right. I'm super impressed, is all. I'm going to wrangle my girls and pick out a few things."

"Sounds good. If you want any suggestions, just ask."

"Well, one of my girls gets these dry, itchy spots on her skin from time to time. Do you have anything for that?"

Bridget stepped from around the counter. "I sure do." They crossed to the left wall of shelves and she bent to pick up two items. "This is a bath soak that has oatmeal and lavender, which will soothe the skin and could help reduce the overall occurrence of the itchy patches. This second one is a lotion that's also heavy in oatmeal with honey to help clear up those kinds of areas."

The woman took both from her. "Perfect, thank you." She turned to the twins. "Lily, Luna, time to go." The girls ran over with their long, black hair flying behind them and big grins across their faces. One was missing her front left tooth while the other had lost her front right.

Something inside Bridget ached. These girls were so darling and her maternal instincts pricked against her organs. Twenty-seven. She was only twenty-seven, for crying out loud. She didn't need kids right now. There were years to go before that wouldn't be an option any longer. *Calm down*, she told her uterus.

As she rang up the items, the door opened again. Bridget looked up and grinned as Jack walked in. She opened her mouth to call out a hello but was interrupted.

"Uncle Jack! Uncle Jack!" The girls screamed and plowed into him.

Wait. Uncle Jack? Then that made... She cut her eyes over to where the other woman stood. This was his sister. No wonder she looked familiar. It was subtle, but the resemblance was there.

"Hey there, girls." Jack hugged them then shot a look at this sister. "I didn't expect to find you all here. I thought you would be at the B&B?"

His gaze caught Bridget's for a moment and a burst of warmth filled her chest. Then he narrowed his eyes at his sister. Oh my God, did his sister know about her? Bridget turned her head back to her.

His sister smiled at Bridget and shrugged. "We thought we'd explore the town a bit. Check out the local shops."

His sister totally knew about her. Bridget swallowed hard, shyness taking hold. That was why the woman had been staring at her.

Jack moved closer. "Hey, Bridget."

"Hi," she squeaked.

He reached out and squeezed her hand. "This is my sister, Allison Thompson-Takahashi, and my nieces Lily and Luna. This is Bridget. She owns the store and lives in the house next door to me."

Lily, the one missing her right front tooth, eyed their joined hands. "Is she your girlfriend?"

Bridget wouldn't be surprised if her cheeks burst into flames. They'd gone on one date and had a hot and heavy make-out session, but that didn't define anything. She wanted to say something, but the words got stuck in her throat.

"What would you think if she was?" he asked.

Luna piped up this time. "Oooh!" She clasped her hands together. "That would be so fun! She makes all of this stuff and she's really pretty."

Jack shot a look at Bridget and lifted one brow. She blinked and gave the tiniest shrug. There was no way she was going to be the one putting a label on whatever this was between them.

He shifted so his fingers interlaced with hers. "Well, that's a relief, because Bridget is my girlfriend."

The girls cheered, making all of them laugh.

Allison said, "I hope you don't mind that we've been poking around. Jack mentioned you had a store and it sounded so great I couldn't resist."

"That's fine," she responded in a soft voice. Damn, she hated being shy. Why couldn't she think of anything better to say? Or at least say it in a more confident manner. "Which B&B are you staying at?"

"The Wild Rose. The pictures online looked gorgeous and Jack told me it seemed nice."

She nodded. "So I hear. I'm sure it's a great choice."

"We should get over there for check-in, but will you be joining us for dinner?"

Her stomach flipped. "Oh, I wish I could, but I can't. I have a huge festival I'm showcasing at tomorrow. I need to pack up my car and get to bed early."

Allison's face fell. "That's too bad. Are you sure?"

She nodded. "It's one of the biggest in the area, aside from the one hosted here in Fallbank at the end of the month. I'm not even sure I'll be able to fit everything in my car, I have so much."

"Why don't you use my truck? I could drive you over and help out tomorrow," Jack offered.

She looked at him with raised brows. "Your sister and nieces are visiting. I couldn't take you away from your family! They came all this way to see you."

Allison shook her head. "It's fine! A festival sounds like a great time anyway. We'll have a lazy morning and meet you guys over there. The girls will love it."

"Really," Jack added, "I want to help. I have something for you anyway." He shot her a grin that made her heart stutter.

"If you're sure? I don't want to derail all of your weekend plans."

"Of course," Allison said. "We didn't have anything set in stone and this will keep the girls entertained." With that, she grabbed up her bag from the counter. "All settled then. We'll see you tomorrow."

Jack leaned in as his sister grabbed her bag from the counter. "I hope this is all okay?" he whispered.

She met his eyes and felt herself melt a little. "Yeah, it is."

He flashed that lopsided grin that did funny things to her insides. "Great. I'll meet you back at your place to load my truck. My sister can pick me up for dinner. See you soon." He pressed a lingering kiss on her cheek. "Girlfriend."

Her blush was uncontrollable and he chuckled as their group headed out. Fanning her face, she vowed to get back at him somehow.

\* \* \* \*

The next morning, Jack was up bright and early and grinning as he drove the thirty minutes to the festival with Bridget's hand in his as she rode next to him. His girlfriend. He had a girlfriend, and the thought made him as giddy as the very first time he'd had one back in sixth grade. Except Bridget was a thousand times better than Sophia de Loughrey. Not a snobby bone in her body and Jack adored that about Bridget. He was tired of fake, self-absorbed women who wanted money and status out of life and nothing more. It was refreshing to find someone down to earth.

"Your sister and nieces seem lovely."

"They are pretty great. I have a lot of friends who aren't close to their siblings. I'm lucky, I guess."

"Yeah, my sister and I used to be super tight, but then she moved to Seattle and it's not the same. We still talk on the phone and text a lot, but the distance makes it challenging."

He squeezed her hand and she leaned her side into his. The road meandered for a few more miles before their turnoff. They parked and Bridget morphed into business mode. He opened the tailgate of the truck and she went straight for the wagon she used to haul things back and forth. He helped fill it to the brim then grabbed the folding table, following her to her designated area.

"You stay here to start setting up and I'll go back to grab the tent and more products." Between the two of them, they had her displays completed within an hour. "I'll go put away the wagon," he said, and took off. He wanted to grab the surprise he had for her that he'd tried so hard to keep hidden. When Jack returned, he cleared his throat to get Bridget to turn around.

She gasped when she did. "Oh my God! Where did that sign come from?"

Grinning, he said, "I made it." Her smile was worth all the work he'd put in to create the replica Three Sisters Apothecary sign she could take to festivals.

"What? You made this? For me?"

For once, Jack was the one blushing. "Yeah. One of the guys from the crew has woodworking tools and he let me borrow them. I did this kind of thing with my grandpa when I was growing up."

"This is amazing. It looks just like the one above the store. Jack! I can't believe this."

"I thought we could stand it up by the front to help draw attention this way." He set up the easel he'd bought and placed the large wooden tablet there. "What do you think?"

She answered by throwing her arms around his neck and kissing the hell out of him. After a startled second, he kissed her back, reveling in the sweet softness of her mouth and the warmth of her body pressed against his. Threading one hand into her hair, he delved his tongue deeper and was rewarded with a humming sigh from her. Before he forgot where he was and how many people were around them, Jack pulled back and brushed his lips against hers once more. "That may have been the best thank you I've ever gotten in my life."

She laughed and stepped back from his arms. "I'm glad I expressed myself well, then. I have no words for this." She turned her gaze on him with such appreciation and happiness, the breath in his lungs froze for a moment. "This is beautiful. I can't thank you enough, Jack."

He shrugged. "You're welcome. I'm glad it made you happy."

She kissed him again, for the space of three heartbeats. "*You* make me happy." She stepped back. "And now I'm going to go find coffee before my admission of feelings gets me all in my head."

He laughed and watched her go. Man, he was so in over his head. They'd technically had a single date, but his heart was already sprinting for a home run. He needed to slow down, but didn't want to. He wanted to go all in and see where this went. He just needed to figure out how this would work with Bridget's entire life here and his in Seattle. But that was doable, right?

\* \* \* \*

Late morning found Jack greeting Allison and the girls, who were dancing with excitement.

"Uncle Jack, did you know there's a petting zoo?"

"There's a whole place with bounce houses!"

"We can get our faces painted! Uncle Jack, are you going to get your face painted?"

"Mommy promised we could each buy one thing!"

Allison smiled indulgently. "All right, girls. Give Uncle Jack a little room to breathe. He isn't used to our high energy, remember?"

A middle-aged couple came in and began examining the displays and Bridget smiled at them. So far sales had gone quite well. Almost a third of the stock was already sold. He watched as she fielded questions from the couple and grinned with pride. She was amazing at this. She knew what to recommend and how to talk about the properties of the ingredients and how they would help with different personal needs.

Allison bumped his shoulder. "She's great, but stop staring so much. You're practically drooling."

The man conversing with Bridget suddenly got in her face. "Are you some kind of witch?"

The unseasonably warm air around them turned icy cold. Every muscle in Jack's body tensed and not in a good way.

"No, sir. I'm not." Her voice was small, but steady. "My family has passed down knowledge of plants and herbs for many generations, that's all."

"So you're all a bunch of witches." The man sneered and his wife glared at Bridget.

"You'll burn in hell for this." The woman crossed her arms and turned on her heel. "We wouldn't dare patronize this kind of evil place."

Lily and Luna cowered by Allison's legs and his sister's face had gone pale. Bridget held her ground, but her eyes shone with unshed tears.

Jack's temper snapped. "You judgmental bastards. How dare you treat her like this. She is brilliant and kind-hearted and wouldn't hurt a fly. I don't know who you think you are, but you can take your self-righteous bigotry and get the hell out of this tent. Don't ever come back."

The couple stormed out and Jack turned to Bridget. "I'm so sorry." He hugged her tight. "Those people were assholes. You are incredible and have a gift to share with the world."

She sniffled and stepped away, wiping at her eyes. "I, ah, just need a second. I'll be fine."

He wrapped an arm around her shoulders again. "I can take over for a bit if you want to take a walk or get some air."

She glanced to where his sister and the girls watched the two of them with sad expressions. "I'm sorry they had to see that. The girls will probably be terrified of me now."

"No, they won't," he said. "I'll talk to them and make sure they understand. No one hates you."

She inhaled a shuddering breath. "Maybe I will go for a quick walk." Bridget stepped around the table. "I'm sorry you saw that. Unfortunately, it happens sometimes."

"Are you really a witch?" Luna asked.

Jack winced as he saw the horror flash across Bridget's face.

"No! I'm not. I just know a lot about plants."

"Oh." Luna frowned. "It would be way cooler if you were a real witch. Then you could zap those mean people!"

Bridget laughed and the sound allowed Jack to exhale. Thank goodness for children's innocence. He couldn't have come up with a better way to break the tension and help them get back to normal.

"I think I'm going to get a hot chocolate. Would you two like to come?"

"Yes!"

"Mommy, please?"

Allison smiled at the girls then at Bridget. "Sure, let's go. Hot chocolate sounds perfect."

Jack watched as Lily grabbed Allison's hand, Luna reached for Bridget's then the two girls linked arms. A sensation of rightness settled over his shoulders as he observed the foursome head out. Yeah, he was a goner for Bridget, but surprisingly, he welcomed these feelings swirling inside him. He just had to hold them back long enough to not scare Bridget off and figure out how to meld their two worlds together.

\* \* \* \*

Despite the horrible moment during the morning, the day ended up being pretty darn great in Bridget's option. She had sold out of products by the close of the festival. Jack's nieces were adorably helpful and brought the happiness back to the festival, while Jack made for the best eye candy. If he kept up with all of the helping at the table and hauling things back and forth, she was going to get spoiled. A small part of her was on alert and anxious. She didn't need to get used to this, because what happened when they broke up?

Wait, why was she assuming they would break up? She was getting way ahead of herself. She yoga-inhaled and pushed the thoughts from her mind. Right now, she needed to enjoy the moment and get to know Jack. And kiss him again. Kissing ranked high on her to-do list. Her hormones were screaming at her for not checking this off the list thirty-seven-thousand times by now.

As they wrapped up breakdown of the booth, Allison wrangled the girls and asked, "So we're having dinner together, right? I'll get the girls cleaned up and meet you two in town?"

"Oh, I don't want to impose on your family time," Bridget said, but Jack interrupted her.

"We'll meet you at the Mexican place on Main Street. They have great tacos that the girls will love." He threaded his hand through hers and squeezed. "Can't wait to spend time with all of the ladies in my life."

Allison laughed. "I'll be sure to leave that out when I talk to Mom next."

Jack grinned sheepishly. "Yeah, maybe I should amend that to *almost* all the ladies in my life. You all keep me running in circles so I can't keep up."

"Go easy on him," Allison told Bridget then waved. The three of them headed off to her car while Bridget climbed into Jack's red truck.

Instead of sitting on the passenger side, she slid over to the middle and was rewarded with a huge smile from Jack. Those eyes of his met hers and her breath stuttered again at how handsome he was. And he was her boyfriend! As in she could kiss him any time she wanted because that was what people did with boyfriends. Wasn't it? Her body lit with heat and she leaned in. Time to test out that theory.

Reaching up, she brushed her hand along the edge of his jaw. His beard was silky and soft as she slid her fingers up and curled them around to delve into the soft hair at the nape of his neck. Her lids dropped closed as she pressed her mouth to his. A sigh escaped her as Jack kissed her back, his lips hungry across hers. Her whole body responded, going from zero to sixty in the span of a few strokes of his tongue. God, she wished they were someplace private. She ached for him in the worst way and needed a release.

After a few more minutes of kissing to the point where she was ready to climb onto his lap, she pulled back.

Jack grunted in protest and cupped her cheek. Resting his forehead against hers, he said, "Damn, honeybee. You kiss better than any other girl I've ever kissed."

She lifted her eyes to his and laughed. "How many girls are on that list?"

He pressed his lips to her once more before settling back. "Doesn't matter, none of them are important anymore." He started up the truck and pulled out of the parking lot. With a sly glance back at her, he said, "But now I'm wishing I'd declined dinner with my sister and was spending my evening alone with you."

The desire in his expression made her shiver. Her heart pounded as she thought of the two of them spending time alone and not in a public place. Heat pooled low in her belly and she swallowed hard. "Maybe after dinner you could come back to my place. We could have a drink or something."

"Yeah," he rasped and flicked his eyes back and forth from the road to her. "That sounds good."

An hour after getting home and changing clothes, she walked over to Cornelius and Jack's place. "Hey, Cornelius," she said as he opened the door. "How's it going?"

"Eh, not great. I heard a rumor today about Timber Lumber Company." He waved her in and she looked around for Jack.

"Where's Jack? What rumor?"

He shoved a hand through the mop of blond hair falling in a wild mess over his forehead. "Jack's on the phone in his room. Word is that some big company is interested in buying us out. I know Paul wants to retire and he's looking for someone to take over TLC."

Shock rocked through her. The logging business wouldn't be a local company anymore? It was one reason people loved Fallbank — they had one of the few locally owned logging businesses left in the state. Logging was the lifeblood of Fallbank and if the company suddenly wasn't around, it could be disastrous for the town. "What does that mean? How will that affect things here?"

The blue of his eyes pierced her down to the marrow and her skin broke out in goosebumps. "It likely means they'll get rid of all of us locals and just bring in crews they already have for the jobs they get. They'd be buying the name and business contacts, but I doubt any of us are keeping our jobs."

"But that would be crushing to all of us!" Her stomach knotted with anxiety. "Logging is how we stay relevant. Fallbank would cease to exist within ten years. Maybe less. How...how are we all going to survive?"

Cornelius shook his head. "I don't know, little B. I really don't."

Footsteps sounded from down the hall and Jack appeared, grinning when he saw her. "Hey, sorry I'm running late. I was talking to my dad."

"That's okay, I understand. Cor and I were just catching up." She glanced at Cornelius with one arched brow to ask if this news had been shared yet. He gave a slight shake of his head. "Anyway. Should we go?"

"Sure." He walked over and kissed her cheek. "You look beautiful, by the way," he murmured in her ear.

A small smile lifted the corners of her lips. She couldn't pretend to have put that much effort into her appearance because today had gone well but was also exhausting. It was nice to know her minimal makeup and cozy sweater dress looked good. "Thanks. You don't look too bad yourself." He wore a simple button-down shirt and jeans, but the way he filled out the shirt with his broad shoulders and chest made her mouth water. And that was before she let her gaze drift down over his thighs and that gorgeously rounded derrière of his. Jack was the epitome of anyone's fantasy lumberjack come to life.

Dinner with Jack, his sister and nieces was entertaining to say the least, but the rumor Cornelius had shared kept swirling around in her head. What would happen to Maria and Manuel who owned this restaurant if the mill closed? What if Three Sisters went bankrupt? How would she ever be able to look Gran in the eyes again if she was the one who let the family business die?

"Bridget?" Jack's voice shook her from her thoughts. "What's wrong? You seem a little distracted tonight."

She hesitated for a second. Cornelius hadn't told her she shouldn't mention this rumor to anyone else, but he also indicated that Jack didn't know yet. A cold pit opened in her stomach. What if Jack found out and left town because of the job insecurity? Would this relationship be over so quickly she never even got to experience the fun honeymoon phase?

His large, warm hand closed over hers. She looked up at him and her tension eased. The depth of feeling she found in his eyes reassured her this wasn't a fleeting thing for him. At least, she hoped.

"I'm sorry. Cornelius told me about a rumor and it's not a good thing." She sucked in a deep breath. "There's a big conglomerate interested in buying out the logging company. It would be devastating for Fallbank and all the people working for the Timber Logging Company. Cornelius said they'd probably let everyone here go and bring in their own workers for jobs when needed. Logging is the only reason this town stays alive. It employs over half the town and the other half thrives because of those jobs. They sponsor the lumberjack competition which helps pull more attendees for the fall festival than any other in the state. We lose TLC and the economy here would shrivel up and die."

Jack and Allison exchanged a look, but it was so fast, Bridget couldn't read too much into it. There was alarm, but also something else. She just couldn't put her finger on it.

"I'm sure it wouldn't be that extreme if someone did buy TLC. A lot of times most people keep their jobs and end up with new management and a new company logo."

"Really?" She wanted so much to believe him, and Jack did have a deep knowledge of businesses. His suggestions for Three Sisters had revolutionized her operations and profits. She couldn't argue that he didn't know his stuff. Which begged the question, why was he working out here as a logger?

He nodded. "I've seen it before. Plus, you never know. Deals like this can be complicated and could fall through at the last minute." He smiled and squeezed her fingers. "It'll be okay."

Relief flowed strong through her limbs. His confidence was infectious and she was choosing to hope he was right. "Thanks, Jack." She kissed his cheek and his nieces squealed with delight.

"Are you going to marry Uncle Jack and be our new aunt?" Luna asked.

Bridget laugh-choked at her audacity. Lune was clearly the bold twin while Lily appeared more contemplative. She knew better than to take that for granted. The quiet ones were always the most surprising.

Jack piped up and saved her. "Bridget and I are pretty new to being girlfriend and boyfriend. Marriage isn't something you rush into, got that?"

The girls nodded solemnly.

Allison jumped in. "I'll take that as my cue to get these girls back to the B&B and into bed. When they're tired, they get punchy and start asking inappropriate questions."

"It wasn't inappropriate," Lily protested and turned her sweet brown eyes on her mother. "They are boyfriend and girlfriend, she kissed him and Uncle Jack made her feel better when she was upset earlier today. Just like you and Daddy. The question was very logical."

Yep, Luna set them on their toes, but Lily was the one who knocked them over.

Allison gave Bridget and Jack a flat stare. "I rest my case. We'll see you before we head out tomorrow? For breakfast or lunch, maybe?"

"Of course," Jack answered. "But not too early, it was a long day."

After they left, Jack scooted closer to her in the booth. "Still up for that drink?"

Even though she'd been bone tired, the thrill from the desire burning his eyes jolted her wide awake. Her whole body tingled with expectation. "Absolutely." She lifted her face up and kissed him. Not wild and frantic, but slow and sensual. She wanted to blow a little life into the embers burning between them so by the time they made it back to her house, they would both go up in flames.

His eyes were glazed when she pulled back. "We should go. Now."

"Mmhmm," she agreed and slid out of the booth. She might have given an extra wiggle of her hips as she stood since she knew they'd be at just about eye level for him.

A low growling noise reached her ears and suddenly his body was pressed chest to thigh up against her back. His big hands gripped her hips as she felt an even bigger bulge press into her bottom.

Teeth nipped her earlobe and she fought not to moan aloud.

"I think there might be some truth to what they say about you. You've bewitched me and damn if I'm not enjoying the hell out of it."

This time a soft, shaky groan passed her lips. She was wet and aching between her thighs. Bridget needed Jack in her bed and she needed him there *now*.

"Let's go, lumberjack." She grabbed his hand and led him out to the truck.

She'd just gotten settled in the cab when her phone rang. A frustrated sigh left her, but she answered anyway.

"Hey, Becca."

# Chapter Nine

Jack should have known when her phone rang that meant the end of their evening. At least from the perspective of ending up just the two of them back at her place, ideally naked and in her bed. Yet his stupid, lust-fueled brain didn't process the ringing as the alarm it should've been. The expression on Bridget's face, on the other hand, hit him like a freight train. A hard rock settled in his stomach as he held his breath.

"Is she all right?" Bridget said. Her voice was so small it hardly filled the truck cabin. She blinked rapidly and her eyes sparkled in the dim light of the streetlamp.

He reached out and slipped his fingers over hers. They trembled beneath him.

"Okay… Okay… I'll be there as soon as I can." She hung up and sniffled. Swiping at her cheeks, she said, "I have to get home. I need to get over to the hospital. Gran had a heart attack."

"I'll take you there now." He started the engine and threw it into drive.

"You don't have to do that." She sucked in a breath and rubbed her palms over her eyes again.

"I want to. You and Gran are important to me. Let me be here for you."

"Yeah. That...that would be good." She sniffled as he rolled through town and toward the highway. "She has to have surgery. They think she might have a blockage. Oh! I need to call my sister."

He held her hand while navigating them to the local hospital and Bridget talked with her sister. When they arrived, she raced out of the truck and he trailed behind as they entered the emergency waiting room.

"I'm Esmerelda Wildes' granddaughter. How is she? Is she in surgery yet?" Bridget wrung her hands as she peppered the front desk with questions.

"Slow down, honeybee." He ran his hands over her shoulders and down her arms. "Give them a chance to answer."

"Bridge! Over here."

They both spun around to find her cousin Becca across the room. Bridget ran over and threw her arms around Becca. "Oh my God, I can't believe I wasn't there for her. I'm a terrible granddaughter."

"She was at her apartment and called nine-one-one. You wouldn't have been able to help anyway, B. Don't beat yourself up for something out of your control."

"Gran should never have moved out. She shouldn't live alone."

Becca leaned back. "You think any of us could have stopped her? This is Gran we're talking about." She looked behind Bridget and saw him standing there and her eyes widened. "Hey, Jack. What're you doing...here?"

He cleared his throat and shuffled closer. "We were having dinner when you called. With my sister and her twins."

Becca lifted her brows halfway up her forehead and Jack almost laughed at her expression. "You" — she turned back to Bridget — "and Bridge were having dinner." She paused for a breath and looked back at him. "With *your family*?"

Bridget stepped back and slid her hand into his. "Yeah, we were. Jack drove us straight here. Sarah's on her way."

The two women launched into a conversation about their family, who still needed to be contacted and who could wait until the morning. All the while, Jack stood there hand-in-hand with Bridget as if he'd done this a thousand times before. As if he was more than her brand-new boyfriend who was fighting off the thin trail of panic in his veins. What was he doing here? He didn't belong with them and it was awkward and uncomfortable for him to even be a bystander to this conversation. Yet at the same time, her small hand in his felt completely right. And when she shifted into his side, he curved an arm around her while she didn't miss a beat in the conversation. It was unsettling to be at odds with himself when he normally wasn't.

Footsteps pounded from behind and they turned. Cornelius skidded to a stop. "Hey, how's Gran? What's the update?"

Becca answered, "We don't know much yet. They did all this imaging stuff and she needs surgery to fix her heart. The doctor hasn't come out again yet." She nodded to the chairs scattered around. "We should sit. I think it's going to be a long night."

They all settled in, Jack and Bridget taking up residence on a small two-seater couch. He wrapped an arm around her, and she nestled her head on his shoulder. They sat that way for hours, alternating between conversing and scrolling on their phones with a small catnap that Bridget took around midnight.

She'd told him to head home at some point during the evening, but while this wasn't exactly how he'd envisioned the night going, Jack was not leaving. Not when he had Bridget cuddled up next to him. Who cared if the couch was uncomfortable? It was totally worth the lack of sleep to have her in his arms and be there when she needed him most. He pressed a kiss to the top of her dark curls and she nuzzled closer in her sleep. Yep, totally worth it.

"Bridget! Becca!" A woman with long blonde hair streaked through the doors and skidded to a stop in front of them.

Bridget jerked awake and jumped up. "Sarah!" She threw her arms around the woman Jack presumed to be her sister. He rose and waited for the two to reunite.

"What's going on with Gran? Why hasn't anyone called me yet?"

"We still haven't gotten any updates or we would've let you know."

Becca grabbed Sarah and hugged her tight. "Glad you're here, cousin."

"Thanks, Becca. Now let's find out what's..." Sarah turned and finally processed his large form standing behind Bridget. "Who are you?" Green eyes a couple of shades darker than Bridget's narrowed at him.

Bridget reached behind her and grasped his hand, tugging him next to her. "This is Jack. I told you about him, remember? The new logger in town?"

"Ohhhh, right." Sarah cut her sister a quick look that was unmistakably "we'll talk later," then glanced back at him. "Hi, Jack. I'm Sarah. Bridge's older sister." She held her hand out and Jack shook it.

"Nice to meet you, Sarah. Wish it was under better circumstances."

She nodded and her blonde hair rippled in soft waves around her shoulders. "Same." She turned to the nurse's desk. "Let's see about an update." Two steps in, she froze and looked to her left. "Corey?" Her voice wasn't the same strong, confident one. This was quieter. More youthful.

"Hey, Sarah." Cornelius waved awkwardly and adjusted his glasses. Jack grimaced for him.

Even without any background, he could feel the tension between them. Clearly they had history together, but what kind was yet to be explained.

"Corey!" She burst into tears and ran to him. He caught her and for a few moments they clung to each other. A few murmured words were exchanged, but too low to be made out.

Jack leaned over to Bridget and whispered, "What's up there?"

She eyed the couple with caution. "They used to date."

Becca snorted. "They were practically engaged."

"No, they weren't," Bridget defended. "It was years ago. High-school sweethearts, that's all."

"Whatever you say..." Becca shot him a look over her shoulder and shook her head. "Engaged," she mouthed.

Okay, then. All he needed to know was they had dated and this was still a touchy subject. Maybe he'd bring it up with Cornelius. Later. When no one else was around.

Sarah stepped back from Cornelius and patted her cheeks dry. After a deep breath, she turned around and aimed for the nurse's desk. They conversed for a minute then Sarah headed back to their little group.

"Gran's still in surgery and they don't know how much longer. They had to wait for the on-call cardiologist to arrive. I guess we just keep hanging out."

Jack sat back on the couch and Bridget joined him.

"You don't have to stay. My sister can drive me home. I'm sure you want to get some sleep and this couch is not exactly comfortable."

He shifted to tuck her into his side. "I'm not going anywhere. I'm fine. There's nowhere else I'd rather be."

"Really?" She wrinkled her forehead.

"Yeah." He brushed his lips across hers and was rewarded with her arm going around his waist as she nestled closer. Leaning his head against the back of the couch, he closed his eyes. Despite this not being the night he'd hoped for, he hadn't lied. His heart was barreling down this relationship path and dragging his head and body along for the ride. Wherever Bridget was, that was where he wanted to be.

\* \* \* \*

Bridget woke groggy, disoriented and with a sharp pain in her neck. She blinked, glancing around the room, then sat up with a jerk. *Hospital. Gran. Heart attack.* The night's events flooded into her mind.

"Hey, you okay?" Jack asked as he sat up.

Her sister, cousin and Cornelius were still sleeping in their requisite chairs. "What time is it?" Bridget's voice was gruff from lack of sleep and her abrupt wake-up call. She glanced at her phone—it was 4:37 a.m. "God, it's so early. Or late. I'm not sure which."

Jack flashed a lopsided smile at her. "Do you need anything? Want me to find some coffee or water or snacks?"

Her heart stuttered in her chest. How had she landed such an amazing boyfriend? A thrill went down her spine as even the thought of him as her boyfriend made her happy. But should she feel this way? Gran was having heart surgery, for crying out loud, and here she was mooning over a guy. An insanely hot guy who did sweet things like make her signs and cat trees and stay all night at the hospital with her and...where had she been going with this train of thought again? Oh, yes. Terrible granddaughter for not focusing completely on her grandmother in the hospital for a heart attack.

"Bridget?" Jack patted her hand. "I think coffee would be good."

She laughed at herself. "Sorry, my brain is a mess right now. Yes, thanks. And some water, too?"

"You got it." He kissed her cheek and headed out in search of the cafeteria.

She stretched and stood, trying not to disturb the others. She paced the length of the room then went to the nurse station. "Hi, I hate to bother you again, but do you have any updates on Esmerelda Wildes?"

"It's no problem, let me check." She typed a few things then smiled. "Looks like she's out of surgery and the doctor should be with you soon."

Relief so strong her legs wobbled flowed through her. "Thank you." She turned and almost ran back to the others. "Becca, Sarah. Gran's out of surgery."

They stirred along with Cornelius.

"That's great news," Sarah said as she stood. Then she plunked her hands on her hips. "Where's Jack? Did he go home?"

Bridget shook her head, annoyed at her sister's assumption. "He's getting coffee and water for us."

The doors behind her opened and a doctor in scrubs and a surgical cap walked through. She pulled the cap off, showing a messy bun of red hair. "I'm Dr. Mayes. Are you the family of Esmerelda Wildes?"

Sarah stepped forward. "Yes, we're her granddaughters. How is she?"

"She's doing very well. The angioplasty and stent surgery went as smooth as it could go. She had two valves that were clogged, but things look otherwise good. She's quite lucky. Ms. Wildes is awake now and in about an hour you can go see her."

"An hour?" Sarah asked. "Why can't we see her now? Why didn't anyone tell us when her surgery was finished?"

Bridget cringed inside. Leave it to Sarah to charge full speed ahead.

Dr. Mayes smiled. "She needs time to not be so disoriented after the anesthesia. Many patients have this done while awake with local anesthetic, but we couldn't this time. That can be hard for someone her age and we want to keep her as calm as possible. We waited until she was awake and not right after surgery finished up because again, we never know how someone will react to the anesthetic. Going under and coming out are two very tense times during surgery.

She'll be here for at least a few days while we monitor her recovery and then she'll have discharge instructions and follow-up appointments, but we'll get to all that later. Right now, the good news is she's doing very well and you can see her soon."

"Thank you so much," Bridget said before Sarah could grill her further. The doctor smiled at them all and went back through the doors. Bridget grabbed Sarah for a hug and reached out to pull Bex in, too. The three of them hugged and Bridget cried a little with alleviation that Gran was okay.

Movement caught her focus and she saw Jack return with a tray full of coffees and a bag of bottled waters. She raced over to him and grabbed the drinks before setting them on a table. "She's okay! Gran is awake and we can see her soon." She threw her arms around Jack and he lifted her up.

"That's fantastic news, honeybee. I'm so happy to hear that."

Her stomach flipped at the pet name. A fuzzy warmth spread in her chest and she grinned against his neck. She'd never had any guy she dated call her anything besides Bridget. Her heart thumped in her chest. She liked it. She liked him. Way more than she should so early on, but there was no stopping the emotional coaster she was on. All she could do was hold on tight and enjoy the ride. "Thanks for being here with me, Jack." She looked up at his brown eyes and her insides went all mushy again. "It means a lot."

She kissed him then because she couldn't not kiss him. Not with all the pleasant, buzzy warmth he created inside her. She stroked her tongue along his once, twice, and forced herself to retreat. This wasn't the time or place for the kind of kisses that heated her blood the way this one was doing.

"You're welcome. Any time you need me, I'm here." He ran a hand over her hair and smiled. "Especially if you kiss me like that each time."

She chuckled and sighed as he lowered her back to the floor. She grabbed a coffee with one hand and laced the fingers on the other one with Jack's. As that first sip danced across her taste buds, she hummed and closed her eyes. Yep, this was exactly what she needed.

A little later a nurse escorted the girls to Gran's room. Bridget's stomach dropped as she took in the sight of Gran, pale and fragile-looking in the hospital bed with tubes and wires hooked up to her.

"Gran," she gasped and rushed over to her side. Tears stung her eyes and she blinked them away. There wasn't time for crying right now. She needed to be strong for Gran. Give her faith that everything would be okay.

Sarah and Becca joined on the other side of the bed.

"How are you feeling? Do you need anything?" Sarah asked.

Gran smiled and gave the finest of head shakes. "I'm just fine, especially with all three of my girls with me now."

Bridget smiled and said, "The doctor said your heart looks good now and you can go home in a few days. You can move back in with me."

"I'll do nothing of the sort." Her grandmother pierced her with a stare. "I do not need you spending all your time either at the shop or taking care of me. I'm perfectly capable of living on my own."

"But, Gran," Sarah protested.

"But nothing," she said and pinned Sarah and Becca with Looks. "Listen to me, girls. I'm a grown woman. The doctor will tell me what I need to do and I'm certain that won't include having to move in with my granddaughters." She crossed her arms and leveled her stare at Bridget. "I will not have you three throwing away opportunities right in front of you just because my health had a little bump."

"A little bump!" Bridget exclaimed.

Gran raised a hand. "I like my independence and I'm not giving it up. That's final."

Bridget held her tongue. She'd well learned the lesson that Gran's word was final when she was growing up. Unless the doctor said otherwise, there was no point in arguing.

\* \* \* \*

Jack yawned as he drove them back in the dark, barely morning hours. As bone tired as he was, Jack still enjoyed having Bridget next to him, her hand resting on his thigh as she dozed against his shoulder. Her sister was somewhere behind them in her car and would be crashing at Bridget's place for at least a week or two. He couldn't tell if she liked him or not and he wasn't quite sure how this might affect his relationship with Bridget. He didn't know how close the sisters were.

He turned off onto their street and parked at her house. With gentle movements, Jack shifted Bridget to the seat so he could climb out and lift her out of the car. Her slight weight filled his arms and he marveled at how much the logging job had enhanced his strength. She mumbled, but her eyes stayed closed. Juggling his way into the house, he managed to get them both inside without letting Candle out, then back to her bedroom. He placed her on the bed and Bridget protested but she rolled to her side as she settled in. He tugged off her ankle boots and pulled her purple and white duvet over her.

The cat meowed behind him. Jack turned and shooed her out of the room. "Whatcha need, fluff ball?" She let out another pitiful yowl and walked toward the kitchen. He followed and found her food bowl empty. "I guess you're hungry, huh?" He squatted down and scratched behind her ears. "I'll get you food."

As he was dishing up cat food, Sarah came in, pulling a suitcase behind her. She jumped a foot when she saw him in the house. "Shit," she said and put a hand over her heart. "You scared me."

"Sorry." He chuckled. "I was feeding the cat."

"I forgot Bridge got a cat. She's precious." She knelt and stretched a hand out to let Candle sniff before running her hand down the cat's back. Sarah stood and sighed. "I'm a zombie. I'm going to grab a few hours of sleep. It was nice meeting you."

"Same here. I'll just go check on Bridget and see myself out."

They parted ways in the hall and he peeked in. Bridget was adorable with her curls splayed out on the pillows. He bent and brushed the hair away from her face, kissing her temple. "Sweet dreams."

Her lashes fluttered and opened. "Stay." She reached out and wrapped a hand around his neck. "Sleep next to me."

How the hell was supposed to say no to that invitation? Not one iota of his body even wanted to say no, so why pretend? "Okay."

She smiled as he kicked off his shoes and joined her under the covers. He opened his arms and she immediately snuggled into him. With her head on his chest, he closed his eyes and fell asleep.

\* \* \* \*

When Jack woke, the light was slanting in at a late afternoon angle and he stretched as much as he could without jostling Bridget. At some point they'd turned so she was spooned against his chest and he couldn't help but notice how good her bottom felt pressed against his groin. His very awake and alert groin. Breathing deeply, he nuzzled her neck and focused on tamping down on his arousal. He would not paw at her like a high-school boy alone with a girl for the first time.

A soft sigh escaped her and she turned in his arms. She blinked her eyes at him. "Hi."

"Hi, yourself. Feeling refreshed?"

"Mmm." She smiled and ran a hand through his hair down to his cheek. She stroked the hairs of his beard. "I like waking up to you. Here. In my bed." Her teeth sank into her bottom lip as pink tinged her cheeks.

His restraint snapped. Leaning up on one elbow, he rolled her onto her back and delved into her mouth. She was so soft and lush and he wanted to sink into her and never surface again.

She twined her arms around his neck and hooked a leg over his hip. When he rocked against her, she shivered and whimpered. She crept her fingers beneath his long-sleeved shirt and splayed them across his back.

He loved the sensation of her hands on his skin, wanted her hands on every part of him. Her dress was bunched around her waist and it took all of his self-control not to pull her dress over her head and her panties down her legs. He wanted her naked in the worst way, but also knew he shouldn't rush things.

"Jack." She sighed and writhed beneath him. "Please."

"I don't have condoms on me. Do you have them here?"

She groaned with frustration and shook her head. "No. I didn't... I haven't needed any in a while and I didn't think ahead."

He kissed her again. "Your sister is just down the hall anyway."

The most adorable little growl vibrated in her throat. "Jack," she pleaded and rubbed against him.

"I know, baby." He brushed his lips over hers. "Just don't get too loud, okay?" Then he kissed his way down...down...down to where he most wanted to taste her.

Later, after he'd given her two orgasms and his body begged to sink into her wet heat, he ignored those base instincts and lay down next to her again. Her whole face and body were soft and relaxed and his grin couldn't be helped. He loved that he'd put that dreamy smile on her lips and the flush on her skin. He traced patterns along the skin of her stomach and licked his lips. "You do taste like the sweetest honey," he murmured in her ear, watching that flush deepen.

She covered her face with her hands and peeked out between her fingers. "Jack! I can't believe you just said that."

"It's true, though. You're my honeybee."

A little yelp escaped her and she clamped a hand over her mouth. The sight threw him back to a few minutes ago when she'd had to do the same to keep her cries of pleasure muffled. He laughed and pulled her closer. "You're making it way too easy to fall for you."

She lowered her hands and stilled, staring at him.

He swallowed and hoped he hadn't just made a fatal mistake with Bridget.

"You're falling for me?"

He nodded, not trusting himself to say the right thing.

Then the corners of her mouth lifted up. "That's good," she said softly. "Me too."

He grinned wide then kissed her again.

# Chapter Ten

"So you and this Jack guy, huh? What's up there?" Sarah asked Bridget while walking around the store and rearranging items on the shelves.

Bridget suppressed an irritated sigh and followed behind her older sister to undo the changes she'd made. "We're dating. What else do you want to know?"

Her sister threw a look over her shoulder, one brow cocked and a smirk on her lips. "I want to know what you two were doing in your bedroom for hours yesterday. You damn sure looked pretty satisfied after he left."

"Sunday Funday." It slipped out of her mouth before she had a chance to realize the gift she'd just given to Sarah.

"Oh-ho-ho! And just what kind of 'fun' was my baby sister getting up to? Dear God, please tell me you were not getting it on while I was just down the hall?" Sarah spun around, her eyes sparkling with amusement.

"Will you leave me alone? We did not have sex." Not full-on. Technically. But Sarah didn't need to know. Bridget smiled and went back to the counter to pretend to look over the expenses. She glanced at her phone to check if the hospital or Gran had contacted her but found nothing. Sighing, she tried to focus.

Part of her brain wanted to concentrate on Gran and what her recovery would look like. Doctor's appointments, meds, even basic things like cooking for her and helping her get around. Chores like cleaning and running errands. And she was now the sole full-time employee at Three Sisters. She'd need to cover Gran's shifts, work longer days then at night make and package products. Plus online orders were picking up, so she'd need to figure out how to get all of those completed and mailed, too.

The other part of her wanted to relive the amazing Sunday she'd had with Jack in her bed. The man definitely knew what to do with his mouth and hands. And his beard! My God, that had been a freaking revelation. She hadn't known how much added sensation all that soft hair would bring. A shiver brushed down her spine at the mere memory of how good he'd made her feel. She could only imagine how explosively good it would be when they were both naked together. Bridget squeezed her thighs together as desire pulsed low in her body.

Ugh, she had to get a hold of herself. Bridget dropped her face into her hands and exhaled. She needed to sort out how to take care of Gran and balance the store on her own and have a boyfriend. Something would have to give. Deep down she knew what would be sacrificed. She swallowed a whimper. Maybe when things improved with Gran, she and Jack could pick things up again.

If he was still around.

And still single.

She was screwed and not in the good way. This sucked so much.

"Hey." Sarah waved her hand in Bridget's face. "What is up with you? I've been moving stuff around all over the place and you haven't chased me away. What gives?"

Bridget pushed up from the counter and glared. "Really? You're doing this on purpose? Stop messing with my store! You're making more work for me and I don't need anything else added to my list." Stomping off, she walked the perimeter of the room and began rearranging everything back into proper order.

"Touchy. Sorry, baby sis. I didn't mean to hit a nerve." She plopped down on a stool and started looking through the new business software. "Seriously, what's going on?"

Bridget spun to pin her with an exasperated glare. "You can't figure it out? You're here for a week. Maybe two. While I appreciate your support, I'm here for the long haul and have to take care of everything. The store is my sole responsibility now. Gran will need care. Products have to be made and online orders need to be shipped. Plus, every Saturday and half of the Sundays for the next month are booked with festivals. How can I go off to these events when Gran would be left alone? I don't have time for everything."

"Whoa," Becca said as she emerged from the back room of the store. "You aren't alone, or did you forget I exist? That Gran is my grandma, too?"

Bridget blinked at her. "Where did you—did you come in from the back door? I didn't know you were coming in today."

Becca pursed her lips as she leaned against the counter. "I gathered as much. Look, I know you're the owner of the store and you and Gran run things like a well-oiled machine, but I'm here. Let me help you. You don't need to take on the weight of the world."

Bridget crossed the room and hugged her cousin tight. "I appreciate this, Becca. I do, but what about the farm? You can't abandon all of your duties there."

"True. I can also help more here. Unlike some people, I do hire employees because I can't do everything. It's fine, I promise."

"And I can stay longer, too," Sarah chimed in. "My boss understands and told me I could work remotely for a few weeks if needed. I'll stay with Gran."

"You'll stay with me. Gran will, too. She can't do those stairs, at least not right away."

Sarah laughed and shook her head. "There's no way Gran will agree to that. And frankly after Sunday, I don't want to be in the house with you and your *boyfriend* while you two are banging."

"What's this?" Becca perked up. "You and Jack had sex?"

Bridget shot Sarah a shut-up-or-die look. "No. Not exactly."

"Mmhmm." Becca smiled slyly. "So he went downtown, then?"

"Oh my God, this is none of your business!" Her cheeks burned like they were on fire. "Since when did the two of you decide you were entitled to all the details of my love life?"

Sarah cocked a brow. "Since forever. We're family."

"I'm curious, how was it with the beard?"

"Becca!" Bridget exclaimed. The beard had been a sexual revelation for her, but they didn't need to know her inexperience. "How would you even think to ask that?"

She snorted. "I bet you a thousand dollars I know more about the intricacies of oral than you."

Bridget covered her ears and sang aloud like a five-year-old. "We are not having this conversation. Jack knows what he's doing. Like really, *really* knows what he's doing. We're leaving it at that."

"What is it that I know how to do?"

Bridget squealed and jumped, spinning around. Jack stood in the doorway. Embarrassment melted her bones and she wanted to find a hole to crawl into and never come out. "Wha— Wh-when, uh…" She shot a glare over her shoulder. Her so-called family had set her up. They had to have seen him walking up and she hadn't heard the door chime. She faced him again and pasted her polite customer smile on her face. "What are you doing here? This is a surprise."

"I'm done at work and thought I'd come say hi. See how Gran is doing." He kissed her cheek and moved his lips to her ear. "Don't think you're getting out of this conversation." He nipped her earlobe and she coughed back a moan.

"H-hey." She squeezed his hand. "I'm glad you're here. How was your day?"

"Nothing to write home about. Same old. How's Gran?"

"Good. I think. I haven't heard from her since this morning. I was thinking of swinging by after I close the store tonight."

"Do you want me to drive you over? We could grab dinner on the way back?"

How was she going to balance all of this? Sure, Becca could help take some of the responsibilities of the shop and maybe Sarah would stick around an extra week or two, but did she have time for Jack? Was it fair to him to only be able to give a fraction of herself?

"You two should go now before visiting hours end," Sarah jumped in. "Becca and I can wrap things up here and you can head out early." Her sister shot Bridget a no-nonsense look and shooed her toward the door.

"I need to get my coat," Bridget said and walked to the back room, pulling Sarah with her. "What are you doing?" She rounded on her sister. "I don't need you managing my life."

"I saw your face and I know you, Bridge. You're overthinking and taking everything on yourself and talking yourself out of a relationship." Sarah put a hand on her hip. "You are not going to dump Hottie McLumberjack because you're freaking out in your head. Let Becca and I help you. Now go! See Gran and enjoy the yummy man-ness waiting out there for you."

"Okay, fine. You win." Despite her reservations, Bridget grinned and grabbed her coat. "See you back at home." She handed her keys to Sarah.

"Maybe. And eventually I'm getting details out of you about all the things Jack is so good at."

Bridget left her sister cackling in the back room as she joined him out front.

Traffic was light getting to the hospital and Bridget hurried as they walked up. She was anxious to see the woman who'd raised her and who she'd seen almost every day of her life for close to twenty years. As they entered her room, Bridget blinked away tears. "Hey, Gran," she said around the lump in her throat.

"Oh, honey, come here." Gran held out her arms and Bridget hugged her.

She had to admit her grandmother looked better than she had just after surgery, but she still had things hooked up to her and obviously wasn't at her peak self. She wanted to squeeze her Gran tight but made sure not to put too much pressure on her. Bridget pulled back and used her sleeve to wipe off her tears.

"Feel better?" Gran asked and she nodded. "That's good. Hello there, Jack. Thanks for bringing my Bridgie to see me."

"Happy to do it. You're looking better, Ms. Wildes."

She waved her hand. "Call me Gran or at least Esme. No reason to be so formal. I am feeling much improved."

"All right, Gran," he said.

"Have you heard anything from the doctors?" Bridget asked. "Any idea when you'll get discharged?"

"They want me here until the end of the week. I think that's unnecessary, but what does an old woman know?"

"Then you'll come back to stay with me." She fixed a stern look on her face when her grandmother opened her mouth to argue. "I mean it, Gran. I doubt your doctor will let you go back to climbing those stairs to your apartment right away, and it will be good to have someone else around. Sarah and I will be there, too. It'll be like old times."

"Lord save me from overprotective granddaughters." She sighed, but a hint of a smile played at her mouth.

Bridget rolled her eyes. "Keep this up and I'll have Becca join in, too. Then you'd have the three of us under one roof. All keeping watch on you."

Gran put a hand to her chest. "Stop that, Bridget! It's not good for my heart." She chuckled and laid her head back on her pillow. "I'll stay, but only for a little while. You need your independence and so do I." She glanced at Jack over Bridget's shoulder. "After all, you have a very dashing boy courting you. You don't need me cramping your style."

"Gran!" She closed her eyes in mortification, unable to look at either her grandmother or Jack.

"It's true." She shrugged. "Now you two go on. I'm tired, and I bet you're hungry for dinner."

Bridget kissed Gran's cheek and stood. "I'll text you tonight to check in. And one of us will come by to visit tomorrow."

She stood and Jack leaned in to kiss her grandma's cheek, too. Her heart melted a little at how sweet he was to her Gran. Maybe Sarah and Becca were right and she was overthinking. There had to be a balance of some kind. Didn't there?

\* \* \* \*

Jack held Bridget's hand as they exited the hospital and walked back to his truck. The look on her face told him how hard this was for her. He wished there was something more he could do, but he couldn't magically fix Gran.

But he could take Bridget to dinner and help keep her going. They climbed in and headed back toward town. The sprinkling of oaks were turning in full color now—the pops of red, orange, and yellow were spectacular against the dark green of the thick firs. He found himself enjoying the surrounding nature far more than expected. His high-rise apartment in downtown Seattle made views this like all the more valuable. He could get used to this kind of beauty all the time.

"Italian food sound good?" he asked.

"Perfect. I could use a massive plate of carbs right now."

After arriving and ordering their food, Jack watched as little by little the tension drained from Bridget's body. He reached across the table and played with her fingers. "Tell me about your day. Everything okay?"

"Sure." She smiled, but the corners of her eyes were tight.

"Hey, talk to me. You're definitely not as relaxed as you were when I left your house on Sunday. Did something happen at the store?"

She refused to look him in the eyes and swallowed hard. "No, nothing specific. There's just a lot going on."

He nodded and laced his hand with hers. "I know this has to be crazy stressful for you. You know I'm here to help, right?"

"I do. It's—there's so much with the store and Gran and it's been just me for so long. Gran helps, but without her... I don't know how to manage everything. Covering all of the hours for the store, making and packaging products, plus all the festivals over the next four weeks..." Tears glittered in her eyes.

Jack moved to her side of the table and put his arm around her. "You aren't alone. You have your sister and cousin and me. I don't mind spending my evenings making your magic balms and my Saturdays selling them. I know you're overloaded, but let the people who care about you help. You're worth it."

Her smile was wobbly but looked genuine. "Thanks, Jack. You're an amazing boyfriend, you know that?"

He shifted in his chair, uncomfortable with her praise. No other woman had seemed to like him for him. They had always liked his money more. Not that Bridget knew about the money, but that was a problem for another day. Today he needed to focus on Bridget and her needs.

He pressed a soft, chaste kiss to her lips. "Keep that kind of talk up and I'm going to get spoiled. Now tell me, honeybee, what is it that I'm really, *really* good at?"

The gorgeous flush that tinted her skin went all the way past the collar of her sweater and he wished he could see how far down it went. He chuckled and kissed her again, lingering a little longer. If he could, he'd spend all day kissing her. The soft sweetness of her made his body hard in all the right ways. The pleasure she gave him was addictive.

"Fine, I'll tell you, but only if you promise to refresh my memory. I might be overestimating your skills."

Heat washed through his limbs and his blood flowed south as he made a low, rumbling sound in his chest. "You're on, baby."

The server brought their food then and he focused on trying to control himself while they ate. He watched as Bridget dug into her food. She must not have eaten much today based on how fast she was inhaling her fettuccine alfredo.

"What's the update on the rumor mill at work? Is there still a big company thinking of buying?"

Jack bit his tongue and winced at the pain. Not that he didn't deserve it. Swallowing, he said, "I haven't heard much else on site."

He had heard a ton from his father each time they talked. Like when was he going to stop messing around out in the woods and come back to real work in the office. It was odd, but Jack preferred the logging work. Yes, he missed negotiating and the thrill that came with closing a new deal, but he enjoyed the physical labor. The camaraderie with his teammates and being outdoors were things he appreciated. He liked the little offshoots of roots he was putting down here.

Plus, Bridget was amazing. He was most definitely not ready to end things with her and go back to Seattle. He wanted to give this relationship a chance and that wouldn't happen if he were three hours away. He knew Bridget would go back to her isolated life and focus on the shop. He loved seeing this brighter, more outgoing side of her. He wanted that to be her all of the time. Her confidence was sexy.

"How are things going with Three Sisters? What about the online orders?"

She tilted her head to the side. "Sales are good. Up from last year, which surprises me. This new software you turned me on to seems to be helping quite a bit. The predictions based on previous years have been helpful in keeping my stock levels stable." She took a sip of her wine. "Online is picking up. The website seems to pull in a good amount of traffic from the tracking I have. I'm pleasantly surprised. And a little nervous. If the web orders pick up too much, I don't know how I'll manage."

"You hire more people. Look at expanding your production. Simple."

"But…" She paused and chewed her lower lip. "I don't know if I want that. I mean, I want to be comfortable and make sure the store does well, but I don't want to be some giant conglomerate. I like the shop big enough to keep the doors open and small enough to keep the local feel. I mainly want to stay in the black and not teeter on the edge of red all the time."

He furrowed his brow at her statement. He'd never met another business owner who didn't have their sights set on expansion and growth and domination. It was weird. And refreshing. What would it be like to simply be content? Safely comfortable with his business stable and steady and not plowing forward? "You could always pull the online ordering if you think it's getting too complicated. The website is still good for recognition and getting actual foot traffic through the door if someone is looking at what's available in Fallbank from a shopping perspective."

"Yeah, I could do that. We'll see how things go through October. I might be speaking too soon. It *is* good to keep sales growing. I just don't want this to get out of control."

"Speaking of keeping things under control, should we go back to your house and you can show me how you package things up? I'm a quick learner."

\* \* \* \*

When they returned to her house, Bridget walked in to find Sarah curled up on the couch with her computer. "Hey, we're back."

Sarah looked up and smiled, closing the lid on her laptop. "Hey, yourself. How's Gran? She texted to say she was okay, but…"

Bridget tossed her purse and keys on the entry table with Jack trailing in behind her. She thought back to Gran and how strange it was to see her in a hospital bed. "She's got her spunk back. She still looks tired and pale and frail—and I will murder you if you ever tell her I said that—but she's in good spirits."

Despite being tired, Bridget knew she needed to package more of her lavender-and-honey body lotion. She motioned for Jack to sit. "I need to grab some things from my shed. Go ahead and get comfortable. I'll be working on products for the next few hours."

She ducked out to her shed and grabbed the bottles and batch of lotion she'd made last night. Hauling it inside, she set it on the coffee table and sat to get to work.

"Hey, wait. Show me how to do this." Jack shifted forward to watch with care. "Put me to work."

"You don't have to," she protested, but he shook his head.

"I want to."

"I'll help, too," Sarah volunteered. "You know I know what I'm doing."

Bridget talked Jack through the process while Sarah moved full speed ahead. After half an hour, they'd gotten into a good groove with the packaging and she was pleasantly surprised at how fast they were going. "At this rate I might not be up until midnight after all." She grinned.

"See what a little teamwork can do for you?" Jack winked and lifted one corner of his mouth. A shiver danced down her neck. Good grief, could he be any sexier?

"So, Jack. Tell me about you. Bridget told me you're from Seattle, but that's it. What do you do?"

He didn't answer for long enough that Bridget looked up. Instead of finding something wrong, she saw him laser focused on the ritual of measuring and pouring into the jars she used for the product.

When he was done, he cleared his throat. "Well, I've done construction mainly. And a friend of mine got me interested in logging, so that's what brought me here." He looked over at Bridget and smiled just for her. "Seems to be a good choice so far."

Bridget was absurdly pleased by his declaration but said nothing. She concentrated back on the task in front of her.

"I can't figure it out." Her sister peered at Jack. "Why do you seem familiar to me?"

Jack looked sharply at Sarah. "I, ah, don't know." He rubbed a hand over the back of his neck and shrugged. "Maybe we have mutual friends or met at some point at some event or another. Hard to say."

"Maybe..." Sarah didn't look convinced.

"Or I could have one of those faces that everyone thinks looks familiar. I get that a lot."

Sarah shrugged and went back to helping with the lotion. "If you say so."

"What do you do in Seattle, Sarah?"

"I work in marketing at a large firm in the city. I went to UW and did an internship there my senior year. It rolled into a full-time position after graduation, so I stayed."

Bridget watched her sister closely as she spoke. She wanted to see if there were any signs she might be growing tired of city life and want to come back home. Yet Sarah never seemed interested. She loved her job and had a high-rise apartment overlooking the Puget Sound. Bridget was forever hearing about the sporting events and clubs and musicals she went to. The friends she hung out with and random dates she went on. Sarah never seemed lonely. Not that her dating ever turned serious. Not since Cornelius.

And goodness knew Cornelius didn't date. He was a confirmed bachelor who kept to himself. Bridget's chest tightened as she thought of him alone in his house. She'd been glad when Jack had moved in with him. Bridget did her best to invite Cornelius over once or twice a week for dinner, but she knew he had to feel isolated.

Focusing back on the task at hand, she pulled her thoughts back to the present. It didn't help to dwell and there wasn't anything she could do about the fact that Sarah and Cornelius, who had once seemed to be the perfect couple, were broken up and not getting back together again anytime soon.

Jack peeked over at her and winked. She couldn't stop her grin. Well, at least she'd found someone. It terrified her a bit to think of how fast she was tumbling into love with him, but she didn't want to deny it. Her life had been empty for years now. Even before Sarah had moved to Seattle and Gran to the apartment above Three Sisters, she'd felt out of place. Like she didn't fit in with this town no matter how hard she tried or how much she loved it here. The people didn't love her back. Well, some of the people. Those who did were friend*ly* but not necessarily friends.

Had that been because of them? Or her? Bridget wondered now if this distance between herself and others in town wasn't at least a little bit her fault. If maybe she'd held everyone at a distance the same way she had when Jack had first arrived.

She watched as he meticulously filled one bottle after another. Slowly. So much so that she almost laughed, but it had taken her time to get faster, too. A pleasant warmth spread across her belly as she watched his concentration. His eyes held the same determination in them that they did when he was between her thighs, hell-bent on giving her what had been the best orgasms of her life.

An ache went through her just thinking about it. Wiggling a little, she filled the last jar and set it with the others. "We finished them all! I can't believe it. In only two hours, too." She beamed at Jack and Sarah. "Thanks for helping. This would've taken me past midnight to do on my own."

Sarah brushed her off. "Like I wouldn't help you with this stuff. We can do more tomorrow or the next night if you've got stuff made. Or whatever you need. This is something I can't do in Seattle. I miss it." She stood and stretched. "I'm going to bed. I'll be working remotely tomorrow, but I can come into the store to help out, too. I'll see you in the morning. Goodnight, Jack."

They both said good night and Sarah petted Candle on her way out of the living room. Bridget began picking up bottles and loading them into the crate she used for carrying supplies to the store, and Jack jumped up to help her.

"Thanks again," she said as he bent next to her. She couldn't help but check out his ass and an appreciative sigh passed her lips.

He straightened and ducked his head to steal a kiss.

It was too quick for her to even respond so she pushed up on her toes and pressed her lips to his. Sinking into the moment, she molded her body against his and lifted one hand to the nape of his neck and the other at his waist. God, but he had abs she wanted to lick. She wanted to explore even farther down his body, but tonight wasn't the night. It was already late and she hadn't gotten the chance to pick up protection yet either. Much to her body's frustration.

"Mmm." She hummed and stepped back.

"Hey, wait a minute," Jack protested with a lazy smile. "Why'd we stop kissing?"

"Because it's late. I know you have to be on site early and I've got to get to the shop, too. Plus, my sister is twenty feet down the hall. And I still don't have condoms. Do you?"

He shook his head. "I know you're right, but I don't want you to be. Not when it comes to you and me together in a bed." He tugged at her waist and kissed her again. "I guess this means I should go."

Frustration and desire flared so hot inside her, she wanted to cry. But she knew if he stayed, they wouldn't be able to stop. She wouldn't want him to. She'd beg him to keep going. To make love to her.

Candle yowled and jumped down from her perch on the cat tower, then walked over to the hall and sat there, staring at her. Apparently, her cat was ready for bed. She laughed. "Yeah, I think this means good night."

They walked to the front door and he kissed her again, slow and sweet. "Night, honeybee."

"Good night." She smiled as he made his way down the sidewalk back to his house.

# Chapter Eleven

Jack's phone rang as he drove home from work. He glanced at the caller ID and grimaced as his father's name popped up. Tapping the answer button on his truck, he said, "Hey, Dad. How's it going?"

"It'd be better if my son stopped playing in the woods and came home to his real job. You've been gone for a month and your reports on the business seem ample enough to know we're buying it out. Time to get back to Seattle and your real life."

"I want to learn more. I think another month or two would be good to make sure I know all the ins and outs. How this would be integrated into our holdings, how to staff it, the risks of the actual jobs and liability we need to have covered."

"Let the lawyers figure that out. It's what we pay them for. We're buying and will reallocate the positions to workers on our teams already. No need to add more headcount."

"Dad, these people are my friends. I can't just take their jobs away." He ran a hand through his hair, irritation bubbling under his skin.

"And what about the people we already employ? Don't you want job security for them?"

"None of them are loggers by training. It takes time to learn this. I'm still making mistakes all over the place despite having a construction skill set."

His father sighed. "I knew working for your grandfather was a mistake when you were younger. You're too hands-on with everything. It will work out. The business case only makes sense if we cut the staff there and use our current people to do jobs as they are booked."

"Grandpa is the one who suggested I come out here and work for TLC. Dig deep to figure out if this was realistic." A wave of nausea rolled over him. How would he tell everyone at work they were losing their jobs? Hadn't Bridget told him the logging company was the only thing keeping the economy in town alive? This wasn't just about those jobs—it was about everyone's livelihood. The whole town of Fallbank would cease to exist in a few years if this happened. His heart twisted in his chest. Bridget would never forgive him. She'd hate him forever. He clenched his jaw. "Dad, I have to go. I'm staying at least through October, that's non-negotiable."

"What is keeping you there? I don't understand."

"I'll call you in a few days with another update." Jack hung up and parked on the street outside Three Sisters. He wanted to hit his steering wheel but managed to refrain. Blowing out a lungful of air, he exited and headed toward the shop. The closer he got, the lighter his mood grew. The prospect of seeing

Bridget gave him a warm, happy sensation in his chest instead of the heavy, jagged weight the conversation with his father had pushed on him.

The chiming of the bell as he entered brought a smile to his face. "Hey, Bridget," he said as her dark curls shifted and she looked up at him.

Her answering grin made him feel like a damn movie star. "Hey, yourself. This is a nice surprise."

Jack walked over with a quick glance to see if they were alone in the store. Grabbing her waist, he tugged her toward him and planted his mouth on hers.

"Mmm." She hummed and her body went soft in his arms as he deepened the kiss. "What was that for?" she asked as they pulled back.

He rested his forehead against hers and closed his eyes. This was what he needed. He needed *her*. And to come clean about who he was and why he was here. She deserved to know. He could trust that she liked him for him, right? He opened his mouth.

Her phone rang and they both jolted. Laughing, she stepped back and said, "Hold that thought, I like where we're heading."

As she answered, he paced the floor, not able to stay still. He admired the pretty fall accent decorations Bridget had placed. Her creativity amazed him. His mind didn't work like this. Finding ways to add touches of whimsy the way she did was beyond his ability. He'd never have thought to add little pumpkins and bright-colored leaves and pinecones as a way to bring the season into the store. He liked how she did the same in her house, too, even when she lived by herself. These tiny things made him wonder what she would be like to live with. Did she have decorations for each season? What about as a mother? Would she do even more if she had children?

He waited for the cold rush of fear to accompany his thoughts about Bridget and motherhood with their own kids, but it didn't show up. Jack relaxed even more, knowing he'd turned that corner with his anxiety. His feelings were still going way too fast, but he couldn't be bothered by it anymore.

"That's such great news!"

Jack turned at her excited exclamation. Bridget beamed and danced from foot to foot, making him laugh. She was too adorable for words.

"Okay. Yeah, I'll be there soon. Bye!" She set her phone down and bounced on her toes. "Gran is coming home today!"

"That's fantastic, honeybee." He hugged her and she squeezed him tight.

"I'll need to go get her and bring her home to my place. She needs to stay at least a week, maybe two, with me and Sarah." She frowned. "I don't know how long Sarah plans to stay."

"Do you want me to drive you? Can I bring dinner for all of you? Tell me how I can help."

She bit her lip and he read the hesitation on her face.

"Tell me or I'll go off and do something anyway. At least this way you'll have a say in it."

Bridget rolled her eyes, but smiled. "Okay, fine. Dinner for us sounds great. Nothing too spicy or greasy. Gran needs bland and healthy food."

"I'll figure it out. You go get Gran. See you back at your place, all right?"

She pressed her lips to his again then locked up the store behind them. Jack hopped into his car and made his way over to the local grocery store. He picked up a rotisserie chicken, salad supplies, a sack of potatoes and a head of cauliflower. Then he headed home and roasted the potatoes and cauliflower together while keeping the chicken warmed in the oven. The salad was the easy part. Jack was packing everything up just as Cornelius walked in. "Hey, how's it going? I thought you'd be back by now."

Cornelius shook his head and threw his keys on the entryway table. "I was talking to Paul. Looks like he really is going to sell." He crossed to the living room couch and flopped down. "I'm not sure our jobs are going to survive."

Jack froze. "What did he say?"

"He's been talking with someone—he won't say who yet, but they're putting together a contract for initial negotiations." Cornelius shook his head. "They mentioned maybe replacing us with their own workers, but I guess that's still up in the air."

Anger boiled in Jack's blood. He wanted to punch something and scream at his father. He'd just had a conversation about not doing any of this, but Dad had jumped the gun. Maybe he needed to go up to Seattle for a weekend and talk to his father face to face. There had to be some way to purchase the company while still preserving the jobs and local economy here.

"That sucks, but I'm sure it'll work out." He hoped his face didn't betray anything.

Cornelius shrugged. "I'm glad you have more faith than I do." He looked over at the stack of food containers on the counter. "What's all that?"

"I'm bringing dinner over to Bridget's. Gran is being released from the hospital today, so I said I'd bring dinner."

"Things are going well with you two, huh?"

He nodded and tried not to grin like a lovesick teenager. "I think so. She's great. I like her. A lot." More than like, but he wasn't quite ready to admit that to himself, let alone Cornelius.

"Dude, you're so far gone for her. I can see it all over your face." Cornelius laughed. "That's good. She deserves it. This town...the guys here haven't always been kind and I think she'd closed herself off. But she's lonely, I can tell." He flashed a smile. "Well, she was."

That warm happiness filled Jack again. He could tell she'd been isolated and too timid to let anyone in. It made him feel invincible to know she'd chosen him to break down those walls around her heart. He didn't even mind that they hadn't been able to be alone together lately. Even surrounded by other people, he enjoyed her company and kept finding excuses to spend time with her. Like bringing dinner.

"Did you want to join us for dinner? I'm sure Gran and Bridget wouldn't mind."

Cornelius paused for a minute then shook his head. "No, but thanks. I don't think I should."

"Is it because of Sarah? What's the story there?"

He sighed and scrubbed his hands over his face. "Yeah, it's because of Sarah. We dated. It didn't work out. It would be awkward if I went over."

"Didn't seem too awkward when she saw you at the hospital. Seemed like she was still into you, if you ask me." Jack arched one brow with a pointed stare. "How long were you two together? Bridget said you were high-school sweethearts?"

"Yeah, we were. Earlier really, but it wasn't like we were able to go anywhere or do anything. She kissed me when we were twelve. Out in her garden when we were looking for frogs. That was it. I never imagined anyone else but her."

"What happened?"

Cornelius shrugged. "She went to college in Seattle. I stayed and started working. I think I already told you I took online night classes to get my degree and then my MBA."

Jack nodded but didn't interrupt.

"I thought I might buy the business when Paul retired, but so much for that. I don't have enough money for a down payment saved up yet." Cornelius shook his head. "Anyway, Sarah wanted me to come to Seattle and I wanted her to come home. In the end, we both went our separate ways." He stood and stretched. "And that, as they say, is all she wrote."

Jack wasn't convinced, but there wasn't anything he could do about it right now. "I'm sorry, Cornelius. For what it's worth, I think there's something there. She still loves you."

He shook his head. "Nah, we've both moved on. Anyway, I'm going to take a shower and crash. I've got some binge watching to do. Say hey to Gran for me."

"Will do," Jack said as he watched Cornelius walk down the hall. An idea was wiggling around in his head. Cornelius wanted to buy TLC but couldn't afford it just yet. Cornelius would have to take out a loan and Jack was almost certain Cornelius couldn't compete against his family's offer. But Cornelius could be useful given his knowledge as a team lead with the lumberjacks and his MBA background.

Jack shook himself from his thoughts and packed up the containers into a reusable bag. Right now wasn't the time to work through all the details. A couple of minutes later, he stood outside Bridget's door and knocked.

Sarah opened the door and her eyes flicked over his shoulder. Her face fell ever so slightly.

Yeah, Sarah still had a thing for Cornelius. Jack was certain of it now. "Hi, Sarah. Have Bridget and Gran arrived yet?" The garage door was closed, so he couldn't tell if her car was here or not. And even though it had only been a little over an hour, he was antsy to see his girl. *His girl*. He almost snorted aloud. Jack had a feeling Bridget might slap him upside the head for thinking something like that. He didn't own her. But there was something possessive inside him that yearned to mark her as his for all the world to see. And if he were honest, he wouldn't mind if she reciprocated in turn. He'd proudly let her lay claim to him.

"They just walked in ten minutes ago. Come on in."

Jack followed her into the kitchen and started unpacking. Gran wandered in. Her skin was pale and she moved a bit slower than normal, but a huge smile graced her features. Her confident grin eased the concern that nagged at him.

"Hello, Jack. I hope you brought tacos!"

His eyebrows shot halfway up his forehead. "Sorry to disappoint you, Gran. I'm under strict orders for something healthy and bland. No spicy food at all."

Gran scowled and crossed her arms. "Well, what good are you to me?"

Jack threw his head back and laughed. He had a feeling he would be in for a long evening. Then Bridget walked in and the sight of her made everything perfect.

\* \* \* \*

A week later, Bridget glowered at Gran and crossed her arms. "So, Dr. Mayes, you're saying it's okay for Gran to live alone and go up and down twelve steps each time to come and go?"

Dr. Mayes chuckled and tilted her head to the side. "Well, she has been cleared by the rehab department. In an ideal situation, someone would live with you, Ms. Wildes. Living alone this close to your heart attack is a bit of a risk. Stairs are okay but try to keep going up and down to a minimum and take your time."

Bridget shot the doctor a narrow-eyed look, then turned back to glare at Gran.

Gran returned the expression. "I'm going home."

"Over my dead body. You heard the doctor. She doesn't want you to live alone yet." Bridget wanted to shout at Gran, but held herself in check. She knew her grandmother wouldn't react well to that kind of behavior no matter how grown Bridget was.

"Sarah already said she would come stay with me." Gran raised a brow, escalating their stand-off.

"Sarah is going home."

"She said she'd stay longer with me so I could get back to my apartment."

Bridget's jaw dropped. She swung around to the doctor. "How long would you prefer someone be with Gran?"

The doctor considered for a moment. "Two weeks if her follow-up appointments go well."

Bridget sighed and closed her eyes. She knew when she'd been beaten. Sarah was going to owe her. "I still don't think this is a good idea," she muttered. "Thank you for your time, Dr. Mayes."

On the ride home Bridget asked, "Why do you want to go home so much? Is living with me such a hardship?"

Gran smiled and shook her head. She reached over and patted Bridget's knee. "No, Bridgie. I just want to get back to my home. My bed. My plants. I want you to have some time alone with that handsome new boyfriend of yours."

She coughed as the air in her throat suddenly stuck. "Jack and I are fine. We have time together." That was a bit of a stretch. True, they'd spent plenty of time together, but usually when she was working on products for the store. She'd taken to spending hours in her workshop out back. It gave her space from Gran and Sarah and allowed her to keep her business anxiety in check. Plus, Jack had come over several times and they'd made out hot and heavy. Sadly, that was all they'd done. It wasn't that she couldn't have him spend the night or her stay at his place, but they'd come to an unspoken agreement that their first time together wouldn't be with other people just a room or two down the hall.

She wanted to have the freedom to be as loud as she wished or laze around in bed with Jack. And have both her sister and grandmother *not* know that she was having sex at the exact moment it was happening. There really wasn't a way to avoid that with them living with her. And Cornelius was practically her brother so it wouldn't be any better over at Jack's place.

Gran hummed, but didn't say anything more. Instead, she changed the subject. "The leaves sure are pretty this year. They look splashy against the firs."

Bridget allowed her gaze to drift over the scenery for a moment then focused back on the road. "They are.

This October is a good month for the color change. The festivals have been booming this year. I've sold out at almost every one of them so far. Three more to go."

She was looking forward to the end of festival season. At least for the fall. So far the weather had been as good as could be hoped for. Light drizzle instead of the heavy rain that kept people inside. She was tired and knew this was the mid-season slump for her. Of course, this year also had more stress than normal with Gran's health and her sister living with her. She hadn't had a day off or any real time to relax. She would swing back up as the Fallbank festival and lumberjack competition grew closer, but right now fatigue and stress were weighing her down.

Once back home, Gran danced inside and announced, "Pack up, Sarah dear! We are downtown ladies now. I'm going home."

Bridget threw her sister a dark look. "Traitor."

Sarah shot her a patented superior big sister I-know-better-than-you expression. "Gran wants to go home and I'm doing as she requested. I can take the time and keep working from here." She turned on her heel to walk down the hall. "I'll be packing," she called over her shoulder.

Bridget growled. "You're staying here tonight. I've already planned for dinner and it's late. Give me one more night to adjust to being abandoned here alone, okay?"

Her grandma must have sensed the turmoil inside Bridget because she folded her into her arms and held her tight. "I'll be fine, honey. You and Sarah and Rebecca take wonderful care of me. It's okay."

Tears slipped past Bridget's shut eyelids. All the pressure and stress of the past week came pouring out of her. Sobs shuddered through her body as Gran rocked her and whispered reassurance. Bridget had come so close to losing the person who'd been her rock for so long. Who'd carried her through the loss of her parents, the taunting from kids at school, the awkward, angsty teenage years and into adulthood. Gran had always been there to pick her up or give advice. Bridget couldn't imagine her world without her.

Eventually, her tears subsided and her breathing evened out again. Bridget stepped back and swiped at her face. "Sorry, Gran." Her cheeks heated to flaming. She hadn't had this kind of emotional outburst that anyone else had seen in she couldn't remember when. Years. She made a point not to show weakness to anyone.

Gran cupped her face in her weathered, wrinkled hands. "Vulnerability isn't a bad thing. It's all right to cry and be sad or scared. To show your emotions to other people. That's not weakness—it's strength. If it means this much to you, we'll stay until tomorrow."

Bridget lifted the corners of her lips. "Thanks, Gran. I love you."

"I love you, too, Bridgie. Now, where are those tacos?"

Bridget barked a laugh and shook her head. "Not tonight, Gran. Not with me watching your diet like a hawk."

# Chapter Twelve

Bridget stared at her phone and willed it to chime. Or ring. Something. Anything. She'd sent Jack a text a few hours ago and she hadn't heard a peep since. What had possessed her to ask him to stay the night? Couldn't she have invited him for dinner and let things unfold naturally? No, instead she had unloaded in a text that Gran and Sarah had moved back into the apartment and did he want to come over tonight.

She dropped her face in her hands with a little groan. What had she been thinking? Way to seem desperate. She was, but he didn't need to know that. Yet they hadn't seen each other in a couple of days and all the making out plus the memory of that one long-ago Sunday in her bed had her primed and ready for the real thing. She wanted to know if the sex would be as good as she imagined. Maybe it would be even better…

A shiver traced down her spine as her hormones spiked once again. God, she wanted Jack like she'd never wanted any man before. She was practically on edge with need. The door chimed with the arrival of a customer and Bridget exhaled a sigh of relief. This would provide a good distraction from her thoughts and fantasies.

"Welcome to Three Sisters Apothecary. How can I help you?"

The woman smiled. "I heard about you from a friend so I decided to pop in. She says you have the best lotions and my skin gets so dry it flakes in winter."

"I've got a perfect option for you." She stepped over to the shelves at the front of the store and plucked up a jar. "This has oatmeal and lavender and should keep your skin super soft and moisturized. No flaking at all."

"Wonderful! I'll take two."

Bridget grinned and rang up the sale. As the woman waved and walked out, her phone dinged. Bridget pounced and almost dropped her phone in her haste. A new text icon taunted her and she punched her finger at the picture.

*Would love to see you tonight. Should I bring dinner?*

Her heart pounded as she reread the words. Jack was coming over tonight. He was going to stay. To spend the night. With her. In her bed. She squealed and did a little dance. Laughter pealed from behind her. Bridget spun to find her sister walking in from the back room where the apartment stairs emptied.

"What was that about?"

"Nothing," Bridget mumbled, refusing to make eye contact.

Sarah continued to stare in silence, a smile playing around her mouth.

"Fine! Jack is coming over tonight."

"I knew it! I knew you wouldn't hold out, you little hussy. Good job, sis. You moved fast." Sarah bumped her shoulder into Bridget's and grinned.

"Since you defected and moved in with Gran, I might as well get some benefits for myself." Bridget grabbed up her purse and coat. "In fact, you can close the store tonight. Oh, and I think I deserve the weekend, too. You can cover the festival in Clear Creek, right?"

Sarah stood with her mouth hanging open. "Who are you and what have you done with my sister?"

She shrugged. "I'm just taking the advice from you and Gran and Becca. I'm putting myself first for once." She waved and headed out. "Enjoy your evening watching *Jeopardy* with Gran!"

After she swung by the store to pick up the *supplies* needed for tonight, Bridget showered and put on a matching bra and panty set. It wasn't some bright, racy color, but a soft peachy-pink instead. Then she threw on a shift dress and waited. Thankfully, Jack had seemed as eager as she was.

He knocked on her door at six pm on the dot and her breath caught when she opened it. He was so damn gorgeous and he was here for her. How in the world had she gotten this lucky? Or rather, was about to get lucky? Her inner teenager laughed at her mental joke, but the grown-up part of her leaped to attention. "Hey."

"Hey, yourself." His gaze drifted over her form, then he looked back at her with a warm appreciation. "You look beautiful."

She flushed and waved him in. He followed her into the kitchen and set down the takeout he'd brought.

"Are you hungry? Should we eat now?" Jack asked.

Bridget stepped closer and twined her arms around his neck. "Later, lumberjack. We should have dinner much, much later." Kissing, they stumbled back toward her bedroom. His shoes were kicked off along the way and she had his belt and jeans undone before they made it through the door. Her whole body was alight with desire for this man. She ached between her thighs and pressed against him to try to get any kind of friction between their bodies. Gasping, she pulled back and let him lift her dress over her head.

"Fuck, you're so gorgeous." He bit his lip and yanked his shirt off while she shoved at his jeans. Then they tumbled to the bed and she gave herself over to the sensations of his hands and lips and body pleasuring her. When they joined together it was unlike anything she'd ever experienced before. The peak of her orgasm hit hard and the waves of her ecstasy washed over her again and again and again. When at last they were both exhausted and sated, she curled up against him in bed. Jack stroked his fingers over her hair as she listened to the steady rhythm of his heart beneath her ear. Three more orgasms and a few hours later, she and Jack got around to eating the food he'd brought over before heading back to her bedroom for round four. It was the best sex and best night of her life. Bridget fell asleep wrapped in strong arms with bone-deep contentment.

\* \* \* \*

Jack stirred and nestled closer to Bridget's warm, soft body, curled up like a little spoon against him. He peeked open his eyes and almost pushed himself off the edge of the bed. It took all of his effort not to jolt at the surprise of a small furry black head with glowing green eyes staring unblinking at him.

"H-hey, Candle," he whispered in an attempt to not wake Bridget up. The cat continued to watch without moving and Jack wondered if he was about to be gouged in the face by a tiny ball of fur he'd thought was his friend.

With painstaking slowness, Candle climbed over Bridget, who mumbled nonsense and rolled onto her stomach, then nudged her head under his chin. He shifted on his back and the cat settled onto him, purring loudly and deeply. Stroking Candle's head, he relaxed again as a sensation of rightness settled into his bones. With a glance at the still-sleeping woman next to him, he smiled. She was adorable, even in her sleep. Her hair was splayed out across her shoulders and pillow and her face revealed an openness she hid from the world. His honeybee's life had been a hard one, and Jack hoped he could ease her path even if it just meant walking beside her.

With a small shake of his head, he twisted his lips to the side. Was he really thinking this far ahead so soon? Long-term commitment with only a little over a month of knowing her? How could he be feeling this much this fast? Maybe he should take a step back and get some perspective, but to hell with that. He didn't want space or time or even thinking. He wanted to rouse Bridget with kisses and love her awake. He wanted to confess this deep, burning emotion inside him that he'd thought he'd felt before, but that had been nothing compared to this ocean of passion and devotion and complete and total infatuation. He was in love like he'd never been before and that scared the shit out of a small part of him. But the majority of him reveled in it and wanted to jump all in. She was caring and kind and pure and good. Her heart was made of gold and he wanted to protect and cherish her gentle, sweet spirit.

She rolled over and snuggled into his side with her eyes still closed. He wrapped his free arm around her shoulders and continued to pet the cat with his other hand. If he could wake up like this every morning, he'd be the happiest guy on earth. He wanted this. All of this. The girl, the cat, the small town, her shop and his logging job. Jack had thought he liked the business side of things, but the daily pressure and stress had been getting to him. Not to mention the notoriety he had in Seattle.

He couldn't go anywhere without being recognized since that asinine article about the wealthiest bachelors in the city that had come out last year. He was still pissed at his mother for ambushing him with that interview. Her desperation to have him "settled in life" had driven her to some very low levels. What would his parents think of Bridget? How would they blend their lives together? He raked a hand through his hair and Candle let out a plaintive meow.

"Sorry, little bit," he murmured, resuming his scritches behind her ears. Her purring doubled in volume and the vibrations tickled his chest.

"Mghrfp." Bridget grunted and sighed heavily. Her lids fluttered and lifted for a moment or two then drifted shut again. Her body stretched against his and his blood stirred. He couldn't lie — sex with Bridget was the best he'd ever had and he wanted more. Lots more. Every day more. Multiple times a day more if he could somehow make that happen. Every touch and kiss and plunge of his body into hers had showered sparks along each nerve in his body. When she had come, it had been damn near transcendental and had dragged him under the waves of ecstasy along with her.

Her naked, pliant body rubbed against his again and she peeked up at him. "Morning."

Color bloomed in her cheeks as he smiled lazily. "Hey, honeybee."

Her lips curled up. "I see Candle kept you company this morning, too." She reached out and rubbed her fingers over the cat's fur.

"Let me take you away for a weekend." His own words surprised even him, but as soon as they were out of his mouth, the idea caught within him. He wanted to take her away from all of her responsibilities, if only for a couple of days. The softness in her face when sleeping was something he wanted to see in waking life.

Wrinkles appeared between her brows. "I'm not sure I can do that. I dumped everything this weekend on Sarah, Gran and Becca spur of the moment. I'm booked every Saturday between now and Halloween with festivals. I can't put it all on them again. It would need to be after that."

A disappointed sigh passed his lips. He wanted to get away with her sooner than that, but he did understand her shop meant everything to her. "Okay, let's see what we can work out." Maybe he could work a little magic of his own and surprise Bridget. "How do you feel about omelets?"

She grinned. "Love them. You sure you're up to that task?"

Humming, he nudged the cat away and rolled to hover over her warm, naked body. "Definitely, but I'm eating first." Then he ducked his head under the blankets and enjoyed her embarrassed, breathy laugh as he kissed and caressed his way to settle between her thighs.

# Chapter Thirteen

Bridget walked into the shop chewing on her lower lip and oblivious to everything around her the following Monday. She was in so much trouble. Like way in over her head, long past the point of no return, terrifying free-fall over the cliff's edge in trouble. Spending the weekend with Jack had cemented his hold over her heart and that thought was terrifying. She'd never felt this much for anyone before, and it had happened so fast it was making her head spin.

"Morning," Sarah chirped.

She jumped just a little and looked at her sister, who was eating a pastry at the counter. "Oh, hey. I, uh, didn't see you there."

"Clearly." Sarah chuckled and took another bite. She nudged a paper bag in Bridget's direction. "I got you breakfast."

Her stomach rumbled awake and she walked faster. "Thanks, I skipped this morning."

Sarah arched an eyebrow. "Busy morning, sis? Did you sleep in by accident? You are a bit late, which is unusual."

Bridget shoved buttery pastry into her mouth and chewed, knowing her cheeks were on fire. "Something like that." Jack had stayed over again and their romp in the sheets this morning still had tingles running through her.

"Mmhm." Sarah pursed her lips. "So how's Jack?"

She coughed and set down her breakfast. "He's good." Bridget looked around at the shelves to avoid Sarah's gaze. "Thanks for restocking things."

"Uh-huh. I didn't hear from you this weekend. What's up with that? What were you doing?"

Now she did look at her sister, whose expression was that of perfect innocence. Bridget narrowed her eyes, not buying the act for one second. Sarah was fishing for details and she wasn't sure if she wanted to share. Her emotions about Jack were very fresh. Too new to know where she even wanted things to head with him. "Jack and I hung out. How's Gran?"

"Gran is just fine." Her grandmother's voice floated from the back door as Gran pushed through it.

"Hi, how are you feeling?"

"I feel like I want to hear about Jack." She leveled Bridget with a smug smile. "Have you two knocked boots yet?"

The bell above the door jingled.

*Thank God!* Saved by the bell. Bridget spun around with her customer smile plastered across her face. Becca walked in carrying a medium-sized box. Oh, damn, she wasn't rescued after all. "Hey, Becca. Are those the goat milk soaps?"

"Yep. I did a couple of different scents this time. Cinnamon spice, sage and bay and pumpkin, too. Plus our normal scents. I thought the fall ones might sell well with the season change." She set the box down behind the counter then looked at all three of them. "What's everyone doing here? Gran, how are you?"

Gran pressed a kiss to Becca's cheek and said, "I'm feeling full of energy today. And we're trying to find out if Bridget here has done the deed with Jack yet. She was unreachable all weekend."

"Gran!" Bridget protested. Three sets of eyes turned on her and she knew she had zero chance of escape. "Fine, yes. Does that satisfy you?"

Becca snickered. "That's what she said."

At the same time, Sarah laughed and said, "I think the better question is, did he satisfy *you*?"

Blood rushed in her ears. Bridget pressed her palms to her cheeks and cringed. "Oh my God, stop it! Yes, we had sex. Yes, it was great. Better than great. He's a spectacular lover. Orgasms galore! There. Now will you three leave me alone?"

A low, deep laugh floated to her from behind. For a split second, Bridget's entire body froze. Her heart skipped a beat. Then she pivoted like someone in a horror movie.

Jack stood in the doorway with a smug grin on his face. He winked and swaggered forward.

She shot a Death Look over her shoulder at the cackles coming from her family. They had distracted her sufficiently enough to miss the bell alerting her to his arrival. Then she turned back to the man who'd satisfied her so many times this weekend, yet her whole body still melted at the sight of him. She almost wanted to throw a bar of soap at his head for being so damn good in bed and now he knew it. As if his ego needed more stroking.

Jack bent and brushed his lips across her cheek and murmured, "Hey honeybee. Glad to know I'm leaving my girl so satisfied in bed." Straightening, he flashed a smile at her family, never missing a beat. "Good morning, ladies. How are you all? Gran, you look lovely and much recovered from the last time I saw you."

Her grandmother batted her eyelashes at Bridget's boyfriend. "You charming young man. Thank you, I am much improved."

"I'm very glad to hear that. You had all of us worried for a minute there."

"What're you doing here?" Bridget blurted out.

"I have a meeting this morning before heading to the job site. I thought I'd come see my girlfriend on the way. I brought you breakfast since I knew you missed it this morning." He held up a white paper bag with the name of a local diner stamped on it.

The playful gleam in his eye made her lips turn up in a smile despite her self-consciousness. He really was the sweetest guy she'd ever met, let alone dated. "Thanks, Jack." Seizing her confidence, she rose on her tiptoes and planted a kiss on his mouth as she took the bag from him.

"Still hungry? You must've worked up quite the appetite this morning. After all, you wolfed down the croissant I brought in for you," Sarah said.

The ten-year-old in Bridget wanted to smack her sister. She was never going to live down this moment. Ever. Years from now, it would get brought up randomly in conversation just to see her squirm. "I'll save it for later." She shot a glare at her sister. "For when I'm hungry again."

"Ha." Becca snatched the bag and opened it up. "I'm famished now. I'll take this breakfast burrito." She grinned and unwrapped the top of it. "It wouldn't reheat well anyway. Thanks, Jack."

"You're welcome." He chuckled.

The door opened again and this time a real customer walked in. Bridget straightened and said, "Hello, welcome to Three Sisters Apothecary. Can I help you?" She wandered over to where the woman stood and helped her pick out two new lotions and a candle. All the while, she kept one eye on her family chatting with Jack. He looked in her direction once and winked. Her lady parts tingled at the sight.

After she wrapped up with the customer, Jack sidled over and slid an arm around her waist. "I gotta run. I'll be late for my meeting if I don't head that way." Leaning down, he brushed his lips to hers.

Despite the lightness of it, the kiss zinged all the way down to her toes. "Thanks for the attempt at breakfast," she whispered. "I'll see you tonight?" She couldn't hold back the hope that filled her at having him with her again.

"Without a doubt. Remember, I'm cooking you dinner at my place." He grinned then kissed her again. "See you then." He nodded to her family. "Have a great day."

A chorus of "Bye, Jack" sounded as he walked out. Bridget spun around to face them and the three of them burst out laughing.

"I can't believe all of you!" Bridget plunked her fists on her hips. "Did you see him walking up when you goaded me into that horrifying outburst?"

Gran waved her off. "Don't worry about that, Bridgie. It's not as if what you were saying wasn't complimentary." She came over and hugged her shoulders. "I'm glad to know you're happy. He seems like a nice boy."

She sighed. "He is. I...I like him. A lot."

"That's not a bad thing," Becca said. "You deserve this. Having a partner isn't a crime. You don't have to be alone all the time."

"I have a business to run," she replied in annoyance. "Boyfriends are distractions."

"You have all of us," Gran reprimanded. "This isn't a store you're running all on your own. You might be the owner, but we all have a stake in keeping our family legacy alive. You can still enjoy life." She looked at all three of them. "All of you need to live a little more. Secure your own family legacy."

\* \* \* \*

Jack sat in the chair across from a large mahogany desk where Paul faced him. He couldn't say he was pleased to be in this meeting, but it couldn't be helped.

"I'm ready to sell," Paul said. "Your company has made a damn good offer."

"My father's company. I work for him." Jack sighed. "How soon do you want to wrap this up? When do you want to sign and be done?"

"End of the month, give or take a week or so. I'm ready to retire and move on. My wife wants to travel more and see our grandkids in Portland." He shrugged. "I've been doing this a long time. I'd prefer to keep this local, but I can't pass up this offer. No one here can match it."

Jack refrained from hunching over and putting his face in his hands. Damn, but how was he going to save the jobs of the people here? How would he save the town's economy source? To exist, Fallbank needed Timber Logging Company. Three Sisters wouldn't survive it. "Would you give me a little time? At least through the end of the month? The fall festival?"

Paul fixed him with a steady stare. "All right, but that's all I can give. Although I'm not sure why you're doing this. Aren't you the one who wanted Thompson to buy TLC in the first place?"

"I did, but I've changed my mind on the execution of how I want us to proceed." Jack stood. "I'd like to keep it local now, too."

Paul nodded and stuck his hand out to shake. "Best of luck changing your father's mind. Or give Cornelius the kick in the pants he needs to step up, but I can't take a sub-par offer. I have to think of my family, too."

"Understood." Jack left the office and walked out into crisp temperatures and light drizzle. He tilted his head up and inhaled. The cool air filled his lungs and cleared his head. He'd figure out something. He had to. But first, he needed to sort out details to steal his girlfriend away for a weekend.

Actually, first he needed to go take down some trees. He hopped into his truck and drove the forty-five minutes over to the work site. Grabbing his hard hat and gloves, he walked over to the yarder. "Where do you want me?"

Niall jerked his chin over to an equipment truck. "Grab a chainsaw and head down the hill. You're on chopping duty today."

With a nod, Jack grabbed a heavy saw and set off down the hill. A mile down he met Cornelius, also cutting trees.

Cornelius grinned and pointed. "All of these trees were damaged in the storm that came through here last week. We need to clear them this week and let the rest of the team haul them up. There's a hundred grand worth of lumber here alone."

"Let's get to it then. I'll take the left." He headed to the far edge and chose a leaning fir another two hundred feet down. Standing at the tree, he cut a wedge in the direction of the slope to ensure the trunk fell in the direction of the pull of gravity. Then he slid around and cut straight across until the wood began splintering and fell with an almighty crash. He stepped to the next one and did the same. By the time he'd felled ten trees, his arms shook with the weight of the chainsaw and the exertion it took to push it clean and straight through the wood in the precise manner needed. One small slip and the trunk could topple in the wrong direction and kill someone. Or himself.

The eleventh tree was leaning at a dangerous slant and a shiver of anxiety slithered through his stomach. Even just the wedge he'd need to cut would be risky and he'd have to be on guard more than the others. He lifted the blade to place it at an upward angle, then set the chain spinning. The edge bit into the wood and the tree swayed. With steady, strong pressure, he guided the metal through the wood until the trunk trembled and drifted closer to the ground. The opposite side of the wood cracked and Jack pulled the saw, fumbling backward as the tree swooped down within seconds. The wind and the debris kicked up in his face and the ground trembled beneath his feet. The air rushed out of his lungs as he realized how close he'd come to having this tree crush him into the ground.

Two loud blasts of a horn caught his attention and he turned around. He tugged his earplugs out and waved to Cornelius as he walked over.

"Time for lunch, but damn good job this morning. That last one was a doozy. Next time have a spotter and you should start on the opposite side. Gravity was in your favor that time."

Hours later he wound his way back through the heavy forests with aching arms and exhausted legs, but buoyed spirits about getting back to Bridget. Tonight, he was cooking dinner for her at his place. She'd felt bad about the two of them spending so much time alone at her place and Cornelius not having company.

After swinging by the grocery store, he pulled into his driveway, hopped out and grabbed the bags. He walked in to find his roommate and his girlfriend chatting on the overstuffed couch. She smiled at him and all the stress from the day eased from his shoulders. That grin made everything worthwhile.

She stood and grabbed a bag as they walked into the kitchen. "How was your day?"

"Better now that I get to see you again. This morning wasn't long enough." He winked as she breathed out a laugh and shook her head.

"You're incorrigible. Can I help with dinner?"

Pressing a kiss to her lips not nearly long enough for him to be satisfied, he said, "Nope. Go relax. I'm doing the work tonight. Let me treat you."

"All right, if you insist. The only thing I'll do is open the wine, but I won't even pour you a glass."

"Cornelius," he shouted over his shoulder then turned back. "Come open the wine. Bridget doesn't understand she doesn't get to do any work this evening. That includes opening the wine."

Laughing again, she took an offered glass from Cornelius and sat back down with an eye roll. "So what do you hear about this takeover of TLC? Is someone buying us out?"

Cornelius flicked a palm in the air. "Who knows? Paul is gearing up to sell, but he's been very hush-hush about who and what the plan is."

"It'll work out, Cor. It has to. Paul wouldn't betray us all by selling out and allowing some conglomerate to outsource the jobs here. He knows it would decimate the economy in town." Bridget put a hand over his forearm. "We'll be okay."

Jack said nothing and tried to focus on cooking, but the dragging weights around his neck were crushing him. He needed to figure out how to keep his family and business needs in balance with what Fallbank had to have to survive.

\* \* \* \*

Bridget was proud of herself for making it through dinner and dessert while still carrying on a conversation with Cornelius and not attacking Jack to tear his clothes off. The whole meal he'd sat by her with little teasing touches along her neck or shoulders, brushes of his fingers along her thigh beneath the table and even once skimming the backs of his knuckles along the curve of one breast. He'd set fire to her blood and she was desperate to get him alone.

As soon as they'd walked hand-in-hand up the sidewalk and stepped inside her house, Bridget pounced on him. Pressing herself flush from chest to thighs, she kissed him hard and deep with a moan rumbling in her throat. She wove her fingers into his hair.

He kissed her back with equal fervor, gripped her hips and lifted her up.

She wrapped her legs around him as he spun to pin her to the door and ground against her. Sparks of pleasure burst through her body and she wriggled for more friction. Jack shifted his lips down to her throat and she sighed at the delicious sensation of his tongue and teeth on her sensitive skin. "More. *Please.*"

He said nothing, but suddenly clothing was shed with alacrity and all Bridget knew were his kisses and caresses, his toned muscles pressed against her softness, his body joined with hers as they ravished each other there in the entryway until they both drowned in the pleasure.

After, when they made it to her bed, she rested her head on his chest and listened to his heart still pounding with the same fierceness as her own. She wondered at how everything was so good.

The ease with which she and Jack got to know one another, the way they talked and disagreed and worked things out like they'd known each other for decades and not less than two months… How he could make her body sing when they made love, giving her such intense pleasure… She hadn't known it existed. No one else she'd been intimate with before had coaxed from her this deep satisfaction that left her trembling from the force of it.

He was so kind and sweet and caring. And how was all of this possible? How had he walked into her life — this perfect partner — and integrated himself with such ease? It was as if he'd been designed to meet every need and desire she'd ever had in life. If she didn't so fervently not believe in magic, she could imagine he'd been conjured up by a spell.

"What's the worst thing you've done?"

"What?" he asked and jerked his eyebrows up.

She covered her face with a hand and muttered to herself, "Sorry, that was abrupt, wasn't it?"

He chuckled and the vibration of it shook through her, too.

"Kind of. Now, why is it that you're wanting to know?" He stroked his hand over her hair and continued down her back in one long motion.

Tingles spread across her still sensitive skin and she snuggled closer in his embrace. "Tell me something about you that makes you not perfect."

His lopsided smile appeared. "You think I'm that amazing, huh? I don't know if I want to disillusion you."

"Oh, come on. There's got to be something disagreeable about you. That's going to irk me?"

"Um, I don't know. My sister always tells me I'm super annoying all the time."

A thought popped into her head. "How long are you staying?"

"Tonight? Did you want me to go home? I thought—"

"No, not tonight. I'll kick your gorgeous arse if you even think of leaving me alone in this bed."

He full-on laughed. "Arse? Are you British now?"

She swatted a hand at that incredible chest of his. "Stop teasing me. I watch a lot of BBC shows. I meant, are you staying in Fallbank? Long term, are you going back to Seattle? I mean, you didn't even move furniture here. You're just renting a room from Cornelius."

He swallowed and caressed her back again. "That's something I'm still figuring out. I didn't think I'd stay here beyond a couple of months, but all of that is shifting in my head. I have a place in Seattle still, but that life is looking less and less appealing to me." He regarded her with a hint of wariness. "What if I did stay? Permanently?"

The weight of what he was asking hit her and she blinked. What if he did stay? If *they* were permanent? That little glowing ember of hope, of happiness at finding another person she could have at her side throughout life, glowed bright within her. "I would like that." Her voice was soft, but steady. No hint of the excitement or that thin trickle of fear that this was all too good to be true leaked out of her. She waited for his reaction. Most men would run screaming from this kind of declaration this soon in a relationship.

Jack smiled. "Me too." He cupped her cheek and kissed her, soft and slow. This wasn't about arousal and seduction, although that was there a little, too. This was romance and love and promise. Even if those words hadn't been spoken aloud, she felt them all the way to the very marrow of her bones.

"Jack." She sighed into his mouth. The kiss deepened and became more. And the way he loved her body became more, too. This lovemaking was fraught with passion and desire, yes, but also unspoken tenderness and caring. Love blossomed between them in a physical way, binding the two of them together in a way she'd not experienced before. This time when she came, it was slow and rolling and shook her to her soul. She let go of all of her fears and gave herself over to him and the emotion building between them. This time, she didn't stop those words from crossing her lips. "I love you."

# Chapter Fourteen

Jack was going to burn for this. He'd led Bridget to think he was staying long term while his family was hounding him to wrap things up and get back home. He wrapped his hands around the thick wire from the yarder and his leather gloves bit into his skin. He welcomed the sting of pain as he hefted the wire and turned to hoof it down the side of the hill. He relished the unrelenting work of running back and forth from the top of the hill and down a mile and a half to where the felled trees lay. Once he dragged the steel cable from the yarder down, he wrapped it around the giant base stump so they could attach the trees and haul them ski-lift-style back up to the top where the machine sat and the trucks waited to be loaded to carry the logs in for processing.

"All set," he spoke into his walkie-talkie. The loud churning of an engine broke the relative silence of the forest and he climbed back up to grab another cable attached to the larger one to wrap around the trees. The work was brutal and exhausting and long. Jack forced his head to be mindful of every moment. He deserved this kind of work today.

Bridget loved him. She'd told him that last night when they'd made love the second time and it had driven him so crazy he'd made her come again just to hear her say it once more. There was no doubt she meant those words. She wasn't the type to throw that around without meaning it with all she was. After she'd fallen asleep in his arms, he'd brushed kisses along the crown of her head but had held those words back. They echoed and ached in his heart, but he couldn't allow them free. He couldn't promise Bridget anything and she was certain to hate him once she learned what his family's company planned to do. He needed more time to convince his father that they needed to change the way they wanted to approach this acquisition. A phone call to his dad was in order.

After securing another wire around a trunk, he pressed twice on the loud horn he had attached to his belt and the line began pulling the log up the side of the mountain. Breathing heavily, he paused for a few moments. Maybe he needed his father to come to the work site to believe that they couldn't reallocate other workers to do this type of job. His background in construction meant nothing when it came to logging. Neither was like each other besides the fact that they were both manual labor. They both required skills that couldn't be easily picked up. A person had to be taught and it took time to master. He was nowhere near where he needed to be and the other guys made him look ridiculous as they worked alongside him.

Yanking his thoughts back to the present, he focused on the work at hand. He had to get through today so he could put his plan into action for stealing Bridget away for the weekend. She needed a break and he needed to pamper her. She might freak out a little, but he felt confident he could persuade her to enjoy their getaway. For once, his money would serve a purpose to help him, not hinder. After all, he'd never met a woman who didn't enjoy his wealth.

Hours later, exhausted from his exertions in the forests, Jack made his way back home. He sent a quick text to Bridget that he was too tired to hang out tonight. It wasn't untrue, and he also wanted to tie up a few loose ends for the weekend.

The next morning he rose, rejuvenated and revived for the weekend ahead. Grabbing his bag, he tossed it into his truck and headed off to work for a half day. Once that was done, he drove over to Three Sisters and walked in. Gran, Sarah and Bridget were there and the smiles they gave him had warmth buzzing inside his chest. They had made him welcome and a part of their family, despite not knowing him for long.

"Jack, what are you doing here?" Bridget walked over to him and kissed his cheek. "This is a surprise. I thought you had to work and I wouldn't see you until tonight."

He grinned at her and wrapped an arm around her waist. "Well, I have a couple more surprises in store for you."

The corners of her smile dipped down and she furrowed her brow. "What do you mean?" She stepped back and he hated the space between them.

For the first time since putting things in motion, he questioned whether or not this was a good idea. "I'm stealing you for the weekend. I thought we could go up to Portland."

"Portland? This weekend." She took another step back and crossed her arms. "I have to work, Jack. We talked about this. There's the store and the festival tomorrow. I can't just up and leave." She closed her eyes and sighed. When she opened her eyes again, they had softened. "I appreciate the gesture, but I can't."

"You can," Gran interjected. "This delightful boyfriend of yours arranged with us to cover the shifts at the store and the festival. Between myself, Sarah and Becca, we have it all sorted."

Bridget looked between Gran and him. "You asked my grandmother to take over my work for me? Who just had a heart attack?" She shook her head and made a frustrated sound before walking off to the back of the shop.

"Shit," he mumbled and trailed after her. He pushed through the door and found her pacing the back room. "Honeybee, I'm—"

"Stop. Don't do that. Don't try to sweet-talk your way out of this. What were you thinking, Jack?"

"I'm sorry. I thought it would be fun to surprise you. We'd talked about going away for a weekend and you were open to that."

"Yes, *after* the fall festival season was done and Gran had more time to recover. I told you that. This store is mine. My responsibility to keep running. *Mine.*"

"And you do a wonderful job of everything, but you're also burning yourself out. I know it's hard, but you have others you can rely on. Trust them, Bridget. Let people help you."

"I'm—"

Sarah came through the door and stood next to him. "He's right, Bridge. You can't do everything all the time. You need to hire an actual employee to help cover the store so you can focus on the big picture. And do things like take a weekend off to run away with your boyfriend. He worked hard to surprise you and make sure all of the responsibilities were covered. We've got this. Go with him. Relax. Enjoy yourself."

She hugged her sister and whispered something he couldn't make out. Then she stepped back and smiled at him. "Both of you have fun. Her bag is in the corner." She pointed to where a large box sat. "Behind there."

After Sarah left, Jack looked at Bridget. Apprehension raced through his veins and his heart thumped fast. "Honeybee?" He put all of his hope into that one word.

"I don't like surprises."

He blinked. "Okay. Then I guess I should fill you in on the others I have planned, huh?"

She sighed and pushed her curls off her cheeks. "No, don't do that. I like little ones, but something like this… It's not my strong suit. I like order and planning in my life."

"I gathered as much, but sometimes it's good to relinquish some of that control."

"I know." She reached out and slid her hand into his. "It's hard for me, but you're right. So I'm going to say thank you for putting all of this together and go get my bag."

He couldn't stop his smile and relief dripped through his limbs when she grinned back. A tiny note of anxiety still remained. Jack needed to be sure he made this weekend worthwhile or she might not agree again. He stepped in and kissed her, wanting her to know how much she meant to him. "Thank you. I'm really looking forward to taking you away for a couple of days."

She bounced on her toes once. "I'm excited, too. Now that I've accepted this is happening, at least."

* * * *

The hour drive from Fallbank to Portland was spent with Bridget peppering Jack for details on what he'd planned for them, but to no avail. She eventually subsided her interrogation and enjoyed the views of the trees and low-hanging clouds floating among them. It gave the world a gothic vibe. When there was a gap in cars, it was as if they were alone in the world.

Soon though, the firs gave way to open farmland and eventually the streets and skyline of Portland came into view as traffic picked up. He navigated while she looked around at the familiar sights of the city. "I haven't been to Portland in a while." She tried to remember, but it had to have been months, if not over a year. Since taking over the store, she hadn't had much time for a day trip to go hiking or shopping or check out the food scene. "I guess I do need to make more time for taking breaks."

Jack smiled indulgently at her. "Then think of this as your first, with more to come. I'll try to keep the bar high to motivate you to come back to see how much better each trip can be."

He navigated through the streets and they ended up in the heart of downtown Portland outside The Nines hotel. She ran her gaze over the Art Deco building as they hopped out of his truck while a valet assistant waited for them.

"This is a really nice hotel, Jack. Spectacular." *Expensive*. The word rang through her head and she couldn't seem to shake it. One night here had to cost a couple hundred dollars and they were staying for two? She swallowed back her apprehension.

He put his hand at the small of her back and leaned in to kiss her. "I wanted to treat you. This is our first trip together." He winked. "I had to make this special for my honeybee."

"You know you didn't have to do this, right?"

Shifting his hand from her back to lace his fingers with hers, he said, "I know. I wanted to. Come on, let's go check out the inside."

He waggled his brows at her and she couldn't help but laugh. "Lead the way, boyfriend." She shook off her nerves and stepped into the opulent modern-met-Art Deco lobby. She turned in a slow circle as Jack checked in. There were statues and paintings and funky art displays paired with rich textured seating and plush carpets and playful wallpaper. It was a kaleidoscope of color and sensory input that came together in a beautiful way.

"All set." Jack walked over and tugged her toward the elevator. "Time to go investigate our room." He flashed her a wicked grin as he hit the button. As soon as they were inside and the doors slid shut, Jack grabbed her close and slanted his mouth over hers.

She sighed and leaned into the heat of his lips and tongue stroking against hers. Lifting her hands, she grabbed his pullover with her fists and held on as her knees trembled. His hands were at her waist, then he drifted the roughened skin of his fingertips along her back. She shivered and pressed her body along his. God, but this man drove her to abandon all sensible thought and action. What was she doing full-on making out in an elevator? Yet she couldn't stop herself. A moan vibrated in her throat as he dipped his hand beneath the waist of her jeans to caress the top of her ass. Her whole being burned with need and when the bell dinged, they stumbled from the elevator together.

Jack glanced up for a brief moment, then walked her backward down the hall.

She wrapped her arms around his neck and let him guide her, giving her trust to him. She nuzzled close and ran her lips along the column of his throat, loving the low, rumbly noise he made when she nipped him with her teeth.

Suddenly she was suspended in the air as he tossed her over one shoulder and raced down the hall. "Jack!" She screeched and laughed. Her hair was a mess hanging down in her face and she bounced against his firm muscles with every step, but his hand on her butt kept her from falling. The urgency thrumming between them made up for any discomfort. The sounds of the key card beeping then the door opening reached her, and she wriggled.

With a grunt, Jack smacked her bottom. It made her ache and throb and turn liquid between her thighs. She stilled at the shocking sensation he'd evoked with one playful move. Before she could think too deeply about it, he plopped her onto a massive, soft bed where she sank into the downy comforter and Jack collapsed next to her. Then he was kissing her and she forgot anything else around her.

\* \* \* \*

Much later, when she surfaced from her sex-induced haze, Bridget blinked and peered around them. "Is this a suite?"

"I got us upgraded at check-in." Jack shrugged and flopped onto his back. He turned and smirked at her. "Damn, honeybee. I'm not sure I'll be much good this afternoon. I thought we could go walk around and check out the restaurants and shops, but my legs are still shaking."

Heat warmed her cheeks and she swatted at him. She had gotten more feisty than normal, but who could blame a girl when she had a sexy-as-sin man in her bed to do with as she pleased? And she was *very pleased*. "Quit embarrassing me," she grumbled.

"I can't. You're too fetching when you blush like that. I especially love when you're naked and I get to watch the pretty pink color spread all the way down to those perfect breasts of yours." He grinned lasciviously at her and stared at her chest.

"Jack!" She covered her face with her hands and rolled onto her stomach.

He swept a hand over her bottom and growled even dirtier words in her ear. With a groan, she grabbed his face in her hands and kissed him again.

\* \* \* \*

The next time they surfaced out of their lovemaking nest, the sky had darkened and Bridget's stomach growled. Jack laughed and brushed his fingers across her still dewy skin. "I need to feed you, huh?"

She batted a pillow half-heartedly at his head. "You did wear me out."

"I thought I worked you out," he joked.

One dark brow rose on her gorgeous face. "Keep making jokes like that and we've never going to end up leaving this bed."

He leaned up on one arm and hovered over her. "Is that a promise?" His cock sure hoped so. Despite their number of rounds in bed this afternoon, he still found himself getting aroused all over again.

Her stomach let out another rumble, this one louder than the first.

Laughing, he said, "Okay, okay. I give. Let's get dinner and then we'll come back for dessert."

She twined her arms around his neck and pulled him in for a kiss. "Promise?" she asked against his mouth.

"Oh, hell yeah, honeybee."

He tugged her out of the fluffy duvet and pillows and she looked around.

"Wow, this is massive." She wandered into the bathroom and squealed. "Holy cow! Look at the size of the tub! And the shower! Oh! The vanity even has one of those stools to sit on while you put on your makeup!" She spun around with wide eyes. "I thought that was something that was just in movies. I don't even wear makeup and I have to try this out."

He followed his gloriously naked girlfriend into the bathroom and watched as she cooed over every detail. He loved it. He loved her. Now if he could figure out how he was going to keep them together, he could tell her those three words, too. She hadn't said them outside of the bedroom and she hadn't brought up the fact that he hadn't repeated the sentiment to her.

A stabbing bolt of guilt shot through him. He was horrible for not being honest with her. He just needed more time. He wanted to come up with a plan to save the town and keep Bridget as his girlfriend. As more than that if things kept going so well between them. He was already picturing them with kids and cats and a massive garden she could fill to overflowing. He'd started looking at land surrounding Fallbank to find an ideal spot to build a house that wasn't too far from town. She'd want to be close to Gran and the store.

His thoughts trailed off as she perched on the plush blue velvet ottoman stool at the vanity. His mind plummeted into all sorts of dirty, sexy scenarios and other parts of him agreed wholeheartedly. Forcing himself to turn around, he called out, "If you don't get dressed, we are never leaving this room. We will be having sex in this bathroom in multiple places, and you will starve tonight."

Her throaty chuckle was his only clue at her approach. She wrapped her arms around him and pressed her still gloriously naked body flush to his back. "Don't threaten me with a good time. I'll hold you at your word."

He swore and started to turn around, but her stomach roaring again stopped him. "Food. You need food. Then more sex."

She kissed his cheek. "Sounds like a plan."

Once they had dressed, they walked out of the bedroom and into the main living area. Again, she fussed over the fireplace and plush couch and mini kitchen with a fully stocked wine fridge. Her excitement over their "upgrade" gave him another pang of guilt. He was trash for leading her to believe they'd magically gotten upgraded to the best suite in the hotel. Of course, Bridget didn't know these were their swankiest rooms, but still. He'd reserved the suite for them. For her. To treat her in ways she'd never been treated before. He would lay the world at her feet if he could. Given the amount of money he had, there was a significant amount he could give her. And she had no idea.

For the first time in his life, being rich was something he was afraid of her learning about. It was a bizarre twist to his money being the main thing women cared about when it came to dating him. Now he had no idea how she would react. And the longer he put off telling her about his wealth, the worse this could backfire in his face.

"Should we go forage for food?" Jack held out his hand and she slipped hers into it.

"I know of this great pub a couple of streets over," she offered. "They have amazing fish and chips and tons of beer options on tap."

"Perfect. Lead the way."

After leaving the hotel, they walked over to the British pub a few blocks away and into the warm atmosphere. Finding a booth, they sat together and she cuddled up against him. "Is this okay?"

"One hundred percent," he answered and looked over the menu that a server slid onto the table as she walked by with a tray of drinks.

"I'll be back in sec," the server called over her shoulder.

Jack skimmed the listings and his own stomach let out a cry for food as he took in all the options. "What are you getting?"

"I'm debating between the pot pie and the veggie pasty. What about you?" She looked up at him and his heart stuttered.

How had he gotten lucky enough to find this woman? How was he stupid enough to find himself on the verge of losing her? He had to find a way to fix the acquisition of Timber Logging. This had been his project from the start. He'd find a way to save the jobs and the town and stay with Bridget. His dad could go jump in a lake if he had a problem with it.

"Jack?"

He cleared his throat and pasted a smile on his face. "Sorry. I was distracted by your beauty."

She rolled her eyes, but he caught the light hint of pink in the apples of her cheeks.

"I'm serious. But I'm thinking the fish and chips since you said it was so good."

"I did say that, didn't I?" She pursed her mouth and looked at the menu again. "I'm getting the same. And a local beer. There're too many great breweries around here to not. Plus, it helps the local economy."

Yep, he was dangerously close to everything blowing up in his face.

# Chapter Fifteen

Portland was freaking magical. And wasn't that a trip for her to even think? Bridget loathed all things magic and here she was waxing poetic about how enchanting this city was. Since their arrival, everything had been wonderful. They'd gone at each other like bunnies, one romp after another, always wanting more. Dinner last night had been crispy, deep-fried deliciousness. Then this morning after another round in bed and in that amazing shower, they'd stumbled out into the world to a cloudy but mild day.

Jack took her to the Rose Garden and the Japanese Gardens and they wandered around holding hands, taking pictures together and enjoying the stunning surroundings. The Japanese Gardens captivated her and they strolled for hours though the lush green world. The trees were massive and created a natural canopy that filtered the low gray light of the world, and the hint of mist in the air made it seem otherworldly. She watched koi fish swim through the little pools and streams with Jack's arms around her and his chin resting on her shoulder. Everything blended perfectly with nature. Even the stone and wood structures grew moss as though the earth were making them its own.

Eventually, they left and found a great local donut shop to stop for a quick bite and warm coffee. Bridget hummed at the sugary, melty deliciousness of her glazed brioche donut. "This is so good." She moaned.

Jack's eyes widened and he coughed on his sip of coffee.

"You okay?" She chuckled and took a bite of her heaven-as-a-donut, another tiny whimper escaping her lips.

"Good. I'm good," he choked out. "I just thought *I* was the only one who could make you make those noises. Clearly I need to up my game."

Bridget licked sugar off her lips and smiled. "I'm certainly willing to let you try over and over again. I'd hate for you to feel you weren't the best thing in my life to make me respond in ecstasy." She nibbled the dough. "But this donut is pretty damn close."

Jack growled and grabbed up their trash, clearing the table with a swiftness that left her stunned. Then he held out a hand. "Time to go. I gotta show my girl how much better I am than some pastry."

She slipped her palm in his and stood. "By all means, feel free to remind me."

\* \* \* \*

Later, after another round or two in bed followed by a nap, Bridget woke to Jack nuzzling her neck with soft kisses. "Mmm, again?" She grinned. "I could be persuaded."

"Much as I would love that, and it does pain me to say no, we have dinner reservations."

"Reservations?" She peeked up at him. "Are we going somewhere fancy?"

He shrugged and a hint of pink appeared in his cheeks. "I wouldn't say *fancy*-fancy, but it's a nice place. You should have a dress or something. I told your sister to pack for it."

"Oh my. Who knows what Sarah would pack for me." She climbed out of bed and showered, then used that plush vanity seat she'd grown so fond of to fix her hair before stepping into the little black dress her sister had packed. At least Sarah hadn't taken it upon herself to buy a new dress that was way more risqué than she preferred. Or more likely, Sarah hadn't had the time to go shopping for her. This dress fit Bridget's style, but she worried it wasn't dressy enough. The sleeveless black sheath was overlaid with black lace that gave a higher scoop neckline and came down to cover her arms. Her silver kitten heels added a little flash of sparkle.

She examined herself in the full-length mirror and chewed her bottom lip. Was it enough? This hotel was already more than she'd imagined and the suite was incredible. She should make sure Jack knew he didn't need to spend this kind of money on her. She had no idea how much this trip was costing him, but it couldn't be easy to cover on what he made from the lumber mill.

A knock sounded on the bathroom door. "You ready, honeybee?"

Her smile was unstoppable. She secretly loved when he called her that. He had given her a pet name. She'd never dated a guy who'd done that before and it made her feel special. Walking out, she clasped her hands together as her stomach fluttered with nerves.

His gaze drifted over her with an awestruck expression. "Wow. You look beautiful, Bridget. That dress"—he slowly smiled—"is spectacular. I'm going to be the envy of every guy at the restaurant tonight." He reached for her waist, pulling her to him.

"You're not so bad yourself." She ran her hands up the midnight blue suit jacket he wore. She wasn't lying—he looked heart-poundingly handsome. The suit had obviously been tailored to fit his wide shoulders and tall frame and damn, did he wear it well. "Come on, we'd better go now or we might not leave at all."

He tucked her hand in his arm and they made their way down to the rideshare car waiting for them. They pulled up outside a small, romantic-looking Italian restaurant and they seated the two of them at a table upstairs, away from most of the other customers.

"What kind of wine do you like?" Jack studied the list and glanced up at her.

"I don't know. Red or white is fine. Although red sometimes gives me a headache."

He nodded and glanced at the list again. "How does the sauvignon blanc from Willamette Valley sound?"

She looked at the menu and the breath in her lungs seized. "Jack," she wheezed, "that bottle costs two hundred and fifty dollars." She ran her eyes over all of the prices. Shit. The cheapest bottle of wine was ninety-five dollars. "I could just get a glass of their house white. I'm sure that would be good." And still probably twenty bucks for one stupid glass. Bridget opened the menu and sweat broke out along her neck. Everything on this menu was priced outrageously. "Jack..."

He covered her head with his. "Honeybee, it's okay. I knew what I was getting into when I made the reservation. Please don't worry about the bill. I've got it."

She bit her lip and gave a slow shake of her head. "I'm not sure I'm comfortable with you spending this kind of money on me. It's just dinner, for crying out loud."

He opened his mouth to respond, but another man called out his name.

"Jack! It is you. Where've you been?" The guy walked over with a bright, perfect smile and a bright, perfect woman alongside him.

Jack stood up to shake hands with this new guy and kissed the woman on the cheek in greeting. The man was in a suit very similar to Jack's and the woman, well, she looked like she'd stepped directly out of a page from *Vogue*. Her red dress, stiletto heels and matching clutch all had to be from some very high-end designer, not that Bridget could even begin to guess which one. Her blonde hair was upswept in a fancy knot and her makeup was flawless, her lipstick a perfect red to match her dress. Then they all turned her way, and Bridget had never felt more out of place in her entire life.

The woman looked her over like a specimen in a science lab and from her expression, she found Bridget lacking. She held out a manicured hand. "I'm Sabrina Van DerKamp, and you are?" She blinked her fake eyelashes twice.

"I'm Bridget Wildes. Nice to meet you." She gripped Sabrina's limp hand and shook it once.

Sabrina's eyes widened. She shifted her fingers to give a light squeeze then leaned in to air-kiss both of Bridget's cheeks. "A pleasure." The pinched expression on her face when she stepped back gave away her lying words. She turned that bemused expression on Jack. "What *are* you doing here?"

Jack stepped closer to Bridget and put his hand on the small of her back. The warmth of his palm radiated through the fabric of her dress in a soothing manner. She leaned back just slightly into his touch. "Taking my girlfriend out for dinner. Stephen, this is Bridget. Bridget, this is Stephen. He and I have known each other most of our lives."

Was this a close friend of his? Anxiety knotted in her stomach. How did he know these people? And if these were the kind of people he normally hung out with, what was he doing slumming it in Fallbank? With her?

"Lovely to meet you, Bridget." Stephen stepped in and kissed her cheek.

She pasted her customer smile across her features. "Yes, um, same here." She cut her eyes to Jack to take his cue on how to proceed.

Sabrina spoke up instead. "We must join you for dinner! It's been too long since we've seen you, Jack, and I'm simply dying to know more about your new girlfriend."

Jack turned to her and she kept her polite mask in place as she said, "Of course, it would be nice to get to know some of Jack's friends."

They all sat and their server came back over to take drink orders. Two bottles of the insanely priced wine were ordered along with appetizers, and Bridget sat with her hands folded in her lap, fake smiling and wondering how long this evening was now going to drag on.

"Jack, what is with this beard on your face? You look like a wild beast!' Sabrina trilled out a laugh.

"Just something different I'm trying out. It helps keep my face warmer when I'm out working."

"Oh yes." She let out that high-pitched giggle again. "You always were one to prefer manual labor over a desk in a corner office." She turned her calculating blue eyes on her. "Bridget, darling, tell us all about you! How did you two meet?"

"Bridget owns her own store. She's brilliant at it." Jack smiled and reached out to cover her knotted hands with his.

"Oh, what kind of store?" Stephen asked. "I always enjoy meeting other entrepreneurs."

She relaxed a fraction and turned one palm up to wind her fingers through Jack's. "It's mostly a body product shop, although we also have candles and teas and other things like that. All herbal based and handmade items. It's been in my family for centuries. That's where we met, actually."

Jack laughed. "I have to admit, I was skeptical at first, but some of the other guys from work dragged me there and she has this amazing beard conditioner. It fixed the itching and makes the hair really soft, like magic. Plus, she was too pretty to say no to."

Bridget flushed and looked down for a moment. When she looked up, Sabrina was peering at her. "How fascinating. You make all of these...items yourself? And your family has been passing these recipes down, you said? Like a coven of witches?"

Sabrina laughed at her own joke, but Bridget couldn't find it in herself to fake it. Thankfully, the server came back with the wine and took their orders. Bridget picked the least expensive meal on the menu. She cringed at what the bill would be at the end. At least they would be splitting it between the two couples.

Jack piped up after the orders were placed. "Bridget is an herbalist. She knows almost everything there is to know about plants and what they can do for people."

An herbalist. She'd never thought of herself that way, but it fit. Like the root workers of long ago, back when medicine study was prohibited to females and the wise women passed down their knowledge. She squeezed his hand under the table.

"How quaint."

Stephen cleared his throat and changed the subject. "So when do we expect you back in Seattle?"

Jack shrugged. "Not sure yet. I don't have a lot of motivation at this time to leave Fallbank right away."

He shot a wink at her and Bridget's smile turned from fake to real in an instant. At least he wasn't acting ashamed of her.

Sabrina rolled her eyes. "You're still out playing lumberjack? And you like it? Have you invested in a flannel company and are trying to make it successful?"

"Logging is really hard and takes a massive amount of skill," Bridget snapped. She wasn't about to let some spoiled rich girl dismiss what her friends did and the industry that kept her town alive. "It's also consistently ranked as the most dangerous job in America. It has the highest fatality and injury rate of any other non-military job on the market. Even higher than the police."

Stephen furrowed his brows. "And your father just let you go off and do this, Jack?"

"He didn't let me do anything. I made this choice myself." Jack clenched his jaw for a second, then changed the subject. "So what's going on with you, Stephen? How's business on your end?"

The topic of Bridget or Fallbank and logging didn't get brought up again. Bridget spent the rest of the meal enjoying the absolutely delicious food, including dessert that was heaven in her mouth. And she had to admit the wine was the best she'd ever tasted. She wasn't sure it was $250 good, but it was far and away better than what she drank at home or at restaurants in town.

When the check came, the two guys argued over it a bit, but in the end Jack paid for the entire meal. Bridget's heart pounded at what must have been well over a thousand dollars. For four people. For dinner. She swallowed down her nausea at the extravagance. She was having trouble drowning out the tiny voice in her head telling her Jack might be loaded and was hiding that fact from her.

# Chapter Sixteen

Jack stood from the table and held out his hand to Bridget. She placed hers in it and he noticed how cold and shaky her fingers were. He wanted to scream with frustration. His friends and this dinner had been the worst idea. Bridget had been uncomfortable the whole meal and her gaze kept cutting back to the thick folio that held the bill inside it. The just-over-a-thousand-dollars receipt. That he had paid in full, like an ass. She wasn't dumb and had to know how much he'd dropped on one meal. He wanted to kick himself. All he'd wanted was to treat her to a nice dinner. Why had he decided the top-rated, most expensive restaurant in Portland was the place to take her? He should've walked out with her when she had questioned the price of the wine. They'd had fish and chips with beer last night, dammit. This wasn't the world Bridget lived in and from her reaction, it wasn't one she wanted to join either.

"You should join us for dancing!" Sabrina exclaimed. "We're going over to this great little jazz club. It's like a speakeasy and they have a live band with a dance floor. You two have to come!"

Mentally Jack facepalmed himself. In no way did he want to continue with this evening with Stephen and Sabrina. He wanted to get Bridget back to the hotel and distract her into bed and hope this all blew over.

"That sounds great!" Bridget grinned.

Shit, he was in such trouble. That wasn't her real smile and she was carrying fine tension in her shoulders.

She shot him a look and nodded. "We should go with your friends. It would be fun."

She was doing all of this for him. Because these were his friends. He loved her even more for the effort she was making to try to join his world, but there was a reason he'd stepped out of it. Why he was drawn to her earthiness and gentle nature. He wanted someone genuine and true. Not fake who only cared about appearances and money like Sabrina.

"Wonderful, let's go grab a cab." Sabrina looped her arm through Bridget's then led them back down the stairs and out into the misty October night.

The club was small and intimate with dark wood furniture and red leather booths lining the walls. Small circular tables filled the space between the bar and the dance floor. On the stage was a six-person jazz band, and couples were already cutting loose to their music. They grabbed a table up front and Stephen offered to get the first round, which Jack gladly let him take. Bridget was already suspicious enough with him paying for dinner. No need to pique her suspicions even more. Maybe another drink and some dancing would help him get this night back to where he'd hoped it would be with the two of them.

She was less tense now, but she was still wearing her customer smile, not a genuine one. Their drinks arrived and Bridget took a long swallow of her Moscow Mule.

Okay, that was enough. He grabbed her hand and said, "Let's go dance, honeybee."

Her eyes grew wide and she gave a little shake of her head as he pulled her to standing. "I can't dance." She cut her eyes to the swing-dancing happening on the floor. "And I really can't move like that."

He pressed his lips to her ear. "Just follow my lead, baby."

They joined the others on the worn, wooden floor and while Jack didn't have quite the skill that some others did, he had enough from the horrible ballroom dancing classes his mother had insisted he take back in high school. He'd hated every minute, but right now Jack had never been more grateful for those lessons. With one hand at Bridget's waist and the other with her fingers in his, he started them off, a simple moving their feet in time with the beat until real happiness took over her expression.

"Jack! You're good at this!"

He swung her out and twirled her back in so she was flush against him. Her laughter was a balm to his soul. Finally, he'd gotten something right this evening. He moved them across the floor, hips swaying, feet sliding and Bridget twirling and grinning. He'd have stayed there forever if he could. Or at least until Stephen and Sabrina left because he didn't want reality to crash through his new world. He wanted this…Bridget in his arms and her smile warming him to his soul. Nothing else seemed as important as this woman and all of the potential a life with her held.

The beat changed into a slower, sexier melody. He spun her again, and this time when she landed against him, Jack pressed his lips to hers and let go of everything around them. He slid his hands up and cupped her jaw as he plundered her mouth and Bridget softened and melted into him. In response, his whole body grew hard. Keeping one palm in place, he shifted the other to grasp her hip as he rocked against her in time to the slow, soulful music that now filled the air.

She pulled back on a gasp and looked at him with wild eyes. Lust-filled eyes. She ruined him entirely. "I love you."

Her eyes widened a fraction and her pupils expanded even larger. "Jack...I love you, too." Bridget ducked her chin. "But you already know that."

He lifted her face back up to his. "That doesn't mean I don't want those words from you again. And I should have told you sooner, because I do love you." Her smile warmed him to his toes. "Honeybee, what do you say we get out of here? Head back to our hotel?"

"Perfect." She leaned in and kissed him again, sweeter and softer. "I'm going to run to the ladies' room first. I'll be right back."

He watched her go, not at all abashed as he stared at her ass in that dress while she walked away. Then he sauntered over to their table and finished his Irish whiskey in one long gulp.

Stephen clapped a hand on his shoulder. "Well, that was quite the display. Practically screwed your girlfriend on the dance floor." His laugh was low and gritty. "I had no idea lower-class girls were so fun to slum it with. I might have to find a nice side piece. Want to introduce me to her friends?"

Jack jerked away and clenched his fists. Hot anger boiled in his blood. How dare anyone—especially a supposed friend of his—speak about Bridget that way? "She's *not* lower-class and she isn't some kind of joke to me. Now get the hell out of my face before I forget that we used to be friends."

He stepped back and held up his hands. "Whoa. Sorry, bro. Really. I guess I didn't realize how serious you were about her. She does seem very…sweet. Wholesome. It's refreshing given the jaded women in our world. I hope it works out for you two. It's an uphill battle, but you're the most determined person I know."

Jack grunted, not trusting he still wouldn't lash out at him for insulting Bridget. He wanted to get the hell out of there and back to the hotel where he could focus on her and forget the rest of the world existed. Then she came out of the bathroom with Sabrina trailing behind her and he knew that plan had been shattered.

She stalked up to their table, grabbed her drink and downed it in three long swallows. Slamming the copper mug to the wood, she said, "Ready to go?" Her eyes were bleary but a little manic.

He took her hand and threw a glare over her shoulder. "Sure, honeybee. Let's go."

\* \* \* \*

As soon as they were in the back of their rideshare, she turned to him and opened her mouth, but Jack closed his eyes, laid his head on the seat and sighed.

"I know we need to talk, but do you think we could table this conversation? For tonight, can we pretend we didn't run into my jerk friends? I promise we can talk about them later, but I don't want them to ruin what was supposed to be a weekend for you to relax and us to spend time together."

He looked exhausted and a little bit of her melted inside. Biting back her words, worry and insecurities, Bridget nodded. "All right." The booze from her drink at the club and the wine from dinner caught up with her all of a sudden. She swayed a little. "I think I'm a bit drunk anyway."

"Yeah, I was afraid that might happen," Jack said and pulled her into his arms.

She relaxed into him and savored his warmth. With a sigh, she let the rhythm of the car lull her into a light sleep. Jack's gentle shaking roused her and she sat up and blinked. "Are we at the hotel already?"

"Yeah. Should we go back to our room?"

She grabbed his hand and let him help her out of the car and up to their room. She shucked her shoes and dress, brushed her teeth and swiped a washcloth over her face. Then she collapsed into the massive bed, tired and tipsy and pissed off that this was the ending to this evening. She'd envisioned a much more passionate and fun way to wrap things up, but instead Jack climbed in beside her and pulled her into his arms.

"I'm sorry, Bridget. This wasn't how tonight was supposed to go."

She nuzzled into his chest with closed eyes and heavy limbs. "I know. I'm sorry, too."

"For what? Why are you apologizing?"

"I don't know." She giggled. "I'm still a little drunk. But this is nice. I like snuggling with you."

She felt him press little kisses to the top of her head. "Same, honeybee. Same."

\*\*\*\*

The next morning, Bridget woke up groggy with a mild headache. When she rolled over, a soft groan escaped her as she winced at the sunlight.

"Morning," Jack said, his voice low and gruff with sleep. He climbed onto the bed and stretched out next to her.

"Good morning. Where'd you go?"

"The room service I ordered arrived. I think I might have woken you when I got up to answer. Want some coffee?"

"Mmm, yes please." She sat up and looked down at the shirt she was wearing. One of Jack's soft cotton T-shirts that came down to mid-thigh on her. Last night came back to her and she winced at the memories. Ugh, how had things gotten so off course from what had otherwise been an almost perfect day? The scent of strong, black coffee hit her nose and she smiled gratefully. She took the mug and sipped. The hot liquid warmed her and helped settle her stomach. "Thanks, I needed this."

"There's eggs and bacon. Toast and waffles, too."

"How many people are you feeding this morning?" She chuckled and scooted out of the bed. "Lead the way. I'm surprisingly hungry."

After breakfast and a shower, she repacked her things into her small suitcase while Jack did the same. When they were both done, she looked around the room. It bothered her that the last memories she'd have of this crazy luxurious suite had been tainted by last night. This weekend's promise had been so close to amazing, then those friends of his had rained all over it.

"No. Not happening," she muttered.

"Huh?" Jack looked at her with furrowed brows.

Bridget grabbed the front of his shirt and yanked him to her. She kissed him hard and wrapped one leg over his hip, letting gravity take them onto the bed. Then they were shedding clothes, lost in each other and their passion.

When they finally re-dressed over an hour later, both of them wore smiles. The valet put their bags into the back of the truck as Bridget settled next to Jack in the cab. Once they were on the road, she nestled close and let the last vestiges of the tension plaguing her fall away.

"So, you want to tell me about those friends of yours?"

He blew out a long breath. "Stephen is someone I've known for years and Sabrina is his girlfriend. They've been dating for a while. She was in our social circle and finally sank her claws into him."

That seemed like an oversimplification, but also startlingly accurate. "Yeah, that sounds about right. With Sabrina, at least."

"What did she do? You came back from the bathroom upset."

"Are you rich?" She shook her head and twisted to look at him. "No, I know you have to have money. How rich are you?"

"Bridget..." He laced one hand with hers. "I'm... *My family* is comfortable. It's not something I like to rely on and I've worked since I was sixteen. But yeah, I'm definitely a rich, privileged white dude."

"That's sort of what she insinuated."

"What did she say?" His voice was gentle, but she saw the way the muscles in his jaw were tight.

"She asked where I bought my dress. I told her Ann Taylor, and she said that was perfect because she needed to get something appropriate as a gift for her maid." The shock from last night had worn off and now she was left with only embarrassment and shame with a dash of anger. Anger at this woman that Bridget didn't know for making her feel so small. And at herself for allowing Sabrina to stir her up like this. Bridget was a typical adult in America. Sabrina was the elitist who lived in a world that most people had never conceived of. The problem was that Jack also lived there, too. Or he had.

She glanced up. His knuckles were white from his grip on the steering wheel. "I can't believe that bitch. I'm so sorry. I've never liked her, but I tolerated her for Stephen's sake. But after last night, I don't think he's someone I want as a friend either. He's changed. Or maybe I have." He looked at her for a moment before focusing back on the road. "I'm not part of that circle anymore. That isn't my world, and as you can tell from meeting my sister, it's not how my family operates."

Jack eased off to the side of the road and threw the truck into park. Rain splattered the windshield in slow drops that soon sped up to a downpour. He turned and cupped her face in his hands. "I don't want that life. I want what we have. I want you, honeybee."

She blinked at the stinging in her eyes. The rough calluses on his hands proved he wasn't afraid to do real work...backbreaking, dangerous work. The sincerity in his eyes, the softness of his expression told her his words were true. "I want you, too." She kissed him slow and sweet, then turned up the simmering heat between them until they were both panting to catch their breath. "Let's go home, Jack."

* * * *

Jack's phone rang and he ignored the call. His father's nonstop calling was taking a toll, but he was stronger than his phone. Over and over and over it rang. He arrived at the work site for the day and shook his head at the massive equipment. Who knew the base of an old World War II tank could be transformed into logging equipment designed to haul massive piles of logs up giant hills so they could be loaded onto the trucks for delivery to the buyers? He pulled his hat over his ears and tugged on his gloves, then joined the crew in charge of arranging the trees into the truck beds. Around him the rumors flew about what was happening to their company. He ignored it as best he could, but the words still permeated into his consciousness.

"I hear the sale is coming any day now. We'll all be out of jobs before Thanksgiving," Charlie griped.

"Shit. Do you think Fallbank will survive? I mean we have the B&Bs and there's some good stores, but this is our only big industry," Jacob replied.

"I hear the witch's store is doing all right."

Jack froze at the mention of Bridget. Did these guys not realize they were speaking about his girlfriend? Or maybe they hadn't noticed he was right here?

Jacob spit off to the side. "I don't know who would buy stuff from a witch, but maybe they don't know what she is."

"Yeah, she needs to be taught a lesson." Charlie grunted as he shifted a log into place on the stack.

"What did you just say?" Jack spun around to face the two guys. He'd done his best to ignore their conversation. After all, fighting with idiots rarely changed anyone's mind. But there was only so much he could take. When someone threatened the woman he loved, he couldn't let it go. "Did you notice I was right here?"

They gave him blank stares. "Yeah, so?" Jacob said. "What of it?"

"Bridget is my girlfriend. You know, the 'witch' you were just talking about teaching a lesson." Jack clenched his fists against the anger pounding inside him. First this weekend with Stephen and Sabrina...now hearing this crap from coworkers was more than he was able to handle.

Charlie sneered at him. "Then maybe you need to get a handle on your bitch. Teach her where her place is, or we will."

"I'm going to give you three seconds to get out of my face and shut your stupid mouth. I don't have tolerance for ignorant, prejudiced jackasses."

"Hey, guys. Let's all calm down." Cornelius walked over. "Everyone back off and give each other space."

"Yeah, sure. Everyone knows you're another witch lover, too. It's disgusting."

Jack let his fist fly. It landed on Charlie's jaw with a satisfying crack. Pain shot through his bones, but he didn't let it stop him. He rocked back on his heels and threw a second punch with his other hand, this one slamming right into Charlie's nose.

All hell broke loose.

Jacob jumped at him and shoved Jack into the ground. The two of them rolled in the dirt, fists flying with insults and swearing slinging back and forth. Charlie dripped blood, his palms clamped over his damaged nose as he tried to kick Jack. Cornelius threw himself into the fray and grappled with Charlie while shouting for others to help pull Jack and Jacob apart.

Jack took a few hits to the ribs and one to the face, but he gave as good as he got. He let all of his rage and stress and frustration with life in general out as he fought to defend Bridget's reputation. And who would've thought he'd be doing something so stupid in this day and age? The thought didn't stop him, though. Being yanked off of Jacob was what stopped him.

His boss stood in front of all of them, red-faced and looking ready to spew fire. "I ought to fire every last one of you. What do you think you're doing fighting like a bunch of juveniles? You are all grown men and could land yourself in jail for assaulting each other. I should call the police and press charges. Not to mention how damn dangerous this kind of stupid behavior is around all of this equipment. The yarder, the saws and the piles of logs could all kill you when you're being careful, let alone acting like clowns. And it wasn't just you who could be hurt or killed!"

Shame flooded Jack as he realized the asinine way he'd acted. What had he been thinking getting into a fist fight, especially on a logging job site? He should be fired. If he were the owner, there was no way he'd tolerate this at all. "I'm sorry, Paul. You're right. This was inexcusable."

"Get off my job site for the rest of the day. You're all on probation. Come back in a week and we'll see how generous I'm feeling."

"I can't go without pay for an entire week," Jacob whined.

"You should've thought about that when you decided to brawl on my job site."

Charlie pointed at Jack. "He started it."

"I don't care who started it!" Paul shouted, his face a mottled purple. "You were fighting. Period. Get out of here, now."

Jack muttered another apology and shuffled off to his truck. Once inside, he blew out a heavy breath and winced as he took stock of his injuries. His ribs hurt from where Charlie had landed a kick and his cheek and eye throbbed from Jacob's excellent right hook. He knew without looking in a mirror that he'd be sporting a black eye for a week or two. Ashamed and angry at himself, he threw the truck into drive and headed back into town. Hopefully his gorgeous witch girlfriend would have a remedy for him. And maybe a little pity instead of ire at his shenanigans?

# Chapter Seventeen

Bridget walked into her shop early on Monday morning in the hopes she could get a bead on how things had gone while she had been away. She entered through the front and stopped short. "Oh, I'm sorry. I didn't realize we had a customer already. Can I help you with something?" She smiled at the girl with gorgeous brown skin and wondered what products she might be looking for. Were Gran or Sarah or Becca here?

The young girl returned her grin. "I'm Arianna. I work here, actually. You must be Bridget?" She walked over and held out her hand.

With a stunned blink, Bridget shook her hand and nodded. "That's me. Ah…I'm not following what's happening. What do you mean, you work here? At this store? Three Sisters Apothecary?"

She nodded, long braids floating around her face and shoulders. "Sarah hired me on Saturday. I'm here part-time while I take classes at the community college."

What? Her sister had hired this girl? Without talking to her? A knot tied in her stomach. How had Sarah done that? She should've been at the festival, yet somehow she was hiring people without Bridget's consent or even knowledge. "I think—"

"Bridget, there you are!" Sarah popped out from the back room with a wide smile. "Did you meet Arianna? She's only been here for a couple of days, but she's such a quick learner."

"Um, Sarah, we need to talk for a minute. In the back." Bridget walked through without a backward glance.

"Arianna, would you mind checking the shelves to see if anything needs restocking? We'll be right back." Sarah said as the shuffling of her footsteps sounded behind Bridget.

Bridget spun around as soon as the door swung shut. "What do you think you're doing? You *hired* someone while I was gone? For two and a half days! On whose authority did you do this?"

"Mine," Gran said as she came down the stairs from her apartment. "I told her the idea was good and she should do it. This girl had stopped in looking for work."

"Gran, I make the decisions like that."

"Yes, I know, but—"

"But nothing. Who ran the festival booth while Sarah was here hiring someone? Has anyone checked the online orders and shipped those out? What about products? Is there a list of things I need to make? Now on top of all of that, I need to worry about finding the income to pay an employee? How much did you offer her an hour? Did any of you consider this before throwing all of my hard work away?"

Gran's Look should have sent Bridget running. "I ran this store for over fifty years, I know a thing or two about it."

Bridget slapped her hand down on the wide table. "I own the shop now. It's not up to you! This is my obligation. I should never have let you talk me into leaving town."

Both Sarah and Gran jumped at her shout. Gran shook her head. "That's the problem, Bridgie. You think of this as an obligation. Not an opportunity. There's no more joy in how you work here. You used to love coming in here and creating new products. Now all I see is stress and anxiety in you." She stepped forward and pulled Bridget into a hug. "Honey, you can't do everything all the time. Asking for help or hiring someone is not a sin. It's not weakness. It's growth and chance and freedom. Live your life *and* love this store. You can do both."

"I can, but on my terms. I do love this store—that's why I sacrifice everything else for it. I will not be the Wildes female who fails this legacy." She stepped back and crossed her arms. "You can't take over just because you think you know better."

"She didn't," Sarah interjected. "I hired Arianna. Gran encouraged me, but the decision lies with me. And I stand by it. You need help, Bridge. I've looked over the books. You can afford a part-time employee and it will help make life easier for you."

Bridget wanted to pull her hair in frustration. "It's like you two aren't listening to me. Stop making decisions for me. I own this store. Not you."

"Fine," Sarah snapped. "If you want to throw everything else in your life away and make yourself miserable working until you die, go ahead."

"Girls, stop it. I will not have you two fighting because of this shop. We are family first and foremost."

Bridget closed her eyes and yoga-breathed. Gran was right. Bickering with Sarah accomplished nothing. She needed to get things back in order with the store. Once she had an idea of how things had gone over the weekend, she'd feel better. Much as she hated to admit it, Sarah was correct that they did finally have the cashflow to hire a part-time employee. They could even go full-time if they wanted, but Bridget was hesitant. At least Sarah hadn't done that. "Okay. I'm sorry I lost my temper. I will give her a few weeks' probationary period to see how she does and if this will work out long term."

Gran smiled, but Bridget held up her hand. "For the record, neither of you has the authority to ever make another decision like this in my stead again." She leveled a stare at her grandmother. "You entrusted this shop to me and I'm the owner." She turned to Sarah. "You might be my big sister, but you don't even work here anymore. You're temporary and I don't know how long you're staying. I took over, not you. Both of you overstepped and I'm not happy about it."

"You're right. I'm sorry." Sarah twisted her lips to one side. "I should've called you and asked or something."

Gran lifted her brows. "While I do know how to run this store, I'll try to do better in remembering you're the boss."

The trio came back out to a very apprehensive-looking Arianna. Bridget gave her a genuine smile.

"I'm sorry I was taken by surprise that you were hired while I was away for the weekend. Let's start fresh. I'm Bridget, the owner of Three Sisters. I understand you'll be working for me part-time?"

Arianna nodded, the morning sunlight illuminating her skin.

"Wonderful. I'll start you on a trial basis and we can chat today about your schedule to get your regular hours set so you have time for your classes. Sound good?"

"Yes, thank you!" She bounced on her toes. "I love this store and I'm so excited to get the chance to work here. I promise not to let you down."

Bridget spent the next two hours showing Arianna the checkout software and her stocking system. Then she caught up on how much had sold at the festival booth Becca had run, as well as the online sales. When all was said and done, she had a list of products she needed to make for restocking and a mental idea of where the shop stood monetarily. She had plopped down on a stool behind the counter to rest for the first time that morning when the door chimed. Bridget looked up to see Jack walking in. "Hey…" Her greeting died in her throat. "Oh my God, what happened to you?"

She jumped up and ran over to him. His cheek was a vivid red and swollen. His right eye was already a mottled purple and inflamed to a mere slit.

He flashed a sheepish curl of his lips. "You should see the other guy. Guys, actually." He flexed his hands and winced.

"Jack! Were you in a fight?" She reached out but stopped herself in case she hurt him. "I don't understand."

"A couple of dudes at work—"

"At work?" She yelped. "You were beaten up at work?"

"I got into a fight. At the job site. They were saying...not complimentary things. About you." He wouldn't meet her eyes.

"Me?" Her voice was small. "I... What?"

"They made derogatory remarks about you. Being a, you know, a witch." He clenched his jaw and tension hardened the muscles in his shoulders and arms. "I wasn't going to tolerate what they said about you. I lost my temper and hit one and then the other. It ended up in a group fight."

This time she did touch him. She cradled his hands in hers. He'd defended her honor and gotten hurt for her? "Jack." She let out a gasping little laugh. "That is the stupidest, most ridiculous thing ever." She laughed harder. "And also weirdly romantic, but it shouldn't be. It's boorish and peak toxic masculinity, but dammit if there isn't some feminine part of me swooning inside, too." She kissed his uninjured cheek. "Thank you for defending me, you sweet, misguided idiot. You better not have gotten fired."

He chuckled and wrapped his arms around her. "I know and I didn't. I got...suspended?" He snorted a guffaw. "It's like being in school again. I'm out for a week, then hopefully Paul takes pity on me and lets me come back. And you're right. I was dumb and barbaric. My inner caveman came out."

She leaned back and shook her head with a half-smile. "Let's see what I have to help patch you up, my well-meaning-but-still-a-doofus boyfriend."

\* \* \* \*

He couldn't help but notice that Bridget had seemed more on edge since they'd gone on their weekend getaway. After patching him up, she sent him home with a few of her salves and lotions and told him to take some ibuprofen and a nap. The next few days when he'd seen her, she was obsessively making and packaging products for the store like she'd sold out of everything and hadn't restocked in months.

He'd done his best to help her however he was able, but she was a little moody and distant and no matter what, he couldn't seem to overcome that gap between them. Worry gnawed at him on all sides now. He thought he might have an answer for the logging side of things. As for the girlfriend part, he was still trying to figure out how to woo her back to where they'd been pre-Portland. He needed her to relax and trust him again.

That Friday, Gran was given a clean bill of health and Sarah decided she was heading back to Seattle. He managed to convince Sarah into letting him into Bridget's house on Saturday before she left town, so he could surprise Bridget with dinner when she came home from the event she was working that day. He knew she'd be exhausted and hoped this would brighten her evening. After throwing together all the ingredients for a chicken and rice slow cooker recipe his sister had given him, he decided to up his game by vacuuming all the rooms and cleaning her two bathrooms. Then he chilled out on the couch with Candle and sent some emails about the idea he had for Timber Logging Company. Eventually, the key in the lock sounded and he jumped up to greet her.

Bridget opened the door and stopped short. She blinked twice. "Hey, Jack. What, ah, what're you doing here?"

She tilted her head in an adorable manner and Jack's grin widened. "I talked Sarah into letting me in so I could make you dinner as a surprise. I know how tired you get after these fall festival events and I thought…"

Her eyes sparkled and she scrunched up her face. *Oh. Shit.* He'd made her cry? How? What? This was not the reaction he'd been hoping for.

She flung herself against his chest and burst into tears, sobbing into his sweater. "Th-th-this is s-s-so n-nice."

He wrapped her in his arms and rocked their bodies from side to side. "I'm here for you, honeybee," he whispered as he ducked his face into her hair. Her small frame shook as she cried and leaned into him. He coaxed her down to the couch. "Do you want to tell me what's going on?"

"I'm sorry. I don't know why I'm bawling and snotting all over you."

"You don't need to apologize. I'm here for you, and I don't mind if you cry."

"It's that I've been so stressed and Sarah went home and I'm tired and here you are. With dinner." She glanced around. "Did you clean my house, too?"

He shrugged. "I vacuumed. And cleaned your bathrooms. And dusted. Candle kept a close eye on me to make sure I did an adequate job."

She snort-laughed. "I can't believe you did all of this. For me." She looked up at him with damp lashes and tears streaked across her cheeks. "Thank you, Jack. You're a great boyfriend."

He thought his heart might stop beating right then and there. She was so gorgeous, even when crying, and so sweet, and he didn't deserve her. He couldn't even find a way to tell her about the possible hostile takeover of the logging company that could be the death knell for this entire town. Pushing away his guilt, he cupped her face and kissed her. "I'm trying. Why don't you go shower and get into comfy clothes while I get dinner ready for us? I'll get a fire going, too."

She twined her arms around his neck and hugged him tight. "You are the best, Jack Thompson." Pressing her lips to his cheek, she rose and headed into her room.

He tossed a few logs in the fireplace and once he had that going, listened to hear if the water was still running. Not hearing it, he went ahead and dished up what looked like delicious, creamy goodness into two bowls and held one out as she padded into the kitchen. Somehow, she made baggy sweats and fuzzy purple slippers look sexy. His blood flow shifted south and he grabbed up his own dinner so he wouldn't pounce on her. "Should we eat?"

With a nod, she led him into the living room, forgoing the kitchen table and curling up on the couch. She patted the space next to her and flipped on the baking competition show they'd been making their way through together. After an episode, they'd both finished their meal and he cleared the dishes. When he returned, he wrapped an arm around and said, "Want to tell me what has you so stressed this week? Or would you rather veg out and not talk about it?"

"My sister hired someone at the store."

"I remember you mentioning that. Are they not working out?"

"Arianna's fine, but I'm worried about keeping the profits from the store high enough to keep her employed. Which seems fine right now, but this is our busy season. Who knows what will happen after the fall? And then the online store has exploded—again, no idea if it will last, and I feel like I can't keep my head above water with how much stock I'm having to make these days. It's never-ending. Plus there are rumors all over town about the logging company getting sold. I don't know what I'm going to do if that happens. If this new owner changes how it's run or outsources the jobs to others..." She sucked in a deep breath. "Fallbank won't survive. It'll maybe take a handful of years, but without logging driving the economy here, the rest of us are on borrowed time."

Bridget tilted her head up to look at him. "Coming home to find you here with dinner *and* having cleaned my house? It overwhelmed me, but in a really good way. You're so thoughtful and sweet and I can't believe you're here with me. I've never had this kind of relationship before."

Jack's stomach rolled and for a moment he thought he might be sick. He was the source, or at least the main source, of all of her stress and she still thought he hung the moon. God, he was an asshole. He opened his mouth to speak, but she kissed him. Then kissed him again before tugging at his clothes. He couldn't stop himself. He selfishly allowed her to seduce him into making love to her right there on the couch.

\* \* \* \*

Monday came around and Jack hauled his butt into the office to meet with Paul like a teenage delinquent at the principal's office. Of course, he'd gotten into a fistfight so, if the shoe fit...

"You ready to come back to work and act like a grown man?"

"Yes, sir. I am sorry for acting like, well like an idiot. I shouldn't have let Charlie and Jacob get to me that way. They weren't speaking very kindly of my girlfriend, but that's not an excuse to resort to violence." Jack winced as he heard himself. He was lucky assault charges hadn't been filed against him.

"Mmhmm. You're on probation. One toe out of line and I'll fire you on the spot. We clear?" Paul crossed his arms and leaned back in his chair.

"Crystal, sir."

"Good. Now tell me what updates you have on Thompson Industries buying me out."

Jack filled him in on how things stood with the contracts but kept it as brief as possible. He was still waiting to hear back from a couple of his contacts to see if he could make changes to this offer or not. Bridget's worry weighed heavy on him. He lived in a constant state of nausea and dreaded anyone in town finding out who was about to upend Fallbank's foundation.

"All right. Keep me posted and go get to work. Don't let me hear even one word about you messing up."

"You got it." Jack stood, headed to his truck then out to the job site. After receiving his work orders from Cornelius, Jack joined the crew on the side of the mountain.

With quiet efficiency, Jack yanked on his gloves and took his place in hefting the massive logs into a position to allow the yarder to scoop them up. He worked with focus to keep out all distractions around him. Unfortunately, that meant he blocked out the warning shout that could have saved him. The last thing he heard was the echoing crack of splintering wood.

# Chapter Eighteen

Bridget hefted the box of lotions she'd packaged last night from the back room and into the main area of the store. She set it down and began unloading them onto the counter so she could group the lotions together by scents. She hummed to herself, her mood buoyant after waking up with Jack that morning. He was spoiling her with all the great sex and his sweet gestures.

Gran popped her head out of the back room. "Bridgie, your phone is ringing nonstop."

"Oh." She grabbed her cell from Gran and looked at the screen. Cornelius' name appeared and she swiped to answer. "Cornelius? What's up?"

"Bridget, you need to get the hospital. Now."

"What?" An icy pit opened in her stomach and she reached out a shaking hand to the counter so she wouldn't fall. "Is it Sarah? Do I need to go to Seattle?"

"No." He paused and his sigh sounded through the phone. "It's Jack. He's been hurt at work."

A low moan vibrated in her ears and she belatedly realized the sound came from her. She hung up and swung to face Gran.

"What's happened?" Gran's face was ashen and her eyes wide.

"J-Jack. He's hurt." Her body snapped to attention. "I have to go. Gran, can you—?"

"Of course. I've got it all covered here, and if I need help, I'll call Becca or Arianna. You go."

Nodding, Bridget snagged her purse and sprinted out through the door. She drove like a maniac to the hospital but when she arrived, it was to frustration and fear.

"Hello," she said to the nurse at the desk in the Emergency Department check-in. "I'm here for Jack Thompson. Can you tell me if he's okay?"

"Are you family?"

She shook her head. "No, I'm his girlfriend."

"Are you listed as an emergency contact for him? What's your name?"

"Bridget Wildes. I-I don't think I'd be listed anywhere."

The nurse gave her a small, contrite smile. "You aren't listed on the paperwork his company sent over. Unfortunately, I can't share any information with you. It's against privacy laws."

"Right." She blinked in a daze. "Has anyone called his family? Are they on their way?"

"The doctors will do that soon, I'm sure."

"Why...never mind. Thank you." She turned and faced the same waiting room she'd been in a few scant weeks ago waiting to hear if Gran would make it through. Now she was back, except this time she didn't even know what was wrong with Jack. How badly was he injured? Was it life-threatening? Bridget sank down onto one of the chairs and with a trembling hand pulled out her phone. She hit the call button for Jack's sister and waited for her to answer.

"Hi, Bridget! What a lovely surprise. How are you?"

"Allison?" Her voice cracked and she swallowed so she could force the words from her throat. "You need to come here. As quickly as possible. Jack's been hurt."

"What? What's happened? Is he okay? How bad is he injured?"

"I don't know. They won't tell me anything because I'm not family or on some stupid emergency contact list. You need to come here."

"I'll call my parents and get in the car right now. I can probably be there in about three hours if traffic isn't terrible. Can you text me the address for the hospital?"

"Yeah. I'll be here. Waiting."

"It'll be okay. I'll call and see what I can find out and let you know. He'll be glad to know you're there, even if he isn't aware of it right now. I'm on my way."

Allison hung up and Bridget stared down at her phone. She sent the address then willed her phone to ring. Allison told her she would call the hospital, then let her know what was going on. She needed to be patient.

Two hours later her phone still sat silent, and Bridget had taken up pacing the waiting room. The door swung open as she pivoted around. Her heart sank as Cornelius and a couple of other guys from the logging company walked in. "Hey."

"What's the word on Jack?" Cornelius asked.

"I don't know. They won't tell me. His sister is on her way and was supposed to call me back with an update, but I haven't heard."

He shoved his hands through his hair. "Damn."

"What happened on site? How did Jack get hurt?"

"One of the trees being cut had previous damage we didn't see. It caused the tree to splinter and the top fell in a way we never expected. Jack was hit and knocked unconscious. That's all I know."

Her heart seized then stampeded wildly inside her chest. "Will he be okay? How bad did he look? Did he wake up at all?"

Cornelius shook his head. "I don't know, little B. I wish I could tell you something, but I don't have a clue."

She wanted to keep asking questions, but would knowing things like 'was he wearing a helmet?' or 'did the tree hit him directly or from the side and just knock him over?' and 'was he bleeding?' ease her worry or add to it? The information she needed would come from his doctors, not the other guys on the job site. Waiting was the only thing she could do until Jack's family arrived and could obtain answers. Any other tidbits would make her fret more. She was strung as tight as she could be without snapping.

She sat and took deep breaths to calm her frayed nerves. Nervous energy leaked out of her in small ways. A tapping foot, clenched hands, rigid shoulders. Still, she refused to cry and wouldn't let the *what if* fears overtake her. If she succumbed, she'd never pull back from the abyss and she didn't want to go there. Not yet. Later, when she was alone, she could fall apart. But now she needed to keep it together.

"Hey, you want coffee or water or something to eat?" one of the local guys asked.

She shook her head. Her stomach was so tied in knots she cringed to think what might happen if she ate. "No, thanks."

"Water. Can you get both of us some water?" Cornelius answered then shot her a look.

She stood and began walking the length of the room, unable to keep still for long. Even though she'd not heard an alert, Bridget checked her phone again. Where was the update from his sister? "She's probably driving," she muttered to herself. Patience was a virtue, but dear lord, it was trying every fiber in her body right now. An update was all she needed. Was Jack alive? Was he awake? Did he need surgery? What kind of injuries did he have?

Turning on her heel, she walked back over to the nurse's station. "Hi. Again. I know you can't give me an update, but is there a chance I can see Jack Thompson? When are visiting hours?"

The woman smiled softly. "There are visiting hours for non-family each day between ten a.m. to four p.m. but we're past those and I don't know if he's been cleared to have any visitors at this point."

Bridget nodded. "Thanks, anyway. I appreciate the information." Dejected, she slumped back into the chair next to Cornelius.

"So you really like this guy, huh?"

She threw him a nervous glance. "Why?"

"Nothing. Just the rumors flying about the company getting sold and Jack's new to town anyway. I don't want to see you get hurt if he leaves. Or have a new neighbor because you leave with him."

"I'm not going anywhere. I have Three Sisters and Gran and…my entire life is here. I'd never up and leave. I can't."

"You can. If you want. Three Sisters could be relocated elsewhere. You already have the online store. Moving a physical location wouldn't be that difficult."

"As if I have the money to do that." She snorted. "No, I'm a townie through and through. I might not be a native to Fallbank, but I'm a local and I'm not moving."

"Sarah did. She seems happy in Seattle." He paused and swallowed.

Her heart broke for him all over again. If choosing a side was ever something she was forced to do, Bridget would pick her sister, but it would rip her apart to lose him as a friend. Cornelius was the brother she'd never had and always wanted.

He opened his mouth again. "You and even Gran could move up there along with the store. Think of how many more customers you'd get."

"Becca is here and Gran wants to be close to Gramps. She likes to visit his grave and talk to him. I do, too." She twisted to face him. "I'm here for the long haul. How long that is" — she paused and shrugged — "that's up to Paul and when and how he sells the company. The life of Fallbank hinges on the logging industry."

He nodded. "Hell, if the company lays us off, I might be the one moving first. Wouldn't that be a trip."

"Stop it, Cornelius. Neither of us is going anywhere. And to answer your original question, yes, I do really like him." She tugged her mouth into a smile. "And I think he feels the same way. We'll just have to see." She sighed. "Worrying is getting us nowhere. Tell me something good. Are you dating anyone?"

He tilted his head toward her and arched an eyebrow. "You think I'm seeing someone?"

"You don't have to be alone forever. You should go out. Meet someone."

The tips of his ears turned pink and he looked away. "I'm on a dating app or two. I'm picky."

"That's great! I'm happy for you. This is a good step forward."

"Can we talk about something else now?"

She giggled. "Fair enough."

The door to the Emergency Department opened and a distinguished older couple walked through. Bridget immediately knew they were Jack's parents. He was almost a carbon copy of his father, and the woman with him had similar features to Allison. She pushed to her feet then stopped. She didn't know these people or even if Jack had talked about her with them. Allison had met her, but beyond that she couldn't say.

Instead, she watched them speak to the nurse behind the front desk, then walk toward the door to the patient rooms. She jumped up again. "Are you Jack's parents?"

The couple turned and pinned her with their stares.

"I'm Bridget"—she paused to see if they would show any sign of recognition, but their expressions didn't change—"and these are the other guys from work." She gestured feebly at their group who also rose and waved. "We're his…friends. Is he okay?"

His mother glanced at their group then back at her. "He's fine. We'll let him know of your concern and I'm sure he'll appreciate it. You don't need to stay, though. I'm certain you all have home lives to get back to you. When Jack is released from the hospital, he can reach out. Thank you!" She smiled and they walked through the door as if they hadn't crushed her heart in the process.

Not that they knew the damage done. Bridget tried to put it into perspective. First, she was sure they were stressed and worried about Jack. Second, they might not feel it was their place to give details on his true status. Third, they were unaware she existed.

She winced and swallowed back her bitterness on that point. Now was not for whining about whether or not Jack had told his parents about her. It was about Jack and if he was okay. What exactly did "he's fine" mean? Her frustration level rose again and she sucked in a deep breath to calm herself.

The entry door opened again and this time Allison walked through. Relief flooded Bridget's limbs and she leaned her hand on a wall to keep upright. "Hi, Allison."

"Bridget! Thank God you're still here." She hugged Bridget tight. "How are you holding up?"

Bridget gave a little shake of her head. "I'm fine. How's Jack? Did you find anything out?"

"He's stable. He has a concussion and heavy bruising from the impact of the tree. The hardhat saved his life. He'll be here for observation for a day or two at least. Last I heard he was in and out of consciousness and conversations were hit or miss with him. You haven't seen him yet?"

"No, they won't let us back because it isn't visiting hours and we aren't family. Your parents came through just a couple of minutes ago. They're back with him." She clasped her hands tight to keep from showing her distress. Jack was *not* fine and she wanted nothing more than to see him for herself.

Allison linked her arm with hers. "Let's go see him."

They walked toward the doors and Bridget glanced over her shoulder. "Cornelius, I'll call you as soon as I leave."

The nurse stopped them before they could get through the door. "I'm sorry, but who are you here to see?"

"I'm Allison Thompson-Takahashi. Jack Thompson's sister. My parents are already with him."

"Okay, you can go on through." The nurse turned to Bridget. "Ma'am, we already talked about who is and isn't allowed in the rooms currently. I'm sorry."

"But she's with me," Allison interjected. "I'm saying it's okay for her to come with me and see Jack."

"I understand, but it's hospital policy. No exceptions."

"But—"

Bridget put a hand on Allison's arm. "It's all right. The rules are in place for a reason and I'm just glad to have any information on how he's doing. I'll come back tomorrow and see him during visiting hours."

She nodded. "I'll FaceTime you if he's awake." Then she glared at the nurse. "I know he'll want to see you."

With that, Allison went back to Jack's room and Bridget turned to go home. Her chest felt like a massive stone was pressing down, crushing the air out of her lungs. She managed good-byes to the others and made it to her car before bursting into tears. All she wanted was to see him and know he was alive. And she did, but knowing versus seeing it were two vastly different things. With shaking hands and wet cheeks, she started her car and made her way back to her house.

# Chapter Nineteen

His head was killing him. And his chest. His whole body was one big ball of pain. Jack peeled his eyes open, winced then closed them while turning his head away. A fresh wave of pain crashed over him. "Turn the light off." He grunted.

"Sorry, dear," his mom responded.

The sounds of blinds closing followed. Wait. Mom? He forced his eyes open again. This time the bright sunlight was muted enough to be tolerable. "Mom?" He flicked his gaze around the room. "Dad? Allison?"

"We're doing this again, huh?" Allison laughed. "You've woken up five times so far and each time you're surprised that we're here. Also, you're in the hospital. Work accident yesterday afternoon. It's morning now."

That explained the pain he was in. He blinked and glanced around again. Where was… "Bridget?"

"Oh, this is different. Maybe it's a sign you're coming out of this cycle." Allison shrugged.

His mom sat next to him on the bed. "I can't get over this beard of yours. You don't look like my son." She chuckled and touched his cheek. "I'm so glad you're okay, Jack. This scared the life out of me."

Guilt assaulted him. He felt like the eight-year-old boy who'd tried to jump a fence on his bike and ended up wiping out and needing thirteen stitches in his knee instead.

"Who is Bridget?" his father asked.

Leave it to his father to be all business, all the time. Jack cleared his throat. "Can I have some water?" His mouth felt like it was stuffed with cotton. A cup appeared in his vision and he flashed a wan smile at his mother. After two sips, he said, "Bridget is my girlfriend."

"Girlfriend?" his mother echoed. She looked to his father, then back to him.

Allison spoke up before their mom had a chance to say anything. "The hospital wouldn't let her in. She's not family and it wasn't visiting hours. Plus, you were unconscious. I saw her on my way in and assured her you're okay. I'm sure as soon as visiting hours start, Bridget will be here."

He frowned then winced. Every time he moved, pain followed. What had happened to him on the mountain? Did the yarder run him over? That was how it felt. Hissing out an exhale, he said, "I want her here now. Where's my phone? And my doctor. I feel like hell."

A trio wearing blue scrubs walked through the door as if he'd conjured them out of thin air.

"Ah, I see you're awake. How are you doing, Mr. Thompson?" the woman in the front asked.

"Terrible. Everything hurts and you all threw my girlfriend out." Jack growled under his breath. "And don't call me Mr. Thompson, that's my father. I'm Jack."

She flashed a placating smile. "Of course, Jack. Let's start with the pain. On a scale of one to ten, with ten being the worst pain you've ever felt, how bad is it?"

Twenty minutes of interrogation and poking and prodding and bright lights shone in his eyes later, the doctors moved on to Bridget getting thrown out.

"I want you to let my girlfriend in when she gets here." Jack shot a glare at Allison. "I want my phone so I can text her to come now." He looked back at his physicians. "She can be here when it's not visiting hours."

"No screens for at least two weeks."

What? Did his doctors not hear him or was his concussion messing with his thoughts this much? "What are you talking about?"

"No screens. No phone, no TV, no computers, no tablets. Not for two weeks. No reading, too. I recommend audiobooks and music. When you feel up to it, light exercise like a walk around the block. Sitting at a park. Nothing strenuous. Definitely no driving." She chuckled to herself. "And of course, you won't be back to work for a few weeks either."

"But my girlfriend. I'm giving you my permission to let her in."

"Sir, hospital policy—"

"I don't care about hospital policy," he shouted and instantly regretted it. A flare of pain throbbed through his head. In a softer voice, he continued, "I understand your rules when you don't have patient permission, but I'm expressly stating that Bridget Wildes can know about my condition and be admitted to my room any time she wants."

The doctor sighed. "All right, Jack. We'll do that." They departed and his parents rounded on him.

His dad said, "Who is this girl that has you so agitated?"

"She's my girlfriend and I don't appreciate that she wasn't allowed back."

"Honey," his mom said in a gentler tone, "you've never mentioned her before. How serious is this relationship if you want her with you at a hospital? You can't have known her long. Unless... Is this the Brizendines' girl? The one you went to high school with? Oh, she is adorable!"

"No, Mom. That's Evette. I met Bridget in Fallbank. She owns a shop here." Exhaustion trickled into his limbs. "Allison, can you tell her to come over now?"

"I can text her, but she might be sleeping. She was here until really late last night. I talked to her when I arrived."

"You know this girl?" His dad looked at Allison with furrowed brows.

She nodded. "I met her when the girls and I came to visit Jack a few weeks ago. Bridget is super sweet."

"Well," his mother sputtered. "I don't know what to say. Is it serious? You haven't mentioned her to us." She waved her hands. "Never mind, that's not important right now."

Jack huffed. "She's a normal girl who thinks I'm a normal guy. She doesn't run in our typical societal circles. And don't you dare tell her who we are, either!" He winced at the spike of pain. His fatigue was bad enough now he was slurring his words. "Don't messs thisss up fo' me." Jack blinked once...twice... On the third time, he couldn't force his lids back up and sleep pulled him under.

\* \* \* \*

Bridget startled awake as Candle stood on her chest and meowed in her face. "H-hey." She swallowed and blinked the blurriness away from her eyes. What time was it, anyway? She rolled her head to check and jumped up, tossing her poor cat from the bed. "Sorry, Candle," she murmured with a quick pet. "I gotta run."

It was half-past-ten and she was late for visiting hours. "Damn!" After throwing on clothes and brushing her teeth, Bridget hopped in her car and took off for the hospital. At least Allison had sent a few texts with updates that Jack had woken up and asked for her. Nerves thrummed in her belly as she realized this would be her real introduction to Jack's parents this morning. She hadn't even showered, which now that she thought about it, was a mistake. But she needed to see Jack. A text that he was okay was different from seeing him with her own eyes. The knot of anxiety she carried around in her chest wasn't going to simply roll away.

She swung into a parking spot and raced to the door. Once outside the entrance, she forced herself to pause and take three deep breaths. Her body stopped vibrating like an electric fence and her heart slowed from a full gallop to a softer trotting pace. Calm, she needed to be calm for Jack. And to not look like a lunatic to his family. With more measured steps, she walked in then went to the fourth floor where she checked in with a nurse. Following instructions, she took a right down the hall and zagged left at the next intersection. Then she counted down to room 4138. Sucking in a deep breath, Bridget walked through the door and stopped.

She darted her eyes around the empty room save for Jack sleeping in the bed. A monitor quietly beeped a steady heartbeat rhythm and all else was silent. Where was everyone? Allison's texts said they were all here with him. She crossed over to a chair by the bed and sank into it.

With a shaking hand, she reached out and touched Jack's fingers. The warmth from his skin soothed her and a trickle of relief ran through her. "Jack?" She whispered, unsure if she should rouse him or not. Deciding not, she curled her palm around his and settled into the chair. Bridget contented herself with watching the steady rise and fall of his chest and the light fluttering of his eyelids. He looked pale and worn out, but she'd take that over the alternatives. Jack was alive and okay and that would satisfy her for now.

She reached up and brushed his hair back from his face with her free hand and he stirred. She froze, half hoping she hadn't woken him and half hoping she had.

His lids lifted and he looked at her.

With all that she'd cried last night, she wouldn't have thought she could cry more, yet tears blurred her vision. "Hi," she choked out.

"Honeybee. You're here."

She nodded and smiled despite the steady flow of water from her eyes. "I'm here. I'm sorry I wasn't here sooner. I really wanted to be. They wouldn't let me in last night and then I overslept this morning. How are you feeling? Do you need anything?"

"Shh. Stop worrying so much." He curled his mouth into a small smile. "You babble when you're anxious. It's cute."

Bridget wiped her cheeks against her shoulders and sucked in a deep breath. "How are you feeling?"

"Everything hurts, but it's manageable. I'm tired."

"Yeah, it'll be a little bit before you're back to normal."

He closed his eyes again and slowly opened them back up. "Glad you're here. I told them you get to stay. You are family. You're gonna be my wife."

A jolt shot through her. Every tiny hair on her body stood on end and a nervous giggle slipped past her lips. This was the head injury talking, wasn't it? Jack hadn't thought about marrying her. They'd been dating for less than two months. Yet somehow his words felt right to her. She loved him in a way she'd never experienced before, and she knew within herself this wasn't a fickle or fleeting emotion. Could he possibly feel the same?

"Wife, huh? Is this your way of proposing? I have to admit, a hospital bed isn't what I expected."

"I'll do it again on one knee when I can stand without the room spinning."

"I don't know, you might need to ask Candle's permission first. She's gotten territorial about her side of the bed."

He snorted then winced. "Don't make me laugh. That hurt."

She jumped up and leaned closer to him. She scanned his face for more signs of discomfort. "I'm sorry, Jack. I didn't know—"

He lifted his head a fraction to press his lips to hers. "Less talking, more kissing."

"You are incorrigible." She brushed her mouth across his again anyway. It helped ground her and keep her mind from wandering too far down paths that weren't real. Voices approaching pulled her back to reality and she stepped back despite Jack's mumbled protests.

The door opened. Allison and her parents walked in.

"Oh, hello," his mother said. "You're the girl from last night, aren't you?"

Bridget nodded as Allison moved forward.

"Mom, this is Bridget. Jack's girlfriend." Allison hugged Bridget tight and asked, "How are you holding up?"

"I'm fine. Relieved Jack is okay."

"I'm Sonia and this is John. We're Jack's parents." His mom stepped closer.

Bridget fought not to fidget as Sonia looked her up and down. A sudden wish to go back in time and take a quick shower and put on more presentable clothes than leggings and a sweatshirt hit her in the chest. She should've given more thought to her appearance this morning. She'd known that she would meet his parents. Yet she'd rushed because all she had wanted was to get over to the hospital as quickly as she could.

Sonia smiled. "Tell us about yourself. Jack said you own a store? What kind?"

"It's been in my family for generations. Three Sisters Apothecary. We sell candles, lotions, salves, teas, soaps. A hodge-podge of things. The recipes for everything have been handed down for centuries. We grow most of the herbs and plants for everything—my cousin has a farm for most of the other products needed for use to hand-make the products."

"Sounds like you're some kind of witch." His father laughed.

"No," both Jack and Allison said.

Jack continued. "She's not a witch."

"I'm an herbalist." She shot a smile at Jack and he squeezed her hand. "I don't do spells or make potions. I offer nature-based products for a variety of personal needs."

"Okay." John shrugged and changed the subject. "So, Jack, now that you've gone and almost killed yourself with this little logging venture, are you ready to come home?"

"Dad, give it a rest. My head is throbbing and I'm too tired to have this argument." Jack closed his eyes.

"I should go," Bridget said and picked up her purse.

Jack's eyes flew open. "Stay. Please. I don't want you to leave."

"I don't want to keep you from resting and I'm sure you want to spend time with your family."

He threaded his fingers with hers. "You're family, too. Remember?"

"Jack…" She warned him with her eyes not to bring up such ridiculous things like marriage in front of his parents she'd met mere moments ago.

"Honeybee." He made puppy eyes at her and she relented.

"Fine, I'll stay a little longer. But if you need quiet, tell me. Okay?"

"Won't happen, but all right."

\* \* \* \*

Three days later, Jack was finally getting discharged. He was able to stand, walk and stay awake for the majority of the day without too much physical pain. The residual headache was faint and he was eager to go home. Or back to Bridget's home since he'd pleaded to stay with her for the remainder of the week. He'd showered and dressed and felt more like a real human being as he emerged from the bathroom. His dad waited in the room.

"Jack, I think we need to talk."

"Not right now, Dad. I'm about to get released to go home."

"That's exactly it. Home. You need to come back to Seattle. Stop messing around with all of this logging stuff and return to Thompson Industries. This is ridiculous."

"It's not and I'm not."

"Not what?" His father crossed his arms.

How was he supposed to explain this to his father? He hadn't prepared to have this discussion yet and Jack had zero desire to hash this out at the moment. He sighed and sat on the bed. "I'm not going to Seattle. I don't want that life anymore."

"The hell you aren't! I haven't spent my entire life continuing your grandfather's legacy and turning Thompson Industries into a billion-dollar company to have my only son throw it all away like trash. You are the heir to this throne and you've always wanted it."

"Dad, I—"

"No, Jack. This is not negotiable."

"It's my life!" Jack yelled. Despite the pulse of pain in his head, he stood and went toe to toe with his father. "You don't get to dictate to me what I'm going to do with my entire life. I'm happy here. I didn't even realize how unhappy I was in Seattle until I came here. This isn't some game I'm playing."

His dad clenched his jaw and glared, but Jack refused to back down. This was his shot at happiness and if he could get a few more things lined up, he'd be able to finally make the move to buy the logging company and stay in Fallbank permanently.

"You will come home. If you think I'm going to allow my son to stay in some no-name town and waste his life cutting down trees, you are dead wrong. You came here to assess if this logging company was worth purchasing. It is and you've done a nice job of building the dossier supporting it. You got Paul Carson to come to the table and negotiate the deal. The contract is on my desk as we speak. I'm signing as soon as we get back to Seattle. Then we'll reallocate the jobs to our crews in Seattle and this will all be a blip on the radar. You almost died and I'll not have my son, Jonathan Ewan Thompson III, snuffed out on the side of a mountain pretending to be a lumberjack. You are above this and you will act accordingly!"

A soft gasp met his ears and Jack turned in horror. It couldn't be who Jack thought it was standing behind him.

Bridget stood there, eyes wide and face pale. She swallowed once.

How much had she heard? He had to fix this. His heart pounded blood through his body and a wave of fresh lightheadedness smacked him. Jack gripped the metal edge of the hospital bed. "Bridget, I can explain."

She raised her brows and her stare turned cold. "Oh, really? Explain how you are the one orchestrating the demise of Fallbank? *You* are the one buying TLC and taking away all of the jobs here. You've been lying to every one of us this entire time! God, you must think I'm so stupid."

He reached for her, but she shied back. "I don't. Never have I thought that about you. Please, honeybee—"

"Don't call me that," she bit out. "You *lied*. About who you are. Why you're here. I don't even know if what we had was real anymore." She blinked away the tears shining in her eyes.

Damn, he'd messed this up beyond anything he imagined. Wooziness assaulted him. "That's not true. I love you. You know that. You love me. Besides, why is this town so important anyway? They all hate you and call you a witch. That is what's stupid."

Her gasp stung him, but not nearly as bad as he feared his words had just hurt her. "I can't look at you anymore." She turned and stormed out.

He tried to chase after her, every fiber of his body screaming not to let her leave. "Bridget, please. Come back." He wobbled down the hall, but a nurse jumped in front of him.

"Sir, you need to go back to your room. You can't run in here and you haven't been discharged."

"Then get my paperwork. I have to leave now."

"I understand, but you have to be checked out by your doctor and they are still doing rounds. They will get to you as soon as they are done."

Jack clenched his fists and exhaled through his nose. Of all the times in his life he'd ever wanted to throw his name and power around, this one was paramount. Yet he knew if he did, it would make him no better than his father, who used the family name and money to get anything and everything he wanted. But he desperately wanted to throw a tantrum of epic proportions. God, he was such an asshole. How screwed up was his head to say that to Bridget? Instead, he gathered his patience and swallowed back his anger. It wasn't the nurse's fault he was in this mess. That was his own doing.

He muttered an apology and shuffled back to his room. His heart felt like it'd been ripped out and shredded with razors. How could Bridget question his feelings for her? Hadn't he proven how much he loved her? He hadn't outright lied—he just hadn't explained the entire truth. He'd told her his name, but never his full name. He'd said he was from Seattle and new to logging, but not why he'd joined the logging team to begin with. And now thanks to his father shouting their business aloud, he hadn't had the chance to tell her on his own terms. Then there was his moronic insult to her about being a witch. Jack knew that was a touchy subject for her, yet his frustration with the town's treatment of her had boiled over in the worst way. All he could do was find her, explain and hope Bridget forgave him. If not...he hated to contemplate the thought of her not being in his life.

He entered his room and stared at his father. Rage filled him, but he'd already had one relationship destroyed today. He didn't need another in shambles. His dad needed to understand what Jack wanted in life and that he couldn't be bullied into changing his mind.

# Chapter Twenty

The insistent pounding on her door made it clear who was outside. "Go away," she shouted. The knocking just grew louder.

Bridget shoved herself off of the couch. Her cat jumped out of the way and raced over to leap onto the cat tree. She shot a glare at the offending furniture that *he* had built. Turning her ire on the door, she stomped over and yanked it open.

"Bridget, please. Hear me out." Jack leaned against the brick wall of her entry while an unfamiliar car idled in her driveway.

She took in his pale face and the way he was swaying on his feet. Her heart thumped in concern despite the betrayal boiling in her veins. "There's nothing to say."

He turned sadness-filled eyes on her. "I can't tell you how sorry I am. I should have told you—"

"You're right you should have. Instead, you lied. You conveniently left out that you're a freaking billionaire business mogul here to buy out our local logging company and decimate the town economy. And called me stupid for caring about a town that hates me. There is no coming back from that. You betrayed the trust we all put in you. That *I* put in you." She swiped at her eyes. A second surge of anger punched through her. She didn't want him to see her cry. He didn't deserve her tears. "You should go."

"I'm not giving up, Bridget. I can't give up on us."

"There is no us. We barely know each other."

"I love you." His voice cracked.

The raw emotion threatened to undo her, but she held firm. "I don't know who you are. I thought I knew Jack Thompson, but Jonathan Ewan Thompson III? He's some rich guy I hear about on trashy society shows. And he's going to destroy the only home I've ever known. Even if everyone in it hates me." She swallowed back the bitterness rising in her throat. "Goodbye."

"Wait!"

But she didn't. Bridget shut the door on him as she slid onto the tile floor, letting her heart break into a thousand shards. She pressed her face into her knees and wept.

\* \* \* \*

By Friday morning, Bridget could tell that Gran's patience was running thin. True, Gran understood her heartache and sympathized, but she also had very little tolerance for moping.

"Bridgie, you need to get away."

"What?" She tilted her head at Gran. "What do you mean?"

"I mean, get out of this store and this town. Take a break. Go visit Sarah or someone else. I can't deal with your forlorn expressions and snippy attitude. It's like living with sixteen-year-old you all over again." Gran shuddered and shook her head. "No. Sorry, my love, but I can't do that a second time. Once was more than enough. Between myself, Arianna and Becca, we'll cover the store and the festival tomorrow. Now leave."

"But…"

Gran shot her A Look.

She held up her hands. "All right, I'm going. I don't know where, but I'm going." Grumbling under her breath, she gathered her coat and bag. She pulled out her cell phone and saw the blank screen. Somehow this was worse than the first two days of dozens of missed calls and texts from Jack. That he'd given up so easily left a hollow sensation in her chest. She wasn't special and he'd moved on, back to his snooty friends and fancy lifestyle. The kind of life she would never fit into. Tapping on the text icon, she rattled off a quick message to Sarah that she was coming up for the weekend.

Her sister sent a response as Bridget was driving to meet Sarah at her office. Bridget navigated the roads and listened to angry, sad girl rock on streaming the whole three-and-a-half-hour drive. By the time she arrived, it was midday and Bridget was starving. Popping into a local deli, she ordered sandwiches for both herself and Sarah. While waiting, she idly perused a small display of newspapers and magazines for purchase and found Jack's face staring back at her. She almost jumped back but caught the reaction before she made a fool of herself. Peering at the cover, she realized this wasn't her Jack. This was Jonathan Ewan Thompson III, clean-shaven with tidy hair and a suit, seated at a table next to an equally posh-looking woman.

"No beard?" she murmured. The image was jarring, but not as much as the title. *Seattle's Most Eligible Bachelor is Back! And already having cozy lunches with an old flame.*

Her stomach twisted and any hunger she had dissipated.

"Order for Bridget!"

"Thanks," she replied weakly then picked up her bag. Back in her car, she slumped in her seat and swallowed away the lump in her throat. No way would she show up at Sarah's office with tear tracks and smeared mascara. But did she mean so little to him? To move on less than a week after breaking up? He'd said he loved her. He had talked about getting married, for crying out loud! Although if she were being fair, he had been concussed when he'd said it, so maybe it shouldn't count.

A breath shuddered out of her and Bridget started her car. She needed the distraction of her sister to take her mind off of Jack and her broken heart.

When she arrived, Bridget parked in the garage under the building and made her way up to the lobby of the skyscraper. As she waited for the elevator, she heard her name called out. On instinct, she turned before she processed the familiar, warm baritone of the voice…and found herself face to face with Seattle's Most Eligible Bachelor.

Up close and in person, this Jack was devastating. He was the epitome of handsome and sophisticated. Hollywood would weep to have him on their big screens. Yet it felt wrong. *He* felt wrong like this. She wanted his silky beard and soft flannel shirts and well-worn jeans. That was her Jack. This man was too beautiful for mere mortals like herself. Too far out of her reach. The sensation left her chilled all over, wrecking her.

"Bridget, you're here." His smile was blinding.

Her heart leaped and sweat broke out along her neck. Why was he smiling? How could he be happy? Maybe he'd just gotten back from another lunch date with his new-old girlfriend. She hated it and his stupid expression. "Why are you in my sister's office building?"

"Your sister? I own..." He cleared his throat. "I mean, ah..."

"You own this building." It shouldn't surprise her, but it did. And underscored how different their worlds were. "Of course you do."

"It's really my family's," he mumbled.

The elevator dinged and she turned on her beat-up tennis shoe heel to enter. She had to get away from him or she would break.

He grabbed her hand. "Please, give me a chance."

She glared and yanked her arm away. "To what? Lie to me again? Play pretend until you get bored and come back to your real life? Stand by and cheer while you destroy the town that hates me? No. I'm done. We're done." She walked into the elevator and pushed the button for the thirty-third floor. "Go enjoy the fancy, rich girlfriend you're already back to dating. She belongs with you and this world. I'm just a small-town witch. We don't fit together."

The doors slid shut as his expression crumpled, and not a moment too soon. She'd been a breath away from bursting into tears and ruining the strong woman persona she was clinging to by the tips of her fingernails. As soon as she reached the floor, she found a bathroom and locked herself into a stall. Taking several deep breaths, she tried to cease the shaking of her hands, but her adrenaline was too high. She couldn't stop the cold, trembling sensation vibrating beneath her skin. After fumbling with her phone, she managed to get an SOS message to Sarah. She stepped out and splashed water on her face. When she looked up in the mirror, Sarah was waiting.

"What happened?"

Instead of speaking, she threw herself into her sister's arms and cried. "J-Jack-k. W-w-we b-broke up-p."

"Oh, Bridgie." Sarah held her tight and let her get it all out. "I knew something had to be up when you randomly decided to visit, but I thought maybe it was good news. When I saw the two of you together in Fallbank..." She paused and sighed. "I didn't see a break-up coming. I'm sorry, baby sis."

"He's here. In the building."

"What?" Sarah stepped back and blinked at her. "What do you mean? Is he stalking you?"

Bridget shook her head. "No. I guess he owns the building. Jack is really Jonathan Ewan Thompson. The Third."

"What?" Sarah shouted. Then she slapped her palm on her forehead. "I can't believe I didn't see it. That's why he looked so familiar."

"Listen, I just found out and...it's a long story. Can we go back to your place and eat ice cream and drink wine and I'll tell you everything? I need to get out of here. I can't see him again."

"Okay. Let me grab a couple of things and we'll go. Give me ten minutes."

Sarah drove Bridget's car to her apartment and once inside the cozy one-bedroom, they hunkered down in the living room. Delivery for dinner was ordered and pre-dinner ice cream straight out of the carton was had. Bridget poured out the whole story to her sister, ugly-crying the whole time. She let go of the tight control she'd held over her emotions the past few days and let herself feel the hurt and betrayal and infinite sadness the loss of Jack detonated in her heart. It pained her so much drawing a breath was a challenge. After eating her emotions, drinking half a bottle of wine and ranting to Sarah, Bridget settled on the couch with her sister and they flipped on a new period drama series to binge watch. After five episodes, Bridget found herself nodding off. In her exhausted state, she curled up against her sister and took comfort in the steady presence that had always been in her life.

"I miss you, Sare-Bear. I wish you didn't live so far away."

Sarah exhaled against Bridget's hair. "I miss you, too. It's lonely here sometimes."

"Come home. You could marry Cornelius and live next door and I could be the fun aunt. God knows I'm going to die alone."

"You are drunk and melodramatic so I'm going to let that last statement go. But you're not going to end up alone."

She stuck out her tongue. "No one wants to marry the town witch. I don't get why I'm the target, but maybe I should just embrace it and terrorize people instead."

"Maybe you should go to sleep, Bridgie. Things always look better in the morning."

Things did not look better in the morning. In fact, they sucked even more. Her head hurt and every time she blinked, it felt like sandpaper scraping over her eyes. Hungover and heartbroken was an awful combination. Bridget wanted to crawl into a dark hole and never come out. Instead, she let Sarah drag her to a local diner a few blocks away. Strong black coffee and a plate of eggs, bacon and avocado toast later and she was feeling a sliver of a human again.

The two sisters strolled along the streets of Seattle arm-in-arm and stumbled upon a block-party fall festival. "Oh, we should check this out," Bridget said. "This could be a good opportunity for the shop next year."

"You never stop working."

She shot her sister an arch look. "I don't have the luxury of not working all the time. If I don't, Three Sisters won't survive." A shiver of fear ran through her stomach. "It might not make it anyway if Thompson Industries has their way. Fallbank might cease to exist."

Sarah rolled her eyes and tugged her over to a booth with handmade reclaimed wood decorative pieces. "You honestly think Fallbank will blink out of existence if the logging company is gone? That seems pretty extreme."

"It's not." Irritation simmered under her skin. "The logging industry is our main job supplier. Without those jobs, the lumberjacks and their families will leave. That takes away at least a third, if not more, of the town's population. With no major industry jobs, we're relying on local businesses. Those won't have enough customers since we'll all have to tighten down on our spending habits with less people around, which hurts all of us even more. Businesses will close. More residents will move away and the cycle spiral until no one is able to keep their doors open and everyone has to go elsewhere to survive."

She grabbed her hair and tucked it into a messy knot on top of her head. "It won't happen overnight, but in five or ten years, maybe fifteen if we're really lucky, Fallbank will be a small note in history. Nothing more."

The bleak look Sarah gave her threatened tears again. But no, she'd had her pity party yesterday. Today was for picking herself up and finding new ways to move forward. "I'm going to see if I can locate the organizers' booth and see how to sign up for next year. This is really well attended."

Bridget walked down toward the other end of the block to find the vendor check-in booth. With a smile, she approached a petite, dark haired woman with a clipboard. "Hi, I'm Bridget Wildes. Are you the event coordinator?"

"Yes, I'm Evalina de la Rosa. Call me Eva. Can I help you?"

Bridget shook Eva's hand and discussed the registration and fees for having a booth at next year's event. The more she heard about the set-up and usual number of attendees, the more excited Bridget got. "This sounds great! Can I sign up today or is there a specific registration time period?"

"You can get set up today. What kind of wares do you sell? We like to not have too many of the same kind to keep attendees from getting bored."

"I run my family's store, Three Sisters Apothecary, in Fallbank, Oregon. We do these kinds of fairs all the time. Our main products are soaps, body lotions and bath products. We also have handmade candles and teas, that sort of thing. We grow most of our ingredients or find small businesses to source from. All of the recipes have been handed down in my family forever. I have a sizable garden behind my house and a workshop to create products."

Eva grinned. "You're a nature witch! Love it." She held out her fist for bumping and Bridget stared at Eva's hand hanging in the air.

"I'm not a witch. I'm an herbalist, but thanks." Bridget tapped her knuckles against Eva's, who shrugged.

"Suit yourself. I prefer the witch label myself. Wise women have been called it for millennia and I'd rather embrace it than let someone else twist the meaning negatively." Eva handed over the paperwork to Bridget and once it was all completed, Bridget waved and set out in search of Sarah.

Eva's words resonated in Bridget's mind as she walked. Maybe Eva did have a point. By running from the label "witch," Bridget allowed bigoted people to warp the work of people who had helped others since the dawn of humanity. She wasn't sure if it felt completely comfortable for her yet, but it gave her food for thought.

Bridget was about to text Sarah to find out where to meet, when she heard her name called out.

"Bridget, wait!"

She turned and saw Allison walking over with her girls and a man in tow.

"Hey, I knew it was you!" Allison threw her arms around her in a tight hug.

The gesture caused Bridget's emotions to rumble beneath the surface, but she held tight to the chain. "Hey, Allison," she said and patted her back. "What are you doing here?"

"We had so much fun when we visited the other fair, I found more and dragged my husband, Hiro, and the girls out."

"Bridget! Bridget!" the girls chanted with bright, happy grins.

"Hi, Luna and Lily." For the first time since the break-up, she managed a genuine smile. These girls were so bubbly and excited it was impossible not to feel the same.

Allison murmured something to her husband and after a quick hello, he led the twins off to another booth. "I hope you still count me as a friend. I know you and Jack..." She trailed off and offered a small lift of the corners of her lips and a shrug. "I'm sorry it didn't work out."

"So am I," she answered honestly. "I wish he'd been up front from the beginning. You could've been, too."

"In his defense, it's stifling to grow up under the Thompson name. People only want to be your friend or date you for your money. Jack had it worse than me, but it means trusting anyone is near impossible."

Bridget gritted her teeth against her anger. "He could have trusted me. I bared my soul to him and he still kept me in the dark. He should have known I wouldn't care about his money." She crossed her arms and looked away. "It's too late now. What's done is done and once the final sale of Timber Logging Company goes through"—she paused and blew out a breath—"it will just be treading water as long as possible to keep Fallbank alive. It'll be a painful, slow death."

"It doesn't have to be this way."

"You're right," Bridget interjected. "It doesn't, but that's not in my hands. Jack made those decisions."

Allison narrowed her eyes and propped her hands on her hips. "You know, TLC was always going to be sold. It wouldn't matter if it was us or another company. The results would be the same either way."

She nodded as she processed Allison's point. "You're right. The difference is, we knew Jack. We trusted him and took him in and made him one of our own. It's one thing for a faceless conglomerate to take over and destroy our lives. It's another for the stab in the back to be from someone on the inside. From someone you loved." Emotion built up and pushed at the bindings she'd trapped them in too close to the surface for Bridget's comfort. She dipped her chin once. "I need to get back to my sister. Nice seeing you, Allison."

"Wait, I want to help. The twins love you! They already call you Aunt Bridget."

The words burned like a wildfire in her chest, but she kept walking. Allison couldn't fix this. No one could.

# Chapter Twenty-One

"I have seven phone messages and your schedule for the day is outlined for you on the calendar app."

Jack took the tablet from his assistant with a brief smile. "Thanks, Lanee." He walked into his corner office and slumped down in the leather chair behind the massive desk. His head already hurt and he'd arrived less than five minutes ago. He still couldn't drive and shouldn't be using a screen yet, but here he was. All work, all hours of the day.

Why did he like doing this again? How had he thought this was the lifestyle he had wanted before going to Fallbank? His entire life was consumed by work and contracts and negotiations. Meetings and phone calls and emails at all hours of every day. This was fun? This was stimulating for him? Buying other companies and consolidating workforces to lay people off?

He'd fallen right back into his old habits. His mother had gotten him a haircut and his father had strongly suggested he shave because it was the more professional choice. Jack had still been out of it enough to agree and go along with whatever they said. As his head had cleared with the passing days, he regretted it all.

"What am I doing?" he muttered, shoving the tablet away. He gazed out of the windows at the snow-capped peak of Mt. Rainier looming above the misty low-lying clouds in the distance. The sight made him ache with the need to be outdoors. To breathe fresh air and be surrounded by nature. He wanted to work with his hands, get dirty, see tangible results before going home. Home to a gorgeous green-eyed, curly-haired witch who'd stolen his heart—and he never wanted it back. He wanted her to have it. Forever.

The ragged hole in his chest hurt with every breath and he couldn't see a way forward. Bridget had slammed the door on them and he couldn't blame her. She deserved to hate him. He'd lied and withheld vital information about himself and his motives for coming to Fallbank. Then he'd added insult to injury by pointing out her town reputation. But nothing about their love had been fake. Not on his end at least. He loved Bridget and if it took him the rest of his life, he'd find some way to win back her trust, or die trying. Too bad it was looking like the latter.

When he'd seen her last week in one of their other buildings, he laughingly thought she was there for him. God, the way his heart had leaped when he'd seen her standing in front of the elevator. Her strained expression had gutted him and the elevator doors closing were the only thing that had saved him from literally getting on his knees to beg forgiveness. Now he continued to rack his brain for how to repair the damage he'd done. And the answer that kept popping up was that he needed help.

Which was how he found himself the recipient of Sarah Wildes' steely glare at the café on the main floor of her building that Monday.

"Talk," she offered as a greeting. Her cool gaze and blonde hair gave her a far less welcoming attitude than Bridget's open and warm vibe. Sarah had mastered the calm and collected façade of a born-and-raised city dweller without an ounce of softness to her.

He sipped his water and cleared his throat. "Thanks for meeting me. I...want to start by saying how much I regret how things ended up between Bridget and me. It was never my intention to hurt her."

"And yet you did. Honestly what did you expect? How could you think it would turn out any other way when you lied about who you were and why you came to Fallbank?" Jaw clenched and nostrils flaring, she gave a small shake of her head. "You always knew your plan was to take over Timber Logging Company and destroy the town economy. That puts you on *everyone's* shit list."

"I know. I think I can fix that. My father might disown me, but I don't care. I can't go back to who I was before. I don't want to be that man anymore." He raked a hand through his hair and grimaced at the residual hair product on his fingers. He'd forgotten about his new-old hair style. "I need your help with Bridget. I can't let her go. I won't. If she really doesn't want me, then I'll accept her decision. I won't stop loving her and I'll always wait for her, but I have to try again. I need the chance to have an actual conversation with her."

Sarah held up her hand and he shut up. "First, what you need to do is figure out who you are. Are you" — she waved her palm in his general direction—"this guy? Rich, eligible, Seattle mogul Jonathan Ewan

Thompson III? Or Jack Thompson, logger and small-town local in the middle-of-nowhere Oregon?"

"I'm not this guy. Not anymore. I was, but it's not who I am inside. My grandfather saw the real me and tried to pull him out. He taught me to work with my hands and be a real part of a team. And I want that life. With Bridget."

"Then the second thing to do is prove you want her. She buries herself in work because she has nothing else. She thinks her life legacy is Three Sisters Apothecary and carrying on the family heritage. But all of that is worthless if there's no one to pass it on to." Sarah's mask cracked for a split second and painful loneliness shone through. "She's never had anyone besides me, Gran and Becca. Not really. Other guys she dated never put in the effort. They didn't treat her like she was special and worthwhile."

She leaned forward on her elbows and leveled her gaze at him. "Bridget has a heart of pure gold. She does nothing halfway and gives all of herself to everything. But for some reason, she hasn't found anyone who sees that. Sees how amazing she is. It's beyond frustrating to watch her date and not have her be appreciated that way she should be. Valued and cared for. I thought you were different. That you saw her worth and pulled her out of her shell. You pushed her into the spotlight and watched her shine." She folded her arms again and glared. "Then you took a baseball bat and smashed the light into a million pieces. And cut her with the shards."

He couldn't refute her words. "I know. I didn't mean to, but I did."

"So fix it. Make it up to her. Prove to her and the world that she is worth the effort. She's your number one and won't ever be anything less. If you can't do that, then you don't deserve her." Sarah grabbed her purse and stood up. "And prove that you aren't going to abandon her or ask her to give up everything for you. She's had a lifetime of giving up every dream that ever crossed her mind to make other people happy and never once tried for herself."

He watched Sarah leave, then picked up his phone. "Hey, Cornelius. Got a minute?"

\* \* \* \*

Bridget spent her week working nonstop. She made massive amounts of new products, reorganized the shelves at the store, cleaned the entire shop from top to bottom, cleaned her house from top to bottom and went shopping for new fall décor to bring to her booth at the Fallbank Fall Festival. She pushed a cart around the local craft store to find items she could combine to create new accents to showcase her products. She grabbed orange and purple-black battery-powered twinkle lights, orange tulle and a garland of glitter-covered black cats. Already, her mind was working out how she could fit the new decorations into her booth displays. The festival was on Halloween this year, so it was bound to be packed. Candy! She needed candy for kids to grab as they stopped in. She found a cauldron-shaped ceramic bowl to put her treats in. Then she rounded a corner to check out.

"There's the witch."

The voice came from her side and Bridget looked over at two women furtively glancing her way. Her patience snapped. Years of ridiculous rumors and whispers and gossip boiled over inside her. How many years had she lived in this town? How long had Three Sisters Apothecary existed? How long would she be talked about and called 'witch?' She was sick of it. Sick of trying to fit in, never stepping one toe out of line for fear it would ruin her business and she would be the Wildes who ended the family legacy. Of sacrificing everything else in life to have a successful business and be a part of a community that didn't want to accept her.

Eva's words rang in Bridget's head. Bridget needed to take back the meaning of witch and live up to the wise women who'd come before. To be worthy of their approval of calling herself a witch.

She spun on those women and glared. "What have I ever done to make you think I'm a witch?"

The two ladies gawped at her for a moment before one recovered. "Well, your store. It's full of witch stuff."

"Oh? Would that be my lotion or soap or tea or candles? It's the candles, isn't it? Because they smell good and no one else sells that kind of stuff." She turned her eyes pointedly at the display of scented candles and body lotions next to them. She arched one brow as she cut her gaze back to them. "Or perhaps because my family has been a member of the town since the founding? There must be a history of us casting spells or making potions and poisoning others. Stealing lovers and causing fatal accidents? Go on. I'll wait for you to tell me. What. Makes. Me. A. Witch?"

"Well... I-it's... You—" The woman stammered in fits and starts.

"Exactly. I've done nothing. I've never harmed anyone. I run a respectable store. I help pull in shoppers for the local economy. I work hard and keep my head down. I've never even gotten a speeding ticket! Yet you still mock me for some reason."

She shook her head. "I'm done. I'm done caring and trying to fit into whatever perfect little mold I need to be in to be accepted as one of your own. You know what, I am a witch! A wise woman who helps others. I'm good with plants and making soap and tea. If you want to judge me, you narrow-minded bitches, feel free. But I'm not going to care about your snobby and worthless opinions anymore. Oh, and keep in mind, it's nearly Halloween and the veil gets thin then. Better watch out for ghosts and ghouls, and any other witches who might be lurking."

She turned on her heel and pushed the cart on, head held high. A buoyancy filled her. For the first time ever, she'd stood up for herself and it felt great. Amazing. Fantastic. She grinned and strutted up the aisle. Sparkly black fabric caught her eye and she paused. Yes, this was exactly what she needed for Saturday. Time for her to put her money where her mouth was. She reached out and added more to her cart.

Walking to her car, she passed the local coffee shop and popped in for a pumpkin spice scone and matching latte. Her friend Serena waved from a table.

"Hey, Serena. How are you?" Bridget walked over with a smile.

Her friend gestured to sit and for once, Bridget allowed herself the chance. If she was going to tell the town to accept her for who she was, Bridget needed to give herself the chance to *be* who she was. That meant fewer late nights at the store or weekends making products and poring over her computer to ensure every penny was accounted for. Online orders were still increasing, and the past couple of weeks at the festivals, she'd sold out. Sales were steady and reaching her income goals for in-person customers, so why not take twenty minutes to eat and enjoy a chat with a friend?

As Gran had always said, there was more to life than the store. Bridget needed to heed that advice if she didn't want life to pass her by.

Serena smiled. "I haven't seen you in so long. How are things? I hear you have a hot new boyfriend." Her smile turned into a Cheshire grin.

Unfortunately for Bridget, all she felt was a sharp stab of sadness in her chest. The thought of Jack still stole her breath and she struggled to recover. "I, ah, I did. Not anymore though."

"I'm sorry to hear that." She put her hand over Bridget's. "I really hoped this one might work out for you. You don't have many serious boyfriends. Do you want to talk about it?"

Bridget shook her head vehemently. "No. I'm not there yet."

"Totally understand. Want to meet for dinner later in the week? We haven't hung out in so long. I miss it!"

It was on the tip of her tongue to say no out of habit. She stopped herself and instead took a breath. Then she opened her mouth. "That would be nice. I need to work less and enjoy life more."

Serena laughed. "No argument there. Want to meet at Bingley's on Thursday at six?"

"Perfect. See you then." Bridget waved and tossed her trash into the bin. Then she continued on her way back to Three Sisters.

Once there she marched in and over to Arianna. "Would you be able to work full-time and still go to classes?"

"Wha—um, yes?"

Bridget tilted her head. "Are you certain? No is an okay answer. I can hire another part-time employee, but I'm going to be making more room for myself."

"Yeah, I can do that. I like working here and could use the extra money, too. Thanks, Bridget. I know you didn't want me here in the first place."

A wave of guilt hit her. Arianna was right, but she'd proved Bridget wrong. "Having an additional employee wasn't in my plans, but I'm glad Sarah hired you. You're great and I'll keep you as long as you want to stay."

"What brought this on?" Becca's voice sounded from the back room as she stepped through the door.

She grinned at her with a shrug. "Just being called a witch one time too many and realizing I give too much of my life to this place."

Her cousin nodded. "You're not wrong about that. I'm happy to hear you're going to make a change for yourself. I can help more, too."

"What about your farm? You do have your hands full there."

"I also have five farmhands to keep things running smoothly. Plus winter is coming so there's less to do and less to grow. I've got more free time. This is my family legacy, too. I want to be a part of it."

Bridget blinked at the stinging in her eyes and rushed forward to hug Becca. "I'm sorry if I made you feel like this wasn't yours. I won't say no to you being here. Not ever."

Becca brought her arms around Bridget and squeezed tight. "I know that. And you didn't make me feel like an outsider. I get that you internalized more of the weight of carrying on the shop and history of the line of Wildes women." She pulled back. "We can at least be two of three sisters here at the store."

"Definitely. Want to help me with the festival booth on Saturday? I have an idea."

Gran popped around the door from the stairs. "Here's two of my girls. Bridget, you're looking better."

She swallowed and nodded. "I'm getting there. It's slow and hard and hurts like a monster, but I'm making some changes."

"Changes?" Gran's eyes sparkled with interest.

"Yep. Arianna is going to work here full-time and Becca is going to cover more shifts. I still love this store so much, but it can't be my whole life. I'm going to find some ways to delegate responsibilities. And I'm done hiding. If people believe I'm a witch, I'm going to embrace that title. I can't let that stop me from having friends and enjoying life." *Even when nursing a broken heart.*

If she were honest with herself, Bridget doubted she'd ever get over Jack. She'd fallen hard and fast, but also deep and solid. This wasn't some fickle love that would fade in a few weeks. It would be years, if ever, before she could think of dating again. Her heart told her it had found its match. Her head replied that the match wasn't real. He'd lied the whole time. Still, her heart couldn't change its rhythm back to the way it had been before. It would beat for Jack for a long time.

# Chapter Twenty-Two

Jack had one last task before he left town on Friday. He stood outside his father's office and steeled his nerves. This could end up ugly. Really ugly. There was no avoiding it, though. If he wanted to move on with his life and be happy, this had to be done. One sharp knock was all the warning he allowed before pushing open the door to his father's office.

"Hey, Dad."

"Jack, I thought you were meeting with..." He stopped as he looked up at Jack. "What are you doing? What are you wearing?"

Jack looked down at his boots, jeans and Henley T-shirt, then absentmindedly scratched at his fresh beard that was filling back in and itched like the devil. He needed Bridget's cream in a bad way. He needed Bridget, full stop. "I'm leaving. I've gotten all the pieces moving to divest from the family company, but I'm...done."

His father rose from behind his desk. "What do you mean, done?"

"I'm branching out on my own. I have money from my own ventures and investments. I bought the logging company and I'm going to co-run it locally. Keep the same employees. Live in Fallbank full-time."

"You are not going to do this." His dad's face turned red and mottled. "I will not have my son abandon the family business to go live in the woods. I've worked too hard for you to throw this all away."

"You didn't even start this company. Grandpa did. Yes, you took the foundation and made an empire, but that doesn't mean it's what I want in life. I want to be happy. Have a family that I see and enjoy spending time with. I want to work hard, but not every minute of every day. That's not a life. That's working until you die. Maybe you love this enough to make that your reality, but I don't."

His father slammed a fist down on the dark wood of his desk. "You can't do this. I groomed you for this role."

"I know, and I've learned so much from you, Dad. But this life? This working every day, at all hours? Never having a real vacation? That's not what I want. I don't love this the way you do. Besides, the world is moving on from this family-owned and handed-down business model. Things don't work this way anymore. Find a new protégé or two or ten for all I care. Someone who is as hungry for this as you are. I'm sorry, Dad. But I'd rather just be your son and not your business partner." He watched as his words sank into his father's head. His dad's entire body seemed to deflate in on itself as he sank back into his chair. Jack's gut twisted, but he held firm. He had to choose his own path in life and he finally knew what it was.

This was what his grandfather had nurtured in him for his whole life…to find where his passion lay. He'd loved working with his hands on the sites Grandpa had taken him to, but something had been missing. He'd found it in Fallbank. Community. A sense of belonging. Love. He needed to love Bridget and if it took him the rest of his life, he would prove that to her. One day, maybe, he could win her back. And he'd start this weekend at the festival.

\* \* \* \*

Four hours later, under the cover of night, he pulled his truck into Cornelius' driveway. He cast one longing glance at Bridget's house, but went inside where his new partner greeted him with a grin.

"Wow, look at that ugly mug. You definitely need to grow your beard back to hide that mess. Can't have you scaring the local kids. Halloween is only one day a year, you know."

Jack guffawed loud and full. "I'm working on it. This is the worst part of it. Itches like mad. I need to get more cream from Three Sisters. I'm all out."

"I've got some in my bathroom. I'll take pity on a poor soul and help a brother out." He left and jogged back out from the hall a minute later. When he held out the jar, Jack snatched it like a toddler stealing a cookie. Within seconds he was smoothing the lotion over his skin and sighing with relief. And fighting against the stinging at the corners of his eyes as the scent he associated with Bridget wafted over him. Lavender and sage. It wasn't as good as burying his nose in the soft spot of her neck and getting the scent straight from her skin, but it would ease the festering ache in his soul.

"You signed me up for the timber sport competition, right?"

Cornelius chuckled and shook his head. "I did. You sure you know what you're getting into? This isn't a joke, my dude."

"You put me in the rookie category, didn't you?"

"I did, but—"

"Then I'll be fine."

"I don't think you get how serious even the rookies are. This is an actual sport. They have world championships that are televised on ESPN. These kids, and I do mean kids, aren't messing around. They've been practicing for years and just waiting to get old enough for the real competitions."

"Well, I might make a complete ass out of myself, but it's for a good cause." He needed the town to accept him back into the fold. He needed to show he wasn't a flash-in-the-pan logger who was going to up and leave again. If he couldn't get the general goodwill of the town back, there was no way he'd get Bridget to forgive him.

"Have you even looked at what the events are? Practiced at all?"

"I Googled it."

Cornelius scrubbed his hands over his face. "You are going to die tomorrow. Figuratively and maybe literally. There is a competition where you stand on a log and chop it in half between your legs. Losing a leg is a real likelihood. I can't believe I'm going to lose my business partner before we even get started. Do we have insurance yet?"

Jack laughed then stopped. "You actually chop wood between your legs?"

"I don't because I don't have a death wish. You are because you're a fool in love."

He stared at Cornelius with wide eyes. "Do you think Bridget will mind dating the guy who came in last for the rookie category?"

A bark of laughter escaped his friend and he joined in. It was either laugh or freak out over the humiliation he was sure to suffer tomorrow.

\* \* \* \*

Saturday morning arrived with clear skies and cool temperatures. Perfect fall weather for Halloween and the festival. Normally, Bridget loved this day. She loved the crowds drawn to Fallbank for the fall fest and seeing all of the booths' wares offered each year. She got to catch up with vendors she didn't see regularly and meet newcomers to the circuit. And the timber sport competition. Every previous year she'd grinned and cheered and celebrated each event.

This year should have been even better with Halloween falling on the same day. Kids and adults would be in costumes and a new level of excitement would sprinkle the air. Yet the hollow sensation in her chest wouldn't go away. She reached for her normal happiness and enthusiasm to find them missing. She sighed and rolled over to where Candle was curled up next to her.

She purred as Bridget rubbed over her ears. "I miss him. Do you miss him, Candle?"

One eye peeked open at Bridget. A tiny chirp escaped the cat's throat. Candle stood and padded closer, rubbing against her chin and flopping down along her side. Then she gave Bridget a very feline 'you are a dumb human' look before tapping her paw over Bridget's hand.

"That's what I thought." She resumed petting her cat and contemplated what to do next. Sure, she was still mad Jack had lied. And that he'd called out the fact that most of Fallbank hated her. Yet that had given her the kick she'd needed to embrace her reputation and change how residents looked at her.

Yeah, it was going to suck when the logging jobs evaporated in town. She wasn't sure where she would go when times turned lean and she needed to close up shop. If she were smart about all of this, she'd let Arianna go and buckle down on expenses to try to keep Three Sisters vital for as long as possible. Instead, she had given her new employee more hours and was trying to balance work and a regular life. Getting a glimpse of what life could be outside her store had made her want more. She'd gone out to dinner and had enjoyed hanging out with Serena this week.

She and Gran could move elsewhere if they had to. Start over in a town more established with a more diverse economy. It would be a challenge to relaunch the store and compete with others in the area, but she now had enough faith in herself and the legacy of what the Wildes women created that they could be successful somewhere else. Seattle rents would be significantly higher, but living closer to Sarah would be nice. That she might catch a glimpse of Jack was tempting, too. Heartbreaking, but tempting.

"Give yourself time. He just ripped your heart out a little over a week ago." Her self-pep talk didn't motivate her. She still felt empty and sad. Lonely. She hadn't realized how desolate her life had been until Jack had walked into her shop. Bridget considered herself independent, yet somehow that had morphed into reclusive. Jack had changed that. Made her feel special and seen. Now that she was back to blending into the walls and simply going about her day-to-day life, it rang hollow. She wanted more. It wasn't that she needed to be the center of attention for the entire town, but having someone care about her day was refreshing. Feeling treasured and worthwhile, that her opinions mattered, had given her a sense of self-worth she hadn't realized was missing.

Forcing herself out of bed, Bridget walked to the bathroom in spite of Candle's meowed protests. After a quick shower, she dressed in her outfit—a mid-calf black tulle skirt, purple and black striped tights and a shimmery and soft purple cashmere sweater. All of it was pulled together with a pair of ankle boots. Then she set her pièce de résistance on her dark curls—a black and purple witch hat with lace and glitter accents. The mirror reflected exactly what she wanted. Sexy, sophisticated and witchy. It was time to claim the role assigned to her by the town and own it with pride.

After loading her car, she drove over to the park grounds where booth set-up was in full swing. She sent a quick text to Gran and Becca, then piled her wagon with her first round of stuff to lug over to their tent space.

"Hey, Bridge," Becca called out as she approached in her own witch outfit. Opting for pants and a jacket instead, Becca had still managed to look every inch the witch despite the non-traditional clothing.

"Morning! You look great." She continued to unload her wares onto the first table she'd gotten into place. "I'm almost done with this first load. Do you mind organizing all of this while I get the second round of products?"

"Sure thing. Gran should be here soon."

The two cousins managed to get the tent set up and decorated to perfection within an hour, giving them a little time to kill before the festival opened and attendees would show up.

"Want to grab a coffee?" Becca asked as Gran walked up.

They hugged hello and Bridget said, "Yes. I need caffeine and something warm sounds heavenly right now. Gran?"

"I'll stay here, but bring me back a hot cocoa?"

"You got it," Becca answered and linked her arm with Bridget's.

They wandered over to the food truck lane and ordered their drinks. Once those were in hand, they sauntered back in the direction of their booth, neither in a major hurry since they still had half an hour to go.

Becca peeked over at her. "How are you?"

"I'm fine." Bridget plastered a smile on her face in an attempt to make herself convincing.

Her cousin lifted one brow. "Really? Because while you look all right, anyone who knows you well can see the sadness in your eyes. I'm worried about you."

"It's been less than two weeks since Jack and I broke up. Can't I be a little sad still?"

"Of course you can. I'd be surprised if you weren't. I'm checking in with you—that's all I mean. Letting you know I'm here for you if you need a shoulder to cry on or an ear to complain to. Whatever you need." She put an arm around Bridget's shoulders and squeezed. "I know you and he weren't together very long, but everyone could see how in love you were. I'm sorry he hurt you."

"Me too." She filled her lungs with the crisp fall air. "It sucks and I'm really sad. And lonely. And heartbroken." Her voice trembled with unshed tears. She gave her head a shake. "But I can't stop living. If nothing else, Jack opened my eyes to what else the world can offer outside of the store and I don't want to go back to living to work anymore. I'd rather work to live and take the time to enjoy life in the true sense. You know?"

Becca smiled and bobbed her head. "I do know."

"Let's head back to the tent. I'm excited to see how today goes. I hope all the tracking with the new business software proves correct for having the right products for max appeal and purchasing." She flashed a real grin. "Maybe we'll sell out before the lumberjack competition begins and we can watch."

Becca shrugged noncommittally. "If dudes chopping wood is your thing..." They both burst out laughing as they made their way back.

\* \* \* \*

The confidence Jack had brought with him this morning was long gone. So far gone, he couldn't even pretend to remember what it felt like. Now his companion was fear. And anxiety. And possibly death, given what he was about to do. What had possessed him to sign up for this competition? He had lost his mind to believe even with the rookie level he could survive these rounds, let alone give a decent showing. Cornelius was right when he said he was going to lose to a bunch of kids. He was surrounded by teenagers just old enough to be legal and he felt every single one of his thirty-one years. The age gap might as well have been a hundred from the look of things.

"I'm going to get my ass kicked," he mumbled and picked up his chainsaw. The worst part was, he hadn't seen one glimpse of Bridget.

Cornelius wandered over to his competition station. "Well, are you ready to just not die?"

He snorted with a nod. "Yeah. That's the goal. Don't die." Jack looked over the line of kids pumped up and waiting to go. "Tell me why I'm doing this again?"

That earned him a look that rivaled the kind Gran gave out. "Because you wanted to impress Bridget and thought this was how to do it. Sorry, dude, but this isn't the way. I tried to tell you this was a bad idea."

"I know, I know." He ran a hand through his hair and scratched at his still-growing-in beard. The salve helped, but this was the itchy stage for him no matter what. "Really, it's that we need to make our announcement to the entire town and what better way to make myself appealing to them all than look like an idiot? How else are they going to accept me as a local?"

"Maybe by you moving here permanently and owning a business?"

"Point taken. Can't change things now."

An announcer began asking for contestants to line up. Jack swallowed hard and looked at his friend. "I guess this is it. Tell my family I died for love."

Cornelius clapped a hand on his shoulder. "Stop being so dramatic. Don't die and I'll see you after. I need you for the bank loan."

Jack watched his business partner saunter over to the lines of chairs where he joined a few other guys from the logging company. He scanned the crowd one more time, but still didn't spot Bridget. He clamped down on his frustration. Cornelius had promised she would be here. Supposedly she always watched the games and he banked on getting her attention this way. If she didn't show up, at least she would hear about the purchasing of TLC and maybe she'd reach out. Maybe.

"Safety equipment on!"

He grabbed his goggles and earmuffs, with a quick check that his heavy bib pants were arranged correctly to protect his legs. The speed chainsaw cut was first on the list. He was given six inches of a massive log to slice one ring from, top to bottom, that was at least a half inch in thickness but no more than one and a half inches wide, then bottom to top immediately after, also within the same thickness. It took incredible muscle control to keep the saw steady for pressure through the wood and also smooth so the cut wasn't jagged. Jack took a wide stance and bent his knees while gripping the idling chainsaw.

A loud horn blared and he squeezed to set the chain spinning and cut a bite through the wood. Tiny splinters spit everywhere and his arms and legs shook with the effort to keep his body as still as possible while smoothly slicing the blade through the log. His first circle fell to the ground and right away he switched direction to an upward motion and cut his second circle. Muffled cheering surrounded him, but the saw's whine blocked out everything else. His focus was solely on the piece of wood and the chainsaw in his hands. With a sudden release, the circle of wood fell to the ground and the tension on the blade sprang away. He locked down on his muscles so the blade didn't swing uncontrolled toward him. He released the power, and the chainsaw shut down.

He stumbled back a step and wiped sweat from his face. Huffing, he looked up to find he wasn't the last one done. A surge of excitement hit. He wasn't the fastest, but he'd take somewhere in the middle as a win.

Cornelius ran up with a huge grin on his face. "Man, that was beautiful! Nice work! Now to get you to survive the next two chops and one giant tree climb."

A wave of exhaustion mixed with terror swept through Jack at Cornelius' words. Three more events? He was supposed to survive three more events? "I need water." He grabbed for his bottle and downed half of it. Then he rolled back his already shaking and sore shoulders and looked at the next station. Springboard chopping. Three cuts, each higher than the previous, and using a board to dig into each cut to stand precariously on while chopping. It was madness. No helmets. No goggles. No safety harness. Just two wooden boards and an ax.

He finished his water and headed over to the next station. Once there, he checked in with the referee and took his place at the log. It stood nine feet high with three spots outlined to chop and two six-inch thick boards strategically placed against the stump for use while making the cuts. Jack tugged at his gloves and hefted the wood handle. The horn blared and he hacked away at the first cut. It didn't need to be wide and deep, just enough to fit the edge of the first springboard so he could jump up and start the next chop. He completed the first and wobbled a moment as he settled into position for the second cut on the opposite side of the stump.

Thirteen chops later and he had enough to shove the second, longer board in place. Jack rose onto it with shaking legs but managed to stay upright. Then he dug into the top of the log. This would be the full cut. He hacked and chopped away making top and bottom diagonal cuts to carve a sharp wedge from one side. Once deep enough, he swiveled to slam his ax into the weak spot on the opposite wall of the log to get a full slice of the log completely cut through. The top foot of the wood teetered and fell to the ground and Jack lowered his ax. His muscles trembled and adrenaline pulsed through his body. He was hot and tired, yet completely on edge and jittery. He felt like an explosion waiting to happen.

He climbed down from the boards and shook off his gloves. Now was his break time and did he ever need it. There was a tent nearby where contestants could rest and wait for their events. He beelined for it. He downed another bottle of water and slumped into a chair, breathing heavily. Closing his eyes, he waited to get control of his body once more. The surge of adrenaline evened out. The trembling in his muscles diminished, though he thought it might be a while before it ceased completely.

"Is this your grand gesture?"

He jerked upright and stared at Becca. "Hey." That was his lame response? "Um, I don't know. Maybe?"

Her expression was distinctly unimpressed. "Glad you thought this out. What are you doing here, then? Bridget will be crushed when she finds out you're here. She's barely hanging on."

Jack winced at the stab of pain that her words brought him. It was killing him that he'd hurt her so much. "I never meant to—"

"Oh, I know. But you did. And killing yourself in some silly competition is not good enough. Not for the town and not for her. You're going to murder Fallbank by leaching it of its economic base, and you think chopping a few logs is going to fix it?" She crossed her arms and glared. "Just get the hell out of town and don't bother any of us, especially my cousin, again."

"What if my grand gesture was *not* stealing the main industry in town and this was to get her attention instead?"

Becca studied him.

He knew if Becca couldn't forgive him, there wasn't a snowball's chance Bridget ever would.

"How are you going to do that?" Becca asked.

He explained his plan and by the end, her begrudging smile gave him hope. "Well? What do you think?"

"It might work. At the very least, you'll win back a bit of goodwill from the locals. Bridget...she may or may not forgive you." Becca whipped off her witch hat and ran her fingers through her wavy chin-length hair. "Bridge doesn't open up to many people. She's guarded and hides behind Three Sisters Apothecary. Trust is hard for her. When her parents died, it left a hole that, try as she did, Gran couldn't fill. No one could. Add in that half the town targeted her as the local witch and she keeps herself as small as possible. Hates attention. You somehow found a way to bring her out of her shell. I loved seeing the cousin I know out in the world for everyone to see. I'm terrified she's going to fall back into her old habits despite her promises not to do so. The wound from you is still fresh and she feels it with every breath. She told me so this morning."

"I never meant to hurt her this way. I was working to find a solution, but it took me longer to see it than it should have."

"I know that now, but she doesn't."

"Will you bring her here? I'm afraid if I see her around town or at her house, she won't talk to me. I could come to the shop, but I don't want to force things. Maybe if she sees me here, if she hears Cornelius' and my announcement, it will smooth the way for us to talk."

"I'll see what I can do to get her to leave the tent for the last part of the rookie competition. She only likes the professional-level stuff. Says the others are too boring and slow."

Jack laughed. Too boring and slow? Well, he guessed in comparison to the expert competitors, he would seem like a sloth in these events, but his body sure felt otherwise. He touched Becca's arm. "Thank you for your help. I know I don't deserve it, but I promise to make it up to her. For the rest of our lives if she'll have me."

She rounded her eyes and whistled. "You do mean business. Two months and she's got you talking about forever." A grin spread across her cheeks. "Bridget really must be a witch."

# Chapter Twenty-Three

"Thank you for stopping by. I hope you enjoy our products." Bridget waved as another customer left her tent. A quick glance told her she was just about out of everything. She should have been more excited, but she couldn't muster up the sensation. Instead, she felt hollow inside. Pasting a smile on her face, she turned to Gran. "Today has gone great! We're almost sold out." Maybe it was the witch costumes they all wore, and the tent décor, that had caught everyone's eye. Most at least popped in to check out the wares and over half of those had left with purchases in hand.

"Yes, it has been a banner day," Gran agreed. "Why don't I see real happiness in you, then?"

Bridget's false smile slipped from her face. "I am happy. Three Sisters has jumped fifteen percent in sales over the past two months. Things are looking great."

"But?"

"No. No buts. I'm happy. I am," she insisted, yet the sting of tears clogged her throat. *Ugh*, she hated everything. The level of loss and devastation tearing her up inside hadn't hit this hard since her parents' death. How had she allowed Jack in so deeply in such a short amount of time? And people called her a witch? Jack was the one playing tricks on her heart, not the other way around.

Gran kept her stare steady on her and said nothing.

"I — I'm sad, too." Tears traced down her cheeks. "I don't understand how this happened. How did I fall so fast for Jack? It doesn't make sense. I don't let people in."

Gran wrapped an arm around her shoulders. "That's why it hurts so much. You let your guard down and he messed up."

She snorted. "He lied to me. And he's destroying Fallbank."

"He was afraid, too. He's been used by others, so he tried to be himself and not let his family name take over anyone else's perception. Both of you saw each other for who you really are. That's how it happened, honey."

"But I don't... I don't know how to deal with this."

"Give yourself time. That's the thing that will help. Why don't you take a walk? Go find Becca or walk around the festival a little bit. I'll take care of things here and I'm sure by the time you're back, we'll be sold out."

"I don't need to do that. I'm fine." She wiped at her face.

"You aren't, and you need to get some air. Take a few minutes."

Gran's voice brooked no room for argument and Bridget gave up any fight. "All right. I'll go for a short walk." She sucked in a deep breath and turned to head out. She wandered out through the different lanes and looked at the offerings until she heard Becca calling her.

"Hey, what's up?" Bridget walked over to where her cousin stood with a grin.

"I was at the timber sport competition. It's pretty good this year. Come check it out with me." She linked her arm through hers and took a step.

"Right now? Are they at expert level? The rookies are too young and slow. You know I don't head over until things get real. I'll watch these kids when they get enough experience to make it up the ladder in a few years."

Becca tugged at her. "There's one you need to see. Trust me, it won't be boring."

A small spark of interest kindled inside her chest and she decided to follow it. After all, nothing had much held her attention in the past two weeks so anything that might take her mind off Jack was welcome. "Okay, you win. Let's go."

They made their way through the crowds, smiling at children dressed up in their costumes and patrons milling through the lanes. The cool air felt amazing in the sunlight—the weather couldn't have been any better. She paused for a brief moment and enjoyed the bright warmth paired with the crisp breeze. She peeked over at Becca and curled her lips into a small smile. "This is nice. Thanks for being here with me."

"We're family. It's what we do. I know it doesn't seem like it, but things will work out. And no matter what, I'm always on your side." She scrunched her face up. "Now let's go watch a bunch of guys flaunt themselves and beat their chests like the alpha males they pretend to be."

Bridget laughed and nodded. "Sounds like your dream come true."

"Ugh, don't remind me of what I'm about to put myself through." Becca joined her laughter as they walked into the arena tent where things were set for the underhand chop. Ten logs sat horizontally on low platforms to keep them stable and in place. Axes rested next to each one. They found a spot a few rows back to watch the event. Bridget settled into her chair as the rookie contestants filed in. She widened her eyes as her lungs arrested and froze. "Jack," she whispered. Then whirled to her cousin with accusation in her expression. "You knew he was here. This is the one you were talking about."

"What?" Becca blinked in perfect innocence. "I had no idea. I meant that one." She gestured vaguely in a random direction nowhere near the contestants.

"Uh-huh." She tried to be mad, but her gaze strayed back to Jack. He put his goggles in place and stepped up onto the log. "Oh my God. He's going to kill himself."

"No, he won't. At worst he'll maim himself and amputate his own foot. There's medical help here so total loss of life is doubtful. They can't have the bad press."

Bridget slapped at her cousin's arm, but ended up grabbing onto it as the refs blew the horn. She held her breath as the wood began flying. They all chopped like madmen, Jack's movements hard yet precise. He held control over the ax as chunks of log fell to the floor. The less than two minutes it took him to hack through the log until it fell in two pieces lasted an eternity to her. Once he dropped the ax, she allowed her body to loosen. "He didn't die."

Becca chuckled. "I told you he wouldn't."

"Why is he here? What is he thinking?"

Becca nudged her elbow into her side. "He's here for you. Duh."

"But why? His family is still going to buy out Timber Logging Company and outsource the jobs. I don't understand."

"Try talking to him, then. Maybe things changed. Maybe they didn't. Either way, is it worth it to you to find out?"

She swallowed and averted her eyes. She didn't know. Could she give him the chance to explain? To have a shot at ripping her heart out all over again? Bridget didn't know the answer and didn't think she would have enough time to figure it out.

The last event was staged and ready to go. Each competitor stood next to a fourteen-inch-thick log of white pine, ax at the ready. The single block chop seemed the simplest of the events, but it still took control and power to get through the wood in less than a minute. The horn blared and axes slammed into the waiting blocks. The rookies chopped over and over and over, each bite of the blade throwing chunks of wood until they made their way to the other side and the top flew to the ground. As Jack let the ax drop, he exhaled and leaned over on his knees. Almost as if he felt Bridget's stare, he turned his head and locked eyes with her.

She froze, captivated by those dark irises that held so much longing she could see it from where she was sitting. His face was scruffy with a half grown-in beard and his hair was in complete disarray. Sweat beaded on his forehead and made his shirt cling to his chest in a way that had Bridget's mouth watering. Despite everything, he was still the sexiest man she'd ever seen. And the way he watched her brought to mind how intense and focused he could be, especially in the bedroom. A shiver traced its way down her back and landed low in her belly. She was in such trouble.

Becca glanced between the two of them. "Yeah, I think you two need to talk." She lowered her voice. "Or get a room. Good grief."

Bridget snapped out of her reverie and shot to her feet. "I think I need some air. And we should get back to the tent. Gran must be wondering where we are."

Becca grabbed her arm. "Gran is fine. I just sent her a text to check in. We sold out. You are staying here. Talk. To. Him."

She grumbled at her cousin. "You're awfully pushy, you know?"

"Maybe, but I'm right."

Bridget rolled her eyes. "Yeah, yeah. I just...I don't know what to do."

"Easy." Becca smiled. "Listen first, then you'll know what to say. Your heart will tell you."

* * * *

Jack was going to die. He sprawled in a folding chair while a handful of other contestants milling around the tent. His breathing evened out and the adrenaline was now a faint buzz in his blood instead of the lightning it'd been during the events. However, since these events hadn't killed him, seeing Bridget might just be the nail in his coffin. The way she'd looked at him back in the tent had eviscerated him. Shock and desire and sadness. And maybe still love? If it took him the rest of his life—and who knew how long or short it might be—he would never stop loving her or wanting her. He would never stop trying to win her again.

Subtly, of course. Like participating in competitions designed to end him or buying things from her store without asking her out. He wouldn't hound her like some dude in a rom-com. Those guys always weirded him out. *"If I just stalk you enough, I'll wear you down until you say yes."* That wasn't the guy he wanted to be. A grand gesture like making a fool of himself sawing wood and trying to save the town's economy was fair because it didn't personally involve her. He just hoped to catch her attention and see if she'd talk to him. Or was that just as stalkery as those other creeps in the movies?

He shook his head and scrubbed a wet towel over his face and hair. His events were done, thank God. Now to wait and see what happened. Would she seek him out? Would she stay until the announcement about TLC at the results ceremony?

The flap to the tent opened a fraction. "Can I come in?"

He spun around to find Bridget peeking through and glancing around. Her gaze landed on him and her cheeks turned pink.

"Sure." He rubbed a hand through his hair. "That is, I mean, if you were asking me."

She stepped through and walked a few feet toward him. "I was. Asking you."

Could this get any more awkward? He flashed a tentative smile at her. "It's good to see you. You look amazing. I love the costume." She looked hot as all get out, but he kept that to himself. No need to make her uncomfortable.

"Thanks. You were…right about the town and how they view me. I decided it was time to stop trying to hide and embrace the witch rep I have. Good witches exist, too." She shrugged and clasped her hands in front of her. "Anyway, I wanted to say you did well out there. I didn't see all of the events, but what I did was great."

Had she just said he was right? She was claiming being a witch now? Holy hell, how'd he get that lucky? "Thanks, Bridget. That means a lot. I think I'll retire from competing after this year, though." He barked out a laugh. "This almost killed me. I had no idea how intense the competition was. Thank God for my time logging or I'd have made a total idiot out of myself instead of just half of one."

She giggled and rocked on her feet. "I thought you looked good."

Then he was out of words. What else could he say? Just start apologizing? Try to explain his plan? The awkwardness was palpable between them and he didn't know what to do.

"I guess I should go. Congratulations again. I hope you did well." She smiled and turned to go.

"Bridget, please wait." He grasped her hand. They both paused and looked down to where their fingers touched. Hers curled around his ever so slightly. That small gesture opened the floodgates for him.

"I'm damn sorry, Bridget. I know I can't make up for what I did, but I promise I am here to fix things. For the town and TLC. My family isn't going to buy it."

"It doesn't matter. Someone will and the results will be the same. Whether it's now or down the line, things will end up the same. We have to face that in Fallbank and find another way. That might mean we move elsewhere or die trying, but we'll figure it out. Your family shouldn't be punished for doing business the way you always have."

"That's very forgiving of you, but it doesn't change that Thompson Industries won't be the new owner. Someone else bought it out before they did."

She swallowed and her skin grew paler. "Oh. Well, like I said, it would happen one way or another."

"Cornelius and I bought Timber Logging Company."

She blinked twice. Then once more. "You and Cornelius did? I don't understand."

"We're business partners now. I divested my holdings in my family business, so I'm out. I took my own money and talked to Cornelius because I needed a partner who knows this industry inside and out. We made an offer and Paul accepted it. TLC isn't going anywhere. The jobs are staying in Fallbank for the foreseeable future. And they'll stay that way whenever we retire." He sucked in a breath. "I'm moving here, too. For good."

Silence stretched between them. Her eyes were wide and vulnerable. Her lips twitched but no words came out. What was she thinking? Was this where she told him to avoid her at all costs when their paths crossed?

"You're staying? In Fallbank?"

He nodded, afraid to speak in case he spooked her.

Bridget's eyes shimmered for a moment, then she looked away and closed her eyes for a long moment. Clearing her throat, she said, "I, um, I don't know what to say." Her hand fell away from his as she gripped her fingers together until her knuckles turned white. "What about that other girl? The one in the tabloid?"

Anxiety nipped at him. "Leah's a friend. Yes, we dated, but figured out fast we were better as friends. I spent the entire lunch talking about you and how I messed up."

Three lines appeared between her brows as she chewed on her lip. "What about your family? They must be livid."

A new voice interjected. "They aren't, actually."

Jack jumped at the sound of his mother's voice. "Mom?" He glanced over Bridget's shoulder. His parents were standing just inside the tent, watching the two of them. "Dad? What are you two doing here?"

His mother smiled and joined them. "We're here for the competition, of course. You did wonderfully, dear." She pressed a kiss to his cheek. "We're so proud of you."

"How did you even know about this?"

His father answered, "Your sister. She thought it might be good for us to see you in action." He coughed and pressed his lips into a thin line for a moment. "Allison was right. You do belong here."

His mom smiled and squeezed Jack's arm. "While we're sad to have you leave the family business, we understand and support your desire to venture out on your own. As long as you love your life, we're happy for you." She turned to Bridget. "I'm sorry our first meeting wasn't under better circumstances, and I hope to remedy that."

Bridget fidgeted with her skirt and pasted her polite customer smile across her face. "That's okay, it was a stressful time for everyone." She glanced between him and his parents. "I should go. Let you all have time together. I'll see you around, Jack."

She rushed to the door, but Jack caught up to her. "Please, wait." He stretched his hand to brush hers but didn't grab hold. He wanted the choice to be hers. Slowly, she turned.

He swallowed and laid it all on the line. "I don't know what to say, except I love you. I'm here for you. Because of you. I won't push or force you into anything but know that if you ever find yourself wanting me again, I'll be waiting. For as long as you need."

"Jack," she whispered and her eyes filled with tears again. "You can't know that. What if in three months you can't stand it here and want to go back to Seattle? To your real life?"

He shook his head and this time he did cup her hands in his. "That wasn't my real life. I was lost and didn't know what I wanted. Then I came here. Working with my hands, seeing the fruits of my labors, loving you. *That* is my real life. I found my purpose and my path when I set foot in Fallbank. This is my home. Not Seattle. It never was. I always felt fake and out of place. I never pretended with you, Bridget. You saw the real me from the first time we met. I love you and I always will."

She opened her mouth right as a guy shoved his head through the tent flaps. He shouted, "Awards time! All contestants to the stage!"

Bridget stepped back and blew out a breath. "I guess you need to go."

"Yeah." Damn inconvenient time for the awards, but he had an announcement to make to the town. "Will I see you after?"

Her lips curled up at the corners. "Maybe."

\* \* \* \*

It wasn't fair. Jack couldn't go around fixing things and saying he loved her and expect her to still be able to be mad at him. And how rude for the awards ceremony to start before she had the chance to say anything. Bridget plopped back into her chair where Becca and now Gran waited.

"Well?" Becca shot an expectant look her way.

Bridget's stomach danced with excitement and nerves. Her heart and her head were once again at odds with each other. Her heart screamed to take this second chance. He had changed his entire life, maybe not entirely for her, but at least in part for her. Jack had walked away from his family business, ensured the legacy of TLC, secured Fallbank's continued existence and planned to stay.

A brush of guilt swept over her as she hadn't considered doing the same for him. It had never occurred to her to leave everything behind and start over in Seattle. To be flexible and give a little to make their lives work together. Did that mean she didn't truly love him? Or he loved her more?

Before she could respond to her cousin, he walked onto the stage and grinned at the audience. Bridget's heart stuttered. Yes, she loved him. More than anyone else she'd ever met. And while she could have changed her world to be with him, she loved this Jack most. The laid-back bearded lumberjack who stole her breath and her heart every time he looked at her. This was the man who'd coaxed her from her shell and showed her a life worth experiencing.

She leaned over to Becca and squeezed her arm. "Yeah, I think we're going to be okay."

"You two better be. I liked having my cousin so happy these past couple of months. But if he messes up again, he's going to answer to me."

Gran poked her head around at the two of them. "Stop that, Rebecca. Anyone can see that Jack is over the moon for our Bridget. I'm glad you two patched things up."

Bridget opened her mouth to tell her they hadn't reached an understanding yet, but the announcer began speaking.

"Welcome, everyone! We're here to give the results of today's rookie competition and then we'll get started with the main portion of today's show, the expert-level events! First though, we have a word from our generous sponsor with some exciting news."

Jack and Cornelius both walked over to the microphone. Jack glanced at Cornelius and gestured, but he shook his head and waved Jack forward. "Thank you all for attending today. Some of you might know me from around town and some of you may recognize me from celebrity news. While I've never considered myself to be famous, my family is well known in the business realm which means from time to time, people are interested in me."

He stared out at the crowd and when his eyes met Bridget's, they stayed there. "I'm Jonathan Ewan Thompson III. Call me Jack. I came to Fallbank two short months ago and you all welcomed me like family. Recently, there were rumors floating around about a hostile takeover of Timber Logging Company. That jobs might be outsourced, and the local economy was going to take a substantial hit. I'm damn happy to say those rumors are dead. Cornelius Hawthorne has agreed to be my business partner. Together we're the new owners and operators of Timber Logging Company."

Cheers and applause broke out from the crowd and even Bridget couldn't help grinning and clapping. The relief that the beloved town that had taken her in as a child would endure soothed her frayed nerves. Plus, the promise of Three Sisters Apothecary's survival for another generation also helped her breathe easier. She would only have herself to blame if things fell apart, and that was a task she was more than up to.

Jack spoke again. "We are sad to see Paul Carson retire but will carry on the legacy he began. And we'll keep the entire business and all jobs here in Fallbank."

More whistles and yells of happiness came from the audience.

"I can't thank you enough for taking me into your fold and making me one of your own. As our first order of business, we wanted to be the top sponsor for today's festival and plan to do so for many more years to come. So thank you again, enjoy the rest of the festival and make sure you stop by all the vendor booths. They could use your patronage. Happy Halloween!"

The announcer came back over and handed out first, second and third places in the rookie category, none of which Jack won. He did, however, place fifth out of ten and Bridget was proud of him. He hadn't trained at all and was brand new to logging. She was thrilled he hadn't killed or maimed himself, in all honesty.

As the rookies filed off stage, she walked over to the platform.

Jack jumped off when he spotted her.

"Want to take a walk?" she asked.

He lifted one side of his mouth up. "Yeah, that'd be great."

They sauntered side by side through the lanes of tents and checked out the wares. It felt reminiscent of their first time at a festival together. "Do you think Candle would be jealous if I came home with another cat?"

Jack threw his head back and laughed. "Yeah, she might be miffed."

She caught his eyes and said, "What if I brought you home instead?"

His smile slipped as he turned serious. "I hurt you, Bridget, and I'm sorrier than I can say. I swear to make it up to you. Take your time. You don't have to make any rash decisions."

"I'm not," she interrupted. "I was scared and hurt. It's hard for me to trust and let anyone in." She reached out and wove her fingers through his. "I understand now it's the same for you, too. People use you for your money and family name. I let you go too easily at the first sign of conflict. I didn't fight for us, but I know what we have together is real. That we can depend on each other."

"I promise to have faith in you and not hide things. I never meant to hurt you and I was trying to find a solution before telling you. If problems come up, I'll talk to you and we can find a solution together. I won't make the same mistake again."

Bridget's heart bounded in her chest and for once her head agreed. "I love you, Jack."

He grinned wide and swung her up into his arms. "I love you, too. My sweet honeybee."

Winding her arms around his neck, she lifted her face up to press her lips to his.

# Chapter Twenty-Four

A six-inch layer of snow blanketed the ground and dusted the towering Douglas firs lining the road as they drove. Bridget looked up at the heavy leaden clouds above. "Looks like more snow."

"Probably, but we'll be back snug at home with Candle before it hits. I promise." Jack winked.

She giggled and leaned closer to him. "I'm sure we'd find a way to stay warm if we ended up stranded."

"Of course we would. I'd never let my honeybee get cold."

"You are quite good at heating me up." She stretched up just enough to nip his earlobe, making him jump. The truck wiggled a hair's breadth under his hands and Jack shot her a look. She flashed an innocent grin and fluttered her lashes.

"Behave. We're almost there," he teased.

"And where is there, again? It's slipped my mind."

"Nice try. You'll find out when we get there."

To keep herself occupied, Bridget connected her phone to the truck stereo and flipped on her holiday playlist. She hummed along and thought about what to get Jack for Christmas. She was stumped on what to get him. So far she had knitted him a scarf and matching cap, plus she'd come up with a basket of skin and hair products with a unique scent of juniper, bergamot and eucalyptus for him. This would be a small batch she could recreate when he needed, but she'd keep it private and not available to customers. A personal scent just for him. But she still felt like she needed something else for under the tree.

The road curved to the left, then Jack turned off onto a dirt drive that had fresh tire tracks in the snow. They bumped down the lane until dirt ended at a clearing encircled by trees. Jack cut the engine and looked at her. "We're here."

"Where's here? What's here?" Bridget looked back and forth between the land and Jack. Bewildered, she cocked her head at him. "What is going on?"

"Come find out."

He hopped out of the truck and she scrambled to follow. Wrapping her scarf around her neck, she came around to the front of the truck to stand next to her lumberjack boyfriend. He grabbed her hand and led her out into the open space. Snow crunched under their boots as they stopped in the center of clearing.

Jack lifted his hand to gesture off to their right. "I was thinking your garden could go back there, with French doors from the kitchen." He pointed slightly to the left. "And your work shed could be there."

She stared at the open space. "What...are you talking about?"

Jack turned to her. "Building a house. Our house. If you like it here. It's only fifteen minutes from downtown, but more secluded. Larger plot of land. More nature to enjoy."

"Our house?" she echoed. She bit down on her lower lip as her chest tightened. He wanted to build a house for the two of them? "For you and me?"

A shy smile crossed his features. "Maybe a couple of kids one day, if you want." He watched her closely and swallowed hard. "What do you think?"

Despite the freezing temperatures outside, warmth filled her from head to toe. "Kids, huh? Yeah, I think I like that idea."

"That's good. Then I can do this." He slid down onto one knee and reached into his pocket.

Bridget gasped and covered her mouth. Her heart took off like a racehorse stampeding in her chest. She blinked against the moisture in her eyes.

He opened a tiny box with a ring nestled inside. A simple square emerald adorning the center surrounded by tiny diamonds embedded into the band winked at her from the velvet. The brilliant green gem wasn't so large that it would look ostentatious on her hand or impede her when making products. It was perfect and breathtaking.

"I know this is fast for some couples, but I don't have a doubt in my mind. You are the partner I've searched for my whole life. You showed me how to trust and how to slow down and enjoy life. I want to hold you in my arms every night as we fall asleep and kiss you awake each morning. Will you marry me, honeybee?"

Her fight against tears failed as she nodded and threw herself at him. "Yes, I'll marry you, Jack!" She twined her arms around his neck and kissed him. This gorgeous, sweet man was going to be by her side for the rest of her life and happiness overflowed within her.

She kissed him hot and hard. "Come on, lumberjack. Take me home and make me fall for you all over again."

# Want to see more like this?
# Here's a taster for you to enjoy!

# So Far, So Good:
# So, That Got Weird
### Amelia Kingston

*Excerpt*

Outside the restaurant after dinner, Jeremy seems as shy as I am, toeing the pavement with his hands in his pockets. Okay, maybe not *as* shy. He can make eye contact without blushing. He's the 'oh, isn't he sweet' kind of shy, while I'm more the 'oh, she has trouble functioning in society' kind. He seems my speed. Slow. Three-legged turtle on a glacier slow. He's nice too. Non-threatening. Safe.

Dinner was only mildly awkward, a raging success in the relative terms of my dating life. But it's the end of the night and this is the part I hate.

What do we do now?

Hug?

Kiss?

Shake hands? *No, that's weird.*

"I had a good time tonight," Jeremy chirps with an innocent smile on his lips. Meanwhile, my stomach is trying to turn itself inside out. *Calm down, Elizabeth.*

He's far from my dream guy, being barely taller than me at all of five foot nothing. He can only be considered 'in shape' if you mean round. He's never going to grace the cover of *GQ*, or even *Wired*. I don't care. I want him—anyone—to sweep me off my feet. I want to feel something—anything— other than this paralyzing fear.

My palms are sweaty. My heart's beating faster than if I'd run a marathon. My brain has unfortunately kicked into hyperdrive.

*What if I have something stuck in my teeth?*
*What if my breath smells like onions?*
*What if my deodorant stopped working?*
*What if I'm a bad kisser?*
*What if I think he's going in for a kiss, but he's actually just going in for a hug and we do that awkward back-and-forth dance, resulting in knocking our heads together?*

My stomach continues its acrobatics, tying itself into knots. I wrap my arms around myself, silently pleading for it to settle. I'm unaware of the pinched shape my face must've taken on when he asks with genuine concern, "Are you okay?"

I can't tell him I'm freaking out, so I lie. Admittedly, not something I'm particularly good at.

"Yeah, I'm fine." I try to pull off a nonchalant shrug and say the first thing that pops into my head. "Just a little gassy. You know, Mexican food..."

*You did NOT just say that!*

Jeremy's soft smile falls into a disgusted frown.

"Right," he says. He eyes his car in the parking lot, undoubtedly eager to get away from my train wreck of a personality.

"I had a nice time, too," I try to backpedal.

He gives me a forced smile. *Now who looks gassy?* This guy's officially lost interest. Can't say I blame him.

"Well, it's getting pretty late." He backs away with a wave, clearly avoiding any physical contact at this point. "Have a nice night, Elizabeth."

"You too, Jeremy." I return the awkward wave and make my way home, my head hanging in shame the whole way.

The second my front door shuts behind me, I beeline for my computer. I pull on my headset and stare at the video chat window, waiting for Jackie to answer. Jackie is my best—and only—friend. With bright red hair and a nose ring, she's also my complete opposite. She's a fierce and feisty woman, the human equivalent of a chihuahua. Small but bossy, Jackie is hellbent on conquering the world. So. Not. Me. I hate being noticed and try to fly under the radar. She loves being the center of attention and ends up bossing everyone around. I count on her for brutal, unabridged honesty.

"¿Qué pasa, chica? That's Spanish for *sup, girlie*? Thought you could use a little culture in your life." Jackie's megawatt smile and flaming red locks light up my screen. The smile fades when she sees the defeat stamped across my face. Or, is it *loser* stamped on my forehead? Or, maybe *twenty-one-year-old virgin*?

"Hey, what's with the sad face?" Her voice drags my brain away from contemplating facial tattoos to commemorate my failures and back to the real world.

"I had my date tonight with Jeremy."

She stares at me blankly. "Who the fuck is Jeremy?"

"You know, CommanderUxorious?" His username finally sparks recognition in her eyes.

"Oooohhhh, that geekalicious noob you've been chatting with for..." She pauses, taking an overly dramatic deep breath before adding, "Fooreeeveeer?"

"Shut up. It hasn't been *that* long. Only six months."

"That's three times the life expectancy of one of my relationships. So, was he hot?"

I try to think of a nice way to describe Jeremy. "He's kinda cute. In a hobbitish sort of way."

"Hobbitish? What the fuck does that mean? Like hairy feet and a fetish for second breakfast?" Jackie asks with a chuckle.

"Well, he's kind of short. And hairy. And chubby. He reminds me of a hobbit. Not in a bad way. Or maybe a guinea pig?"

"Sweet baby Jesus, stop. No. Just no. You can't be *hobbitish* in a *good* way. No one wants to fuck Frodo. Could you imagine screaming *Harder, Baggins, harder!*"

She makes crazy sex noises, moaning and slapping her desk à la Meg Ryan in *When Harry Met Sally*. I'm desperate to hold back my smile, but I can't. The second she sees me cracking, she goes full tilt.

"*Oh, your feet are so big and hairy. Give it to me, baby! Take me to Mordor. Destroy that ring!*" We both burst out laughing. I laugh until my sides hurt and my eyes are watering.

"*My precious! My precious!*" Jackie finishes with a flourish, leans back in her chair and smokes an imaginary post-coital cigarette. "So, what happened? Did you show him your hobbit hole?"

"Not exactly."

Jackie knows me well enough to hear the embarrassment in my voice. And, in true Jackie style, she calls me on it.

"Lizzy, what did you do?" She uses the nickname she knows I hate just to be a brat. Like I'm the family dog that got into the trash. She's disappointed, a twinge angry maybe, but in no way surprised.

This isn't my first colossal disaster of a date. Epic failure is kind of my thing.

"I-I..." I stutter, thinking of how to explain. "I might have told him I was gassy." I hide my face in my hands, sure I'm turning redder than Jackie's hair. She's still laughing when I finally peek through my fingers.

Keeled over in hysterics, she nearly falls off her chair. Luckily, almost cracking her head open sobers her a bit.

With a few deep breaths, she composes herself. "What, and hobbits aren't into that? Guess you won't be hearing from him again any time soon."

"Seriously, Jackie, what's wrong with me?"

"So many things, my child. So very *many* things."

"I'm serious. We had so much in common. We spent two hours debating AMD versus Nvidia."

"Oh, gee. Graphics cards. What a panty dropper."

"I thought he was perfect. Respectful. Sweet. Mild-mannered—" Jackie's obnoxious fake snore interrupts me. "And even with him, I freak out and ruin it! Why am I so pathetic?" I drag my fingers through my hair and tug at the roots until it almost hurts.

"You're not pathetic," Jackie assures me, albeit with derision and frustration in her voice. "You spent six months building this spectacularly boring guy up in your head and you're surprised when he comes up short? Pun intended."

"Why can't I meet a nice guy and not freak out when it comes to the physical stuff? I can't even *kiss* a guy." I bang my head on my desk in classic toddler-meltdown fashion.

"Darling, sweetie, beautiful, light of my life, you know I love you, right? I mean in the strictly BFF way. I don't do Taco Tuesday."

"I love you too. And, eww."

"Lizbit, listen to your momma Jackie. You don't need a nice guy. You need a sexy filthy *man* who won't just pop your cherry—he'll obliterate it. You need to get fucked. Then it won't seem like a big deal."

I shake my head, almost losing my headset in the process. "It's not that easy."

"Yep. It really is." Jackie holds up one hand in a circle and moves the index finger of her other hand back and forth through it. *Classy.*

"It's not. Not for me. I get stuck in my head and overthink things. I get all panicked and say something stupid that ruins it. Like *I'm gassy!*"

Jackie lets out a quick chuckle at the reminder of my ineptitude. "That's because you're going out with hobbits! But yeah. Don't say that again. You need someone so fucking hot you turn your brain off and think with your pussy for once."

"What the hell does that mean?"

"It means dress slutty, go to a bar, find a guy who gives you a lady boner and ride him until he's dry." She gives me a shoulder shrug. "Easy."

"That's so not me. That's *never* going to happen." I shudder, panic trickling up my spine at the idea.

I don't do slutty.

I don't do bars.

I don't do *riding.*

"Well, I guess you'll be a virgin forever then. Is it too late to switch your major from pre-med to religious studies? You'd make an awesome nun."

\* \* \* \*

I hate Jackie. I mean, I love her, but right now I rue the day I ever accepted her stupid friend request. *'Just go to a bar and find a guy.'* It's that easy. I can walk right up to the bar and order one. I'll have a margarita and a sexy surfer. Beer and a muscled jock. Whiskey sour and a frat boy. Nope. I'll have a rum and cola—hold the rum—and an ever-growing sense of inadequacy. There's a bunch of guys here all right, but they're all chasing after the hot blonde in the short miniskirt. No one is lusting after my awkward smiles and self-conscious fidgeting.

My butt is asleep from being perched on this stupid bar stool for the past hour. I'm a complete loser sitting in this cramped campus bar by myself, sipping my soda and waiting for someone to ask me for a *ride*. The looks I'm getting aren't of the come-hither variety. They're more of the what's-her-deal kind.

Who comes to a bar alone on a Friday night? Weirdos. And serial killers, who I guess, by definition, are weirdos. Their own species, but same family. The point is, nobody approaches the creepy loner unless they want to be chopped into little pieces and buried in the desert. That's the level of weirdo I'm flirting with. I'm sitting alone. Strike one. I'm in a T-shirt and jeans, not a low-cut top and skin-tight leggings. Strike two. I came here to meet people, so Jackie made me promise not to stare at my phone. No selfies for this girl. Strike three. *Total weirdo.*

A group of girls take up residence next to me at the bar. I give them my token swear-I'm-not-a-psycho wave and get a lukewarm chin-raise in response. Sadly, this is the most positive interaction I've received from anyone tonight. What I wouldn't give to teleport back in front of my computer right now, safely swaddled in my footie pajamas.

A few more minutes go by and I'm trying not to be too obvious while eavesdropping to find an in on their conversation. It's about the Kardashians. Not my forte. I angle myself toward them so people might think I'm part of the cool crowd. Part of *any* crowd.

My mouth goes dry, my heart stops and my breath catches in my throat when the unthinkable happens. A guy—a hot guy—staggers up to me, gestures to my chest and says, "Cool shirt." He's talking to me! He's actually talking to me. Out of all the girls in this bar, he chose me. A wave of idiotic, giddy pride washes over me.

I blush, smile and glance down at my black T-shirt that reads 'There are only 10 types of people in this world. Those who understand binary and those who don't.' Jackie told me to wear something sexy. Black is sexy, right? Being funny is sexy too. This shirt is a twofer.

His eyes don't leave my chest while he sips his beer. He must be a slow reader. "Do you get it?" I ask him, trying to keep my tone un-insulting. He doesn't have to be a genius. I'm searching for my first time, not my soulmate.

He puts his arm on the bar behind me and leans in close enough that I can smell the alcohol oozing out of his pores. I have the urge to scream 'Personal space invasion!' but I bite my lip and keep silent. My back stiffens and I lean away as far as I can until it hits the bar behind me. He pushes his thumb inside the sleeve of my T-shirt, massaging my biceps intimately.

His hot breath is on my ear as he pants, "You know what'd make it better? If it were on the floor next to my bed."

Bile rises in the back of my throat and panic surges through my body. Sure, this guy is hot, but I don't want this. This isn't me. I pull my hands into my chest. "No, thank you." My voice is shaky and it comes out a question. That only seems to encourage him.

He moves his other hand to my knee. Condensation from the beer he's got pinched between two fingers seeps into my jeans. I feel violated by the cold, wet, unwanted sensation.

"What nice manners. I'd love to hear you say pretty please. On your knees," the stranger croons into my ear.

I want to tell him to fuck off. I want to shove him away. I can't. I'm frozen in place. He moves his hand up my thigh. My entire body goes rigid and my eyes go wide. I look to the girl next to me, silently pleading for help.

She sees the sheer terror on my face and snaps, "Hey, creep! Leave that poor girl alone."

"I'm just being friendly," the guy answers. He pulls away from me, a lecherous grin slashing across his face.

"Why don't you go make friends with your left hand? I think it's getting jealous," she quips.

The guy just holds up his hands in surrender, shakes his head and walks away.

Once I'm able to breathe again I turn to the patron saint of hopeless women and thank her for intervening.

She gives me a tight smile. "You know, if you don't respect yourself, no one else is ever going to respect you either."

"Ah, okay," I answer, not really sure why being harassed by an asshole at a bar is somehow my fault now. Trying not to seem ungracious, I add, "Thanks again." I give her a shaky smile and a quick wave. She just nods and returns her attention to her friends. I down the rest of my warm, flat soda before making my way to the nearest exit and into an Uber faster than I can say 'Friday night fail'.

"Jackie, you're an idiot," I tell my best friend as soon as I get home.

She rolls her eyes at me and sighs.

"No, I'm a genius. You're just doing it wrong."

"Oh, gee, thanks. I didn't realize there was a wrong way to get *molested* by a stranger in a bar!"

Jackie quirks an eyebrow. "There certainly is. And if you weren't enjoying it, then you were definitely doing it wrong. Was he hot?"

"Yes, he was hot. And he was also crass, overbearing, drunk and had a serious misconception of my personal space boundaries."

"Jesus, you and your Goldilocks vagina are impossible. *This guy is too shy. That one's too aggressive*," she mocks in a high-pitched voice that is epically condescending. "They're boys, not bowls of porridge. Just pick one and dig in already."

I can't form a response. Creepy fairytale analogy aside, she's totally right. The guys I like are too shy to ever make a move and the guys who do make moves go too fast. It's the same every damn time. Either they run away or I do. Fizzle or explosion. I can't find a middle ground. My just-right Mr. Right.

It seems hopeless. I'm doomed to wander the earth untouched and unloved forever.

"I guess there *is* one other thing you *could* try." Jackie's tone has a familiar deviousness to it. She's waiting for me to take the bait. And, because I'm an idiot, I do.

"And that is?"

"Hire an escort."

An escort? That's crazy. Extreme. Ridiculous. Flat-out insane. *Isn't it?*

I pull up my web browser and type 'male escort' into the search bar. Big mistake. Huge. Massive. Throbbing. Mistake! I close the browser and try to purge the last thirty seconds of G-strings and gyrating-hip pop-up ads from my memory banks. Why do men think leopard print is sexy? I don't want to be mauled by your penis, thank you very much.

Dialing it down a notch, I have better luck searching 'college hookups.' The first few links are all *Maxim* magazine-type articles explaining the dos and don'ts of the college hookup. Spoiler alert, vomiting on a guy is a turn-off. I'll file that gem away for later reference. Halfway down the page I hit pay dirt.

Scoreyourscore.com.

It's a website designed for people to rate their sexual partners. You can sort by campus, age, gender, sexuality, kinks, etc. It's sexual Yelp. Too much nipple play. Nimble tongue. Sloppy kisser. Ridiculous stamina. Micro penis. Two-pump chump. Meat curtains. *Do. Not. Google. That!* It goes on and on. Men and women both detailing their exploits. This handy website is a goldmine of data.

I don't know how to read people, but data I get. Data speaks to me in a language I can understand. Right now, it's telling me, somewhere in all this hay, I will find my needle. That special someone to take my virginity. A brilliant if slightly deranged idea begins to form in my twisted brain. I don't need a professional — more of an experienced amateur. I open up a spreadsheet and go to town, more optimistic than I've ever been about taking the next step in my womanhood.

# About the Author

Cass is in love with love, and has been since she peeked at her first romance novel at age fifteen. When an unannounced romance hero walked into her imagination presenting his heroine and pushing her into the spotlight, Cass knew she was destined to become a romance writer. The adventure of a new book and the comfort of an old favorite are two of her most cherished pleasures. When she's not writing or reading, Cass explores the world with her spouse and two kids. She loves chocolate, the Texas Longhorns, and the Oxford comma.

Cass loves to hear from readers. You can find her contact information, website details and author profile page at https://www.totallybound.com

# TOTALLY BOUND

Home of Erotic Romance

Sign up for our newsletter and find out about all our romance book releases, eBook sales and promotions, sneak peeks and FREE romance books!